PROMISE ME FOREVER

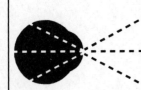 This Large Print Book carries the
Seal of Approval of N.A.V.H.

Promise Me Forever

Diane Amos

THORNDIKE PRESS
A part of Gale, Cengage Learning

GALE
CENGAGE Learning®

Detroit • New York • San Francisco • New Haven, Conn • Waterville, Maine • London

GALE
CENGAGE Learning®

LIBRARY OF CONGRESS CATALOGING-IN-PUBLICATION DATA

Amos, Diane.
    Promise me forever / by Diane Amos.
        p. cm. — (Thorndike Press large print core)
    ISBN-13: 978-1-4104-4615-2 (hardcover)
    ISBN-10: 1-4104-4615-8 (hardcover)
    1. Ranch life—Montana—Fiction. 2. Large type books. I. Title.
    PS3601.M67P76 2012
    813'.6—dc23   2011045174

Published in 2012 by arrangement with Tekno Books.

Printed in the United States of America
1 2 3 4 5 6 7 16 15 14 13 12

A12005 967311

My mother, Aurore Labonte
My grandmother, Marie Boilard
My mother-in-law, Caroline Amos
I admire your strength, your courage
and your passion for life.
You are greatly missed!

CHAPTER 1

May 1898

Life wouldn't be worth spit if he lost his ranch. But after herding longhorns for twelve hours and working half the night at the Gold Nugget mine, Benjamin Ricker was too doggoned tired to dwell on his troubles.

Ben gazed at the clear blue Montana sky through the hole in the roof of the Golden Harp Saloon. It was a wonder the entire place hadn't burnt to the ground. When the lightning struck, Pete, the owner, had slammed a mug against the cedar bar and shouted, "Free drinks for anyone who helps to save my place."

After twenty-four hours of free liquor, the wooden establishment rocked with crude jokes, off-color language, and endless drunken laughter. Pete told a raunchy story that stirred the noise to frenzy. Then everyone grew quiet.

Ben's spine stiffened as the swinging wooden doors behind him creaked back and forth.

"My good Lord," Pete muttered, eyes wide, as if the Man Himself were standing there.

Ben swung around and stared in disbelief. What was a nun doing in a saloon? She was a little thing, wearing a long, black habit. Ben blinked twice. Could two beers make a man hallucinate?

Pete hurried across the room and wiped his hands on the stained white apron tied around his waist. "Good day, Sister. What can I do for you?"

"How kind of you, sir. I'm Sister Elizabeth. It seems I've gotten lost." The nun pulled a tattered newspaper clipping from her pocket. "I'm looking for Welcome, Montana."

Ben felt sorry for her. Little did she know she was standing smack dab in the center of Welcome. One night three months ago, Pete had dictated the words for the advertisement that would encourage new families to move to their small community. After adding a few embellishments of his own, Ben signed his name to the piece of paper. When he read the finished masterpiece aloud, everyone in the bar shared a good laugh.

On a whim three days later Pete mailed the article to a newspaper back East.

Pete cleared his throat. "Well . . . Sister Elizabeth, you aren't lost."

She barely blinked. "This is Welcome?"

"Well, yes."

She unfolded the clipping and glanced down. "This article was written by Benjamin Ricker. Do you know where I may find him?"

Pete pointed an incriminating finger toward the bar. "As a matter of fact, that's Ben over there."

Sister Elizabeth stepped toward him, her blue eyes blazing with anger. A tendril of russet hair had escaped her black habit and hung limp over her damp forehead.

She inhaled a sharp breath. "Are you Mr. Ricker?"

Ben settled his hat more firmly on his head. "Yes, ma'am . . . er, Sister."

She waved the paper in front of his face. "You wrote this article?"

"Yes."

"Where's the church, the library, the Golden Harp Theater?"

He remembered coining the term Golden Harp Theater and how hilarious it had seemed at the time. He shrugged. "It's all here, Sister, if you use your imagination."

She tapped her laced black shoe impatiently against the saloon's sawdust-covered floor. "In other words, Mr. Ricker, this entire newspaper article is nothing but fabrications."

Ben met her tempestuous blue eyes and smiled. "No Sister, I don't lie, but sometimes I do stretch the truth a bit."

Elizabeth O'Hara glared at the foolish grin plastered across Ben Ricker's unshaven face. The town was a far cry from what she'd envisioned when she'd read the newspaper article. Disappointment twisted inside. Welcome, Montana, had seemed the ideal place to escape.

Her nose wrinkled in disgust as she detected the smell of beer on Ben Ricker's breath. The even stronger stench of alcohol in the room mingled with the odor of deviled eggs, sweat, and Heaven only knew what else.

As Elizabeth glanced around the room, she slid the toe of her shoe over the sawdust littering the wooden floor. In the corner stood an ornate, chrome-trimmed cast iron stove, a bucket of coal nearby. She tried not to notice the two spittoons strategically located by the bar. Signs on the wall at opposite ends of the room advertised beer for

17¢, applejack for 20¢, redeye or corn whiskey for 25¢.

Excluding the stained apron around his waist, the bartender was the only neatly attired gentleman in the room. He wore a crisp white shirt, a deep red silk bow tie, matching suspenders, garters on his sleeves and gray trousers.

Leaning against the banister of the staircase leading to the second floor stood a woman whose large bosom threatened to escape from the bodice of her violet silk dress. The garment sported a fashionable bustle and layered ruffles and was as nice as any dress Elizabeth had seen back East.

Eyes lined with kohl and lips a deep crimson, the bold woman anchored one hand to her shapely hip and winked. "Good day, Sister."

She stepped forward and directed Elizabeth to an empty table away from the bar. "Call me Queenie. Sit down, Sister," she said while waving a hand toward the bartender and taking a seat. "Pete, a couple tall glasses of lemonade would be nice."

Nothing was turning out as Elizabeth had hoped. When she'd pulled into town, she heard an ungodly racket, saw its source and felt panic for the first time. Until then, she'd told herself nothing could be as bad as what she'd run away from.

The wooden saloon vibrated with deafening noise. The crude comments coming from inside turned her stomach. As her wagon rolled along the dung-covered street, she saw three drunks on the wooden walkway. Another lay facedown between two horses hitched to a rail. Worse still was the one relieving himself beside Luke's Trading Post while he sang a little ditty that reddened her cheeks. She rounded the corner of the next building, shoved her beaded reticule beneath the wagon seat, and quickly donned the black habit she'd brought along for such an occasion. For years she'd noticed how men treated nuns with respect.

"What brings you here, Sister?" Queenie asked.

Elizabeth assumed a pious pose. "My parish saw the article in the paper and thought Welcome would be the perfect place for Sister Agnes and me to establish an orphanage."

Queenie glanced toward the door. "Is Sister Agnes outside?"

"No. She's going to meet me here in another month or two. Until then, I need to find work and a place to stay."

Pete arrived with two mugs of lemonade and set them on the table. Elizabeth felt a moment's panic. Her money was gone.

Queenie batted thick lashes at Pete. "Honey, add it to my tab."

Elizabeth reciprocated with a gracious smile. "Thank you."

"It's nothing, Sister. Just put in a good word for me with the Man Upstairs."

Pete lifted a shaggy brow. "If you ask me, she'd better put in a hell of a lot more than a good word."

Queenie let the comment roll by. "Do you know of anyone who's hiring? Sister Elizabeth doesn't want to twiddle her thumbs while she waits for her partner to arrive."

Pete scratched his chin and glanced toward the spring sky through the gaping hole in the roof.

Elizabeth tried to appear calm. "Maybe some of the local children need tutoring in reading and arithmetic."

Pete met her eyes reluctantly. "Not many children in Welcome. There's a baby, still not weaned, and Clyde, but he can't even talk, much less learn to read."

Desperate, Elizabeth glanced around the room and spotted the piano in the corner. "I could sing for my room and board."

"Though I'm sure you have a right nice voice, the songs you know belong in the Lord's house, not in this rowdy bar. If I could, I'd give you free board, but my upstairs needs fixin', and the rooms won't be ready for another few weeks."

"Where else can I stay?" Elizabeth took another sip of lemonade and tried to hide her anxiety.

Pete's face brightened. "I have an idea. Ben," he shouted above the racket. "Come over here a minute."

Ben Ricker sauntered across the room. In need of a shave and a haircut, he wore a tattered cowboy hat, torn jeans, and a western-style shirt caked with dust. When he looked up, his deep amber eyes warmed Elizabeth's insides and reminded her of the whiskey her stepfather stocked in his liquor cabinet.

"Aren't you looking for a cook?" Pete asked after a pause. "Sister needs a job for a few weeks."

Although Elizabeth didn't want to work for Ben Ricker, she was desperate and would take any job, even shoveling horse dung off the streets of Welcome.

Looking dazed, Ben hesitated a moment. "You cook, Sister?"

She tilted her chin with confidence. "Certainly."

"Can you make beef stew?"

"My beef stew stands alone."

"I can't pay much. Just room and board and let's say . . ." The hint of a smile resurfaced. "One dollar a week."

Never mind that her time in any kitchen was next to nothing. Indignation rose in her voice. "That's robbery. No decent cook would work for so little money."

A victorious look claimed his face. "You turning me down?"

The skunk wanted her to refuse his offer. "Will my room be near the kitchen?" She'd need to be close by.

He hesitated. "Yeah, I suppose so."

"Can I keep everything that's in my wagon in my bedroom?" She prayed the liquor had dimmed his brain enough not to ask pointed questions.

He lifted one shoulder in an easygoing shrug. "As long as you can cook, it doesn't matter to me what you keep in your room."

Elizabeth hoped he was a man of his word.

"I heard you telling Queenie about your plans to start an orphanage. Make sure that waits until you're off my place. I can't have a bunch of children running amok on my ranch."

An innocent smile seemed the most prudent answer.

Satisfied, he nodded. "We better be moving so you'll have time to fix supper. Oh, one other thing. Can you make biscuits?"

"Do birds fly?"

A moment later, Queenie and Elizabeth followed Ben Ricker's broad back through the swinging doors.

He looked over his shoulder. "Where's your wagon, Sister?"

"Around the corner," she replied as a scream pierced the air from the direction she'd pointed.

Drawing his gun, he took off with Elizabeth at his heels and Queenie huffing and puffing several yards behind. As they turned the corner, Ben Ricker's expression changed from disbelief to fury.

Six-year-old Joshua sat in the only wagon in sight, dangling a harmless snake in front of his nine-year-old sister's terrified face.

"Joshua, throw that down this instant or I'll take a switch to you." Elizabeth tried to ignore the wrath on Ben Ricker's face.

Not easily daunted, Joshua sent Elizabeth a sidelong glance and tucked the grass snake in his shirt pocket.

"I'm warning you, Josh. Get rid of that snake right now."

With a mischievous grin, the boy took a flying leap out of the wagon, landed on all fours, hopped around like a stallion, and after a minute set the snake loose in a clump

16

of grass.

Elizabeth nodded approvingly. "That's a good boy. Now climb back in the wagon. We'll be leaving soon."

Ben lifted his hand in protest. "Whoa, I'm not so sure about that. Five minutes ago, we agreed no children."

Elizabeth stepped closer until they stood toe to toe. "If you recall, I never said a word."

Queenie elbowed Ben Ricker in the ribs. "Looks like the Sister also knows a little something about stretching the truth."

Ben Ricker's eyes turned cold. "Dammit all to hell, this isn't stretching the truth, it's downright lying."

"Mr. Ricker, I'll not have you speaking that way in front of these poor orphans. If someone's at fault, it's you for fabricating that advertisement."

"I mentioned children to you."

"Maybe so, Mr. Ricker, but you never asked if I already had any in my care."

"What do you aim to do with them?"

"They'll stay with me in my room, of course. You already said they could, remember?"

He fell silent and seemed to mull over the matter.

"If I couldn't almost taste the beef stew

we're having for supper, I'd send you on your way. You keep that boy and girl out from under my feet, you hear? I'm giving you one chance. One," he said, waving his forefinger in her face. "I don't want any more surprises from you, no more omitting facts."

As Ben Ricker gave her meager belongings a cursory glance, Elizabeth spotted movement beneath the old burlap bag under the wagon seat. She casually pulled at the worn cloth, tucked Bernie's tail out of sight and met Ben Ricker's suspicious gaze.

"Sister, have I made myself clear?"

"You have nothing to worry about."

CHAPTER 2

As the buckboard rolled along the rutted road, Elizabeth flicked the reins and cast a worried glance toward her sister. Looking forlorn, Cecelia blinked several times and nibbled her fingernails. Elizabeth put her free arm around her sister's delicate shoulders. "Pumpkin, everything will be all right, you'll see."

"Was that Welcome back there?"

"Afraid so." Including the Golden Harp Saloon, she'd seen six wooden structures, seven if she counted the lean-to that housed bales of hay.

"But what about the newspaper article you read to us?"

Elizabeth had committed the piece to memory.

Tired of city life and hankering for the country? Escape to Welcome, Montana, where people stand with hands outstretched in friendship. The article listed the town's attributes and employment opportunities that had turned out to be nothing more than a figment of Ben Ricker's vivid imagination. She'd been drawn to Welcome because of its name and the powerful visual drawn by the article. All lies. Every last word. The only outstretched hands were wrapped around mugs of beer.

Elizabeth inhaled several deep breaths before she trusted herself to speak. "The article was a mistake."

Cecelia pulled damp fingers from her mouth and stared ahead with a stark expression. "I don't think Mr. Ricker likes me very much," she whispered in a soft, vulnerable voice.

Anger coiled in the pit of Elizabeth's stomach. She knew Ben Ricker wasn't responsible for Cecelia's anguish, but the disgruntled look on his face when he'd spotted the children had rubbed raw wounds. "He's grumpy. It has nothing to do with you." Elizabeth tipped her sister's face up. "Now I want to see a smile."

When Cecelia managed a half-hearted attempt, Elizabeth tweaked her nose. "That's better, Pumpkin. Try to forget what's happened, and for now, ignore Mr. Ricker. He's a crabby old grouch."

"What's a crabby grouch?" asked the

inquisitive, high-pitched voice behind her.

"Never you mind." She cast her brother a serious look over her shoulder. "Do you remember what you're supposed to call me?"

"Yes, Sister Elizabeth," he replied with a thick dose of respectability and then ruined it by sticking his tongue out at her.

She ruffled his hair. "You little rascal, behave yourself."

Joshua giggled and dropped down beside Bernie.

Cecelia reached behind the seat and pushed a hand beneath the burlap to pat her pet. As her fingers wound their way around the long ears, Bernie emitted a doggy sigh of content, stretched onto her side, and extended a brown paw beyond the tan cloth. "What's going to happen if Mr. Ricker finds out about Bernie?"

Elizabeth didn't want to consider that. The eighty-pound basset hound was due to have puppies any day, one more problem to add to her growing list. "He won't find out," she said with false confidence for Cecelia's sake.

"But how are we going to hide her?"

"Don't worry. I'll think of something."

Cecelia bit her lower lip and glanced at

21

the man astride his horse. "Mr. Ricker looks tired."

Drunk was more like it, but before Elizabeth could say anything, she remembered what her mother had told her numerous times over the years. *Elizabeth, if you can't say anything good, don't say anything at all.* Unfortunately, Elizabeth was better at speaking her mind than she was at remembering this proverb. Somehow she managed to clamp her lips together and move her head in a half-nod.

About twenty feet in front of the wagon, Ben Ricker sat in the saddle atop his mare, his broad shoulders either slumped forward in fatigue or weighted down by the alcohol he'd consumed. Lean and lanky with a loose-jointed swagger hard to ignore, he was a man who could turn women's heads. Not hers. His easygoing smile and whiskey-colored eyes held some appeal, but she'd never allow herself to become involved with a drinking man. She'd seen what alcohol did to men. Worse, she'd seen what alcohol had done to her sister.

A breeze stirred her skirt, reminding her that she probably smelled worse than Ben Ricker. First thing on her agenda was a clean change of clothes and a bath.

Forty minutes later as the buckboard

bounced along the rocky dirt path, a white two-story farmhouse with a wraparound porch came into view. Worry knotted Elizabeth's stomach. If Ben Ricker didn't allow her and the children to stay a while, she didn't know what she'd do. She'd spent her last few dollars on train tickets and this wagon; everything they owned was packed in the boxes behind her. She sighed nervously and glanced at the Ponderosa pines that towered on either side of the narrow winding drive. Swinging overhead, a weathered gray sign with the words *Gold Nugget Ranch* creaked back and forth as their horse plodded underneath.

Ben Ricker's drooping shoulders and bobbing head indicated he'd fallen asleep in his saddle, probably too inebriated to remain alert. Five minutes later his trusty horse stopped suddenly several feet before the wooden farmhouse that was in dire need of paint.

Ben Ricker jolted awake.

In slow motion, he swung his leg over his mare and dismounted. He yawned, stretched his arms above his head and smiled at an elderly man with a pipe clamped between his teeth, sitting in a rocker on the porch.

Elizabeth could tell by Mr. Ricker's expression that he cared deeply for the individual frowning at them. She watched with apprehension as the old man pushed himself up and squinted. He took a deep pull on his pipe and blew out a puff of smoke.

"That you, Ben?" he asked in a raspy voice. He wore thick glasses that magnified his eyes, patched denim overalls, and a red-and-white checked flannel shirt. His gray hair was parted down the middle and combed behind his ears.

Mr. Ricker hopped onto the porch. "Sure is. Did you miss me?"

"Can't say that I did." The creases on the wrinkled face deepened. "Did you buy me any tobacco?"

"Yes, but I've got a surprise for you, too."

The elderly gent pursed his lips. "Spit it out. I could die before you get around to tellin' me." Then he cocked his head to the side. "Is it raining out?"

Elizabeth twisted around and spotted Joshua peeing off the back of the wagon. She cringed. It was too late to do anything about her brother's bad manners. After checking that Bernie was still covered, she gave her sister's hand a comforting pat. Then, determined to salvage what little chance remained to make a good impression, she hopped down from the wagon and marched onto the porch. Not waiting for an introduction, she extended her palm and took the parchment-like hand in hers. "Pleased to meet you, sir. I'm the new cook."

She saw anger spark in the clouded gray eyes, noticed how the face pinched with bitterness. Throwing the pipe aside, the old man aimed his hand toward the buckboard. "I ain't ever had any help, ain't gonna need any neither. Go back where you came from."

Ben Ricker's mouth curled into a wide grin. "I'd like you to meet Granny Ricker."

When Granny spun around and scowled at the post to Ben's left, he knew he'd been right to hire someone to do the cooking.

"Ben," she said with her finger pointed off target. "Hightail it inside now if you know what's good for you."

He hated to see Granny lose her independence, but she needed help. Her failing eyesight deteriorated with each passing week, and he couldn't be here to watch her every minute.

Seven days ago she'd unknowingly dropped a towel on the cook stove. When he arrived home, she was asleep in the kitchen rocker with flames licking the back wall. No significant damage was done, and Granny wasn't hurt. But he might not be so lucky the next time. Ben's fingers had barely touched Granny's elbow to guide her inside when she gave him a prideful look and yanked her arm away. "My eyes are a mite dim, but my mind's still sharp so you needn't herd me like some daft steer."

"Granny . . ." he started to say but stopped when she stormed into the house.

Not anxious for a showdown, Ben decided to kill some time and give Sister Elizabeth and the orphans a tour of the ranch house before facing his grandmother. He stepped off the porch and ambled toward the buckboard where Sister Elizabeth was unloading her boxes. Down on his hands and knees, Joshua did a fair imitation of a rambunctious pony scampering on all fours. "WINNN—EEEEEEE." With a playful toss of his head and a wide grin, the boy made Ben smile. The kid was a real pest but cute. As Ben approached the wagon, the girl slid to the other side of the seat and started to gnaw her thumbnail. She kept her gaze on her shoes; her breathing came in short spurts like someone who'd run a mile. He speculated at the cause of the hollow look on her young face.

Sister caught him studying the girl and immediately went to her side as if the child needed protection from the likes of him.

She squeezed the girl's shoulder reassuringly and met his eyes. "Where should we store our belongings?"

"Maybe I've changed my mind about hiring you." He was ribbing her, but she didn't take it that way.

"You, Mr. Ricker, are a lowdown scoundrel, a dirty skunk. If I were a man, I'd introduce you to my knuckles."

"Introduce you to my knuckles? Is that convent talk for punching someone in the nose?"

Her lips parted and then clamped shut.

"Sister, would you really punch me?" he asked with a wink and a smile.

She closed her eyes and appeared to whisper a silent prayer.

"Isn't it a sin to hit people for nothing?"

The freckles on her nose ignited as sparks flew from her eyes. "Darn right it's a sin, but I'd do it and worry about the consequences later." She inhaled an audible breath and picked up a medium-size box. "Now, cut the bull, Mr. Ricker, where do we put these?"

He hooked one arm on the side the buckboard. "Instead of letting your temper get the best of you, shouldn't you be saying a prayer or something?"

She swung around and deposited the box

on the porch, then turned and shrugged hopelessly. "As far as you're concerned, Mr. Ricker, one prayer would not suffice." Ben enjoyed baiting Sister Elizabeth because she refused to be intimidated by him. He chuckled and grabbed the largest carton, directing her inside. "Sister, did anyone ever mention you have a sassy mouth?"

A blush tinted her cheeks as she looked him square in the face. "Many times, Mr. Ricker. Many, many times."

The mischief in her eyes surprised him. That paled compared to what he felt when he noticed how truly pretty she was, with a face that would make any cowboy sit up and take a second look.

"Damn," he said to himself, or thought he had until he saw the quizzical look on Sister Elizabeth's beautiful face. Ben halted his line of thinking, wondering if he'd go straight to Hell for just noticing.

He glanced away and led her to the room off the kitchen where she and the children would be staying. Once they had unloaded the boxes, Ben pulled the wagon into the barn and wiped down Sister Elizabeth's horse. Then, figuring he'd given Granny enough time to calm down, he headed inside to do his damnedest to get her to see reason.

As he walked in the back door, he spotted no one around, but he was pleased to see that Sister Elizabeth had already taken out numerous ingredients, bowls, and utensils. When Ben cooked, he made do with a bowl and one pan. Evidently, the Sister knew her way around the kitchen more than he did. For once, they'd have a meal he didn't need to supervise, and with a little luck, Granny would stay away from the kitchen until the food was ready to serve.

Making his way up the stairs, he tapped on Granny's door. When she didn't answer, he inched the door open and peeked inside. She'd fallen asleep in her rocker by the window. Her glasses sat on the sill, and the light breeze stirred a wisp of her thinning gray hair. For a moment he saw her as she once had been, a strong woman who'd done a man's work without complaining.

She'd raised him with sound words and a strong hand, which she didn't hesitate to use on his backside when needed. Her gentle touch had wiped his tears and comforted him through the rough times. She'd loved and cared for him all his life. Now it was his turn to do the same for her, if only she would let him.

As he bent to kiss her cheek, her eyes fluttered open, and she smiled at him. Then her back stiffened. She stared at him as though she could read his mind. Even as a little boy, he'd felt the penetrating gaze from her gray eyes.

"Are you daft? Bringing a woman here to cook? Can't afford it! Don't need it! I'll quit cooking when they bury me, not one minute sooner. You hear?"

"Granny, you know I love your cooking, but . . ."

"No ands, ifs, or buts. Get rid of her."

Ben sat on the bed opposite his grandmother. "I thought you'd be glad to have someone around to talk to during the day while I'm working."

"I ain't. Send her away." Granny grabbed her glasses from the windowsill and angled them over her nose. "Besides, with these on, I can see you sitting there with that doggoned look on your face, trying to sweet-talk me into changing my mind. It ain't gonna happen."

Granny's eyes focused on a spot above Ben's shoulder. According to Doc Cartwright, at most she was seeing shadows. By summer's end, she'd be blind. The thought sickened Ben.

"Granny," he said, taking her hand. "I felt sorry for the woman. She was down on her luck and needed a break."

"Two women in the kitchen is one too many. And where do you expect to get the money to pay her, huh? You got some growin' in the garden waitin' to be picked?"

Lying was something Ben detested, but he knew by the stubborn look on his grandmother's face that he had little choice. Ignoring the bitter feeling rising in his gut, he blurted, "She's not here to cook. You misunderstood. She's here to learn from you. I mentioned you might be willing to teach her. If you feel you can't, I'll understand and ask her to leave."

Ben stood and strolled toward the door.

"Where you think you're going?"

"To repack her wagon."

"Horse feathers! You think my eyesight's so bad I can't teach some poor woman how to cook?"

As he stood by the clear stream, Ben Ricker shed his clothes and got a nose full. Beer, sweat, and the dank smell of the gold mine that penetrated his pores were a powerful combination. In desperation, he'd started working the mine last month. Each night after sleeping a few hours, he'd stumble out of bed and drag himself to the dark tunnel where he put in a full six hours of back-breaking labor before joining Granny for breakfast.

They were destitute. Granny realized finances were tight, but she had no clue how bad. He'd been pinching pennies for the last two years, and no matter how many corners he cut, the money never stretched far enough. He'd lost a third of his long-horns to the brutal cold this past winter and more last summer to the drought. If things didn't turn around, he'd lose the ranch. That would ruin him and kill Granny for sure. At times, he wanted to say to hell with it all, but he couldn't. The ranch meant almost as much to him as it did to his grandmother.

He lathered his body and washed his hair. Ben was so tired he shut his eyes for a few seconds and felt himself nodding off. The frigid water rippling along the bank soothed his body and mind until he started to shake and feel his legs going numb. He climbed out of the water, rubbed himself dry with a worn towel, and shrugged into a clean shirt and jeans. After he washed his dirty clothes with the lye soap his grandmother had made last fall, he hung them to dry over the limb of a nearby tree.

He heard an ear-piercing screech that reminded him of an animal in distress. As Ben stood and listened, he recognized a familiar voice. Water splashed and several yips followed. Curious, he edged closer toward the sound and got an eyeful.

Sister Elizabeth was crouched along the water's edge with her back to him. Her black habit lay nearby. He ordered himself to look away but stood rooted to the ground. A curtain of fire-red hair draped over the Sister's shoulders and covered her bottom. He'd seen a wisp of that magnificent mane against her forehead in the saloon, but he'd assumed a nun would either be bald or keep her hair cropped close to her head. Never had he envisioned the silken strands that cascaded over her small, naked frame.

Unable to stop himself, he watched her work the soap up one leg and down the other, up one arm and back. Consumed with guilt, he continued to stare. He barely heard the scream when she lowered herself for an instant below the surface of the water and then quickly soaped her hair and ducked under for a last rinse. When she stood, she was facing him. Droplets of cold water shimmered on her wet arms and legs. Her long hair draped over her body and prevented him from seeing much, but what he did see was enough to confirm his earlier suspicions.

On the day he died, he'd be rubbing elbows with the Devil.

CHAPTER 3

Clad in a clean, damp black habit, Elizabeth hurried across the backyard and entered the dilapidated farmhouse. Seeing no one around, she breathed a sigh of relief. She could do without a confrontation with either Benjamin or Granny Ricker to increase her growing anxiety. She'd begun to panic soon after her bath. Now that the moment had arrived, could she pull off this hoax?

Though she wasn't a nun, at least, she'd observed enough to copy what they did and how they acted. Unfortunately, cooking was boring. The kitchen was hot. Meals took time and handling meat was such an unpleasant task. Back in Boston, elaborate meals had appeared on her table without her lifting a hand, and the dirty dishes had vanished in much the same way. The one time she'd attempted to brew tea for herself and Cecelia, she'd become distracted and the kettle had boiled dry, filling the house with smoke and an acrid smell. Her carelessness had ruined a good kettle along with any desire to ever reenter the kitchen.

Elizabeth's natural optimism came to her aid. She'd never made beef stew, but she'd eaten it several times. Beef, potatoes, onions, carrots, she ticked off the list and immediately started to feel better. She could do this, she told herself, with a smile and a push of the bedroom door.

"Hi, you two. Any problems while I was away?"

Joshua pointed to wooden boxes piled in the corner. "Nope. I fixed Bernie a really good house to hide in."

"I can see that." Elizabeth peered inside at the pregnant dog, whose distended belly looked ready to pop. Refusing to dwell on that problem, she stepped away and walked to her sister.

Cecelia glanced up and smiled timidly. "I've been doing what you told me to." She lifted her hand from the ceramic bowl at her side and displayed fingers coated with biscuit dough.

Elizabeth hugged her sister. "I'm proud of you, Pumpkin. You're a big help."

"Do you think Mr. Ricker will let us stay?" Cecelia asked in a tremulous voice.

If all went as Elizabeth fervently hoped, Benjamin Ricker would taste one bite of their mouth-watering biscuits, declare them the best he'd ever eaten, and then double her wages. "He won't want us to leave once he samples these biscuits. Now, you better let Joshua have a turn kneading the dough. I might need your help in the kitchen."

Earlier that day Elizabeth had scoured the kitchen for a cookbook but had found only brief notes scrawled on cards. Fortunately, the one she'd tucked in the pocket of her habit held a list of ingredients for biscuits; otherwise, she didn't know what they'd have done. The missing directions didn't concern her. Even a fool could figure out everything needed to be thrown together in a bowl. Determined to make the best biscuits that ever graced Benjamin Ricker's table, Elizabeth had instructed her sister and brother to work the dough nonstop. Their future depended on this meal, and she intended to do everything possible to ensure its success.

Confident the biscuits were well on their way, Elizabeth headed to the kitchen to start the stew. Cecelia followed close behind with head hung low. With a purposeful stride, Elizabeth marched across the room and stopped suddenly, giving a wary glance around. Her sister bumped into her.

"Cecelia, do you see an icebox?"

While chewing her thumbnail, Cecelia shook her head.

Elizabeth lifted a disdainful brow. "Something tells me this isn't good news, Pumpkin."

Cecelia slipped wet fingers from her mouth and whirled around. "It's not here, Betts."

Slipping an arm around her sister's thin frame, she whispered, "Call me Sister Elizabeth, remember?"

Cecelia glanced down, planted her fingers back in her mouth, and mumbled, "No faucets, either."

Elizabeth heaved a disgruntled sigh. She gave herself a silent pep talk and made great strides until she peered around the room: no icebox, definitely no running water, no knobs on what she'd assumed was a gas stove. She looked out the kitchen window and found a well complete with hand pump and a bucket a hundred feet from the kitchen door. Upon closer inspection, she saw that the black cast-iron stove was heated by wood kept in a basket a few feet to her right. She brought her hand an inch above the stovetop. Warmth radiated toward her palm. Smiling confidently, she lifted the circular lid and threw two hefty logs onto the glowing coals. She set a large cast-iron kettle on the stove and was glad to hear the wood crackle as she left the kitchen to find the root cellar.

"Let's go, Cecelia, we're really cooking now."

"We are?"

"The stove's roaring, and we are, too, two sisters about to cook beef stew," she said in singsong fashion that brought a brief grin to Cecelia's face.

"Things are going good?"

"Good?" Elizabeth scrunched up her face. "What kind of dumb word is that? We're doing much better than good, Pumpkin, even better than great. How's stupendous sound to you?"

Cecelia's eyes widened. "Stupendous," she whispered, trying the word for the first time. "Yes, I like that. Stupendous means Mr. Ricker will let us stay, and we won't have to go back."

"Pumpkin, don't you worry. No matter what happens, we aren't ever going back."

They found the wooden door to the root cellar underneath the main part of the house. The scent of musty earth drifted upward when the rusted hinges creaked open.

Cecelia tugged at Elizabeth's hand and

stepped backward. "Don't go in there."

"There's nothing to be afraid of," Elizabeth said with more bravado than she felt as she lit the kerosene lamp inside the door. She stepped inside tentatively, but when a large hairy spider zipped down its web and dangled inches from her nose, she leaped back with a muffled scream.

Cecelia was poised ready to flee.

Elizabeth laughed. "Take it easy, Pumpkin, it was only a spider." The biggest spider she'd ever seen. And though she made light of the matter and concealed her fear, she wasn't about to reenter without a weapon.

After searching for a minute, she found a thick branch. Wielding it over her head like a sword, she swung the limb back and forth while grasping the lantern with her other hand. When she felt a tickle on her cheek, she screamed, gave the branch a mighty whack, and heard the sound of rolling vegetables bursting open on the ground.

Cecelia shrieked.

Within seconds, Elizabeth heard the pounding of feet. The lanky silhouette that soon blocked the daylight spilling in the doorway had to be Benjamin Ricker. In the wavering lantern light, she made out his mouth set in a grim line.

"What's going on, Sister?"

A spider seemed a lame excuse for all the fuss. She needed something bigger.

"Something furry came at me. It was big and came up to here," she said with her hand at eye level.

"That's impossible, Sister. We keep the door shut tight. Whatever spooked you couldn't have been very large."

"That's what you think."

He glanced around. "No real harm done, except for that one cracked winter squash. Just add it to the stew so it won't go to waste. What's that in your hand?"

She looked down at her fingers, still wrapped tightly around the branch. "Oh, that," she replied as if she'd just now noticed the limb.

A taunting grin lifted a corner of his mouth. "Yes, that."

"It's a branch, Mr. Ricker."

Benjamin Ricker eyed the limb and the squash split open on the ground. "Now that you've beaten the squash into submission, I bet the other vegetables have taken notice. You're safe. Why don't you put your weapon aside and allow me to help you?"

After searching thoroughly overhead and finding no signs of the spider, she reluctantly leaned the branch against a wooden shelf.

His hearty laugh echoed inside the root

cellar, stirring the Irish temper beneath her black habit. "I hope you're enjoying yourself, Mr. Ricker."

Another chuckle. "Earlier today you were ready to take on an entire saloon." He cocked an eyebrow for her benefit. "Yet a tiny spider sends you into panic."

Not wanting to encourage him further, she started filling the nearby basket with carrots, potatoes, and onions. As they worked elbow to elbow, she noticed he smelled like fresh air and springtime. His clothing, though old and worn, was clean and hugged his body in ways that set her heart drumming. Mr. Ricker was a looker, no denying that. She inhaled a deep appreciative breath and dropped another potato in her basket.

"Have you taken out the beef for supper yet?" he asked in a friendly tone.

"Back in Boston we had an icebox. I didn't know where to find the meat," she said, thinking he'd appreciate her honesty.

The smile slipped from his face. "You aren't in Boston anymore," was all he said, flipping the lid off the wooden barrel in the corner.

Elizabeth directed the light toward the barrel.

"What's that?"

"Beef, what else? You needn't wrinkle your nose. This brine keeps our meat from spoiling. We Montanans may be backward, but we make do."

She hadn't meant to insult him, but it was clear that he thought she had.

He threw a hunk of beef in a metal pan and, taking the basket, made a visible effort to regain his composure.

"Sister," he said, after a minute. "I shouldn't have raised my voice just now. It's not your fault you're an Easterner. Grab your weapon and come outside. There's someone I'd like you to meet."

Easterner, he'd sneered in a way that made Elizabeth see red. Boston had lots over Montana as far as she was concerned. Piped-in gas lit their home and provided fuel for their stove. She and her sister had even ridden the subway, a marvelous underground series of tunnels that connected the entire city. There were theaters, automobiles, and nice clothes. Boston was on the cutting edge of civilization, and if it hadn't been for her stepfather, Robert T. Hines, she'd still be living there with her brother and sister. Montana, however, did have one huge point in its favor. No one would ever think to look for her here.

After Benjamin Ricker walked out the

43

door, Elizabeth searched the dirt enclosure one more time for signs of the spider before darting out with her head held low. Unable to help herself, she gave her habit a violent shake and surveyed the black folds of the skirt for any sight of her eight-legged attacker. She hoped Ben Ricker hadn't noticed the shiver that racked her body as she checked behind her and then brushed nervous hands along her arms. Finally, she glanced up and saw a small boy, approximately five years old, clinging to Mr. Ricker's pant leg.

The ragamuffin was filthy from his head to the big toe protruding from the sole of boots about to fall apart. An oversized shirt held together by a safety pin hung loosely on a small frame hunched forward. Clenched tight in his dirty hand was what at first looked liked a soiled sock. Upon closer inspection, Elizabeth spied two frayed, stitched eyes and a painted mouth. Her heart twisted. She pulled her gaze away from the youngster and lifted it back to Mr. Ricker.

Wide grin on his face and looking pleased, Benjamin Ricker ruffled the boy's disheveled hair. "Sister, meet Clyde."

The boy covered his face with the crude

cloth doll; one large brown eye peeked at her.

"I know I was rough on you in the saloon earlier today, and I'm truly sorry for what I said about your collecting orphans." Benjamin Ricker wiped his boot against the leg of his faded jeans. "Clyde's mother died shortly after he was born. Not a soul around here knows who his pa is."

Elizabeth couldn't understand why he was telling her this. "Sister, what you're doing is commendable, and I want to support your efforts." His smile widened and enveloped his face. "Clyde's an orphan, and I figured you'd want him for your orphanage."

When Elizabeth entered the kitchen, the pot she'd left on the stove was glowing red. She instructed Cecelia to fetch water and then started to dice vegetables for the stew. Walking across the room was a challenge with Clyde's arms wrapped around her leg. Once more, she bent down and lifted the boy's chin.

"Let go, honey. No one's going to hurt you."

With a blank look, Clyde bit down on his doll and tightened his fingers around her leg.

He'd managed to hike her skirt halfway

up her calf. The child was terrified. Elizabeth was, too. She could barely take care of herself and her brother and sister, and now she was responsible for this boy.

A growling noise came from deep within his throat as he snatched a carrot from the counter.

Elizabeth was appalled by his condition. He had no social skills and smelled as though he hadn't been near soap and water in weeks. She didn't know if she could help him emotionally, but physically he was going to smell sweet as spring flowers when she got through with him. For now, she did her best not to breathe too deeply and continued dicing vegetables.

Cecelia arrived with a bucket of water and tugged at Elizabeth's sleeve. "What's wrong with him?"

"Pumpkin, no one ever gave Clyde a chance. No one even took the time to talk to him. Sad, don't you think? Would you be willing to amuse him while I prepare supper?"

Cecelia eyed Clyde warily, stuck her thumb in her mouth, and smiled down at the pathetic child gnawing on a carrot and smacking his lips. The boy was noisier than even Bernie when she ate.

Cecelia extended her palm toward the

frightened child. "Clyde, come with me. I will be your friend. You'd like that, wouldn't you?"

He grunted and Cecelia jumped back. Her nervous laugh brought a silly grin to his face. Timidly, he reached for her hand. Cecelia led the boy into their room and closed the door.

Concentrating on the chore, Elizabeth sliced the beef into long, thin strips. She was especially careful to follow the grain of the meat. Once she'd accomplished this unpleasant task, she scooped handfuls into the hot pan, which sizzled on impact. Before adding water, she stirred the beef with a long wooden spoon only to find the meat had stuck to the bottom of the pot. She jabbed at it, poked it with a knife, but it wouldn't budge.

She began to panic. Hoping water would solve her problem, she lifted the bucket and poured its contents over the burning meat. Satisfied for the moment, she added the vegetables and stirred. The beef held fast. Upon closer inspection, she spotted dead ants and a spider floating on top of the pot. Before she could do anything about the unwelcome intruders, she heard someone behind her.

"You be needin' some help?"

Granny Ricker had slung a pink floral apron over her denim overalls and flannel shirt. She eyed Elizabeth suspiciously and peered into the pot. Elizabeth glanced over her shoulder at the spider and ants floating in the broth and waited for Granny to comment.

"You'll be needin' flour to thicken the gravy and lard for flavor. Let 'em vegetables cook for a while first."

"Yes, I will," Elizabeth replied, thankful for the assistance.

Granny removed a tin of lard and a tin of flour from the shelf over the dry sink. She eased herself into the rocker where she fell asleep a short while later.

The old woman looked so vulnerable that Elizabeth's heart swelled with compassion. It was terrible to lose one's eyesight but worse to lose one's independence. Never again would Elizabeth or the children rely on another human being for their welfare.

She turned her attention to the boiling stew. After waiting ten minutes for the vegetables to cook, she threw in several heaping spoonfuls of lard and watched the grease melt and swirl on top of the broth. She wasn't sure what to do with the flour. Did she need a little or a lot? Should she just pour it in? She considered waking

Granny but decided against it.

Elizabeth lifted the flour tin over the boiling kettle and dumped half its contents into the water. Too late, she saw the words baking soda. The mixture bubbled, rose, crested, and then overflowed onto the stove's surface where it spit and sputtered.

As Elizabeth eyed the blackening mess, one redeeming thought kept her from total panic; at least she'd mixed plenty of dough for the mouth-watering biscuits.

She heard the creak of the rocker, and from the corner of her eye she spotted Granny leaving the room. The stench of burnt stew wrinkled Elizabeth's nostrils. She forced a long breath into her lungs as she leaned against the kitchen counter and glanced out the window at the snow-capped Rocky Mountains in the distance.

She prayed Ben Ricker would allow her to stay long enough to save some money. She intended to travel to California, where she'd find a job as a seamstress and support her brother and sister. Unlike her mother, Elizabeth would never rely on a man to care for her or the children.

She'd learned a valuable lesson from her mother's two dismal marriages: first, Elizabeth's father, a dreamer unable to accept reality even when it meant starvation for his family, and then, after his death, Robert T. Hines, who'd seemed to be the answer to all their problems. But Mr. Hines's true nature soon surfaced, causing Cecelia to quake in her shoes at the tone of his booming voice.

Elizabeth never intended to marry.

Not only would she be self-supporting, but also unlike her mother, Elizabeth's pride would never permit her to bow down to the demands of any man.

Elizabeth breathed a sigh of relief. They'd escaped from Boston and their domineering stepfather.

A shiver sluiced down her spine.

To Elizabeth, even the 2,400 miles that separated them was not distance enough. By now, he'd discovered the empty safe behind the leather-bound tomes on the third shelf of his bookcase. By now, he'd be fighting mad. By now, his men would be scouring the countryside for her and the children.

Elizabeth frowned.

Would she ever truly be free of Robert T. Hines?

CHAPTER 4

The smell was nothing compared to the sight that greeted Ben when he entered the kitchen. A thick black crust coated the top of the stove. Gray smoke poured from the opened oven door. Sister Elizabeth's black shoes crunched as she bent to retrieve what looked like blackened pellets on a baking sheet.

When Elizabeth swung around and spotted him, she was taken by surprise and heedlessly flipped the biscuit tray upward. Several hot, charred discs slipped from the baking sheet and hurtled toward Ben. He ducked, but not soon enough. One pelted his right cheek like a hot poker. He reached up and rubbed the sensitive spot to the right of his nose with his finger.

He met her wide, blue eyes.

"Don't you know better than to sneak up on a woman when she has hot biscuits in her hands?"

He rubbed his face. "I do now."

She looked as if she'd waged war with a bag of flour and lost. Her eyebrows were barely visible beneath a powdered mask. The perspiration on her upper lip formed a batter of its own. Her hands were caked and several fingers were stuck together. He couldn't detect fingernails, and it was impossible to know where her wrist ended and her sleeve began.

There were no tears on Sister's white face. Quite the opposite. What galled Ben was the way she looked him straight in the eye and dared to beam an innocent smile.

"I've had a slight setback," she announced in a voice ringing with sincerity.

He should fire her, Ben thought, but he couldn't. His conscience had been giving him a devil of a time all afternoon since he'd seen what he had no business seeing. It was one thing to peek at a naked woman without her knowledge, quite another to stare at a naked nun.

He'd looked, all right. He'd memorized the mole above her right breast and the dimple over her navel. Unlike Granny, there was nothing wrong with his eyesight, and he'd capitalized on his keen vision. After he'd batted the matter around a while, he smelled no better than this grimy kitchen.

The truth was he was guilty.

He studied the stove before turning back to her. "You call this a small setback?"

She waved her hand matter-of-factly. "This looks worse than it really is."

"You can't cook, can you, Sister?" he asked, since the proof was right before him.

She laughed nervously. "Mr. Ricker, I can see how you'd jump to that conclusion. I've always cooked on a gas stove. I had a little trouble adjusting to wood, but take my word, I've ironed out the kinks, and tomorrow, you'll have your stew."

He noticed how the hazel flecks in her eyes twinkled in the lamplight. The flour outlining her full upper lip pulled his gaze downward, and he watched her tongue dart nervously from one side to another.

"Tell me, Sister, are you hiding any other secrets I should know about under all that flour?"

Sister Elizabeth reached up and swiped a hand over her forehead, leaving behind crusty fingerprints. "Mr. Ricker, I'd tell you all my secrets, but I think you've been through enough for one day."

He joined in when she started to laugh but couldn't figure out how he could feel so happy while on the verge of certain starvation.

His mood swung dramatically when Josh's high-pitched voice resonated from upstairs. "Come quick, Bernie's having her babies!"

"What's going on now?" Ben asked, noting the guilt on Sister Elizabeth's face.

She spun around and ran from the kitchen, through the living room, and up the stairs to the second story with Ben at her heels. Wide-eyed, hand over her mouth, Cecelia stared into Granny's room. Clyde ran in circles in the hallway while Josh jumped up and down, flapping his arms in excitement. "Bernie's having puppies! Can we keep them?"

Elizabeth threaded her fingers through Josh's hair. "We'll decide later."

Ben followed Elizabeth into Granny's room, anger knotting his jaw. Every man had his limits, and he'd reached his some time back. Once everything settled down, he'd send the good Sister packing. He saw the hound with its distended belly, lying on its side in front of Granny. "What in the hell is this?"

Elizabeth knelt on the floor and turned to Granny. "How is she?"

"She's fine. What's her name?"

The children stampeded into the room and skidded into one another. "That's Bernie," Josh said, his face flushed.

Clyde grunted and clapped.

"Short for Bernadette," Cecelia added in a low voice.

Granny shook her head in bewilderment.

Wanting to spare Granny the confusion and noise, Ben dropped onto his haunches and clutched his fingers around her arm. "Here, let me do that."

Granny yanked her arm away. Her shoulders stiffened. "I ain't gonna be mollycoddled anymore. For months, everyone's tiptoed 'round here waitin' for me to croak. If someone wants to ask me a question, they ask you instead of me. 'How does Granny like her tea? Would Granny like to go to town?' I may be going blind, but I ain't feeble-minded."

She pushed her forefinger into his chest. "Now get so I can help this poor varmint have her pups."

He strode across the room and leaned against the door casing. The doctor had warned him to reduce the stress in Granny's life. Thanks to the Sister and her tribe of orphans, that was no longer possible. Silently, he cursed Sister Elizabeth's foolish shenanigans.

Sister Elizabeth gazed at him innocently. She'd lied to him one too many times. As their eyes met, he scowled. Worry streaked across her face.

Granny stood, hurried to the bureau, and grabbed her sewing basket. The constant fatigue that had plagued her for months seemed to vanish. Wanting to help and afraid she would trip, Ben started toward her, but her warning look stopped him.

Granny continued across the room, knelt, and felt for the dog's hindquarters. "You're doing good. Don't you fret none, I'll be right here in case you need me."

The dog licked Granny's hand. "I used to be the best," she said, in a soothing voice, speaking to the dog. "With your help, I'm gonna prove I still am, even with my eyes going bad."

When Bernie groaned, Granny ran a comforting hand over the dog's belly and cooed softly, "Don't worry, old girl, I'm here."

Spellbound, Josh dropped to his knees and peered at the dog's backside. Clyde followed suit. Cecelia stood like a statue with her fingers in her mouth.

A wet pup slipped out between the hound's hindquarters. The dog nuzzled the small furred creature and licked the sack from the tiny animal.

"Yuck," Josh shouted, sticking out his tongue.

To quiet the boy, Sister Elizabeth nudged him with her elbow.

The next puppy came quickly, but it lay limp even after being prodded by the hound's snout. Granny snatched the tiny creature from the damp blanket and rubbed her warm hands over its small body.

The puppy didn't stir.

Ben's chest felt as though it were caught in a vise. Unknowingly, his hands fisted. Damn the woman who'd brought this trouble into his house. If this puppy died, Granny would bear the pain.

And she'd already suffered too much.

Granny wrapped soft cotton from her sewing kit around her little finger and wiped the puppy's mouth. She brought the animal up to her ear and listened.

The troubled look in her eyes wrenched Ben's heart as she lifted the puppy to her mouth and blew air into its lungs. When the tiny creature yelped weakly, Ben's heart almost exploded with relief.

Hugging the animal to her chest, Granny blinked away tears of joy. "I did it," she said, sounding more alive than she had in months.

Ben relished Granny's contented expression until Josh shouted, "Yippee, now we gots three dogs!"

Confusion clouded Granny's face. "What are all these young'uns doing in my house?"

Sister squeezed Granny hand. "God's entrusted these children to my care. I'm hoping you'll allow us to stay a while."

Granny rubbed the dog's ear. "I ain't the one who makes decisions 'round here anymore. I don't think I'd remember how."

Ben tapped his booted foot on the pine boards. "Granny, I assure you the children won't be here long. If you find you can't nap, let me know, and there'll be hell to pay."

Granny frowned. "All I do is nap."

Ben turned to Sister Elizabeth. "You've stretched my generosity to its limit. First, you trick me into letting you bring orphans into my house, now a dog and puppies. Look at this room, children and animals everywhere. How's Granny ever going to rest?"

"They're good children," Sister Elizabeth replied, talking directly to Granny. "I'll see they don't bother you."

Before Granny could answer, Ben intervened. "See that they don't. Where do you expect to keep the dogs?"

Sister Elizabeth stood and planted her hands on her hips. "In my room, of course."

"Like hell you are."

"Mr. Ricker, you promised."

"That was before I knew all the facts." Ben pointed at the hound and her litter. "Those animals are staying in the barn tonight."

Cecelia stepped forward. "You can't do that. Bernie hates being alone. She'll have nightmares."

"Bernie has her puppies to keep her company," Ben reasoned, noting how both Granny and Sister Elizabeth stared at him as if he'd sprouted two horns.

Granny rose, her chin inching upward. "Didn't you hear the child? Bernadette hates being alone. The rest of you can hightail it right out of here. But while there's breath in my body, this dog and her puppies stay right here."

For someone no longer able to make decisions, Ben noticed Granny was catching on fast. He recognized a losing battle when he saw one.

Later, Ben was on his way across the front yard when he spotted Lefty, who whipped his Stetson from his head and slapped the dust from his hat against his thigh.

He rubbed his hands together. "I can hardly wait to eat some of that stew."

Lefty was one of the few hands who'd

stayed behind when things had gotten rough. Ben owed him big, but each time he mentioned it, Lefty would wave away his concerns and remind Ben that he had given him a chance when no one else had. A man could have no better friend than Lefty. Trampled by a stallion years earlier, his right arm had limited mobility. Because of a sharp mind and natural ingenuity, Lefty did pretty near anything with one arm that other men did with two.

Ben tapped his friend on the back. "Don't go in there. It'll give you nightmares."

"Are you telling me there's no stew?"

"I'm afraid so. Worse than that, Sister Elizabeth's baked some buckshot that would drop a grizzly from a hundred yards if you fired it from a gun."

"You're kidding, right?"

Ben rubbed his face. "Take my word for it."

"What'll we do now?"

"Throw ourselves on Zack's mercy, what else?"

Lefty rolled his eyes skyward. "Not beans again."

Without answering, Ben strode toward the bunkhouse where Zack would be preparing his evening meal. Zachariah was a cantankerous old man, a creature of habit with a heart of pure gold. Every day at five o'clock, he'd head to the stream and remove the waterproof tin he kept under the icy water. He'd carry the tin back to the bunkhouse and scoop out a generous serving of baked beans and salt pork. On good days, he ate with his plate on his lap while sitting on the rock wall that bordered the property. On cold or stormy days, he ate inside on a stool by the window.

Ben yanked open the door of the bunk-house. Lefty followed him inside.

Zack eyed them suspiciously. "Well, well, what brings you two mangy varmints here at mealtime?"

Ben sat on the edge of a bunk. "Lefty and I were thinking you might like some company for supper."

He pointed a leathery finger at Ben's nose. "More than likely, you two no-goods are here to eat. How's an old guy like me supposed to save any money when I have to spend my hard-earned cash keeping your empty bellies filled? What happened to that beef stew you two were jawing about earlier?"

Ben heaved a deep sigh. "It isn't a pretty story." He paused before continuing, "I think I made a big mistake when I hired Sister Elizabeth."

Zack leveled Ben a stern look. "I told you as much this afternoon. I even offered to take her and the kids back to town. But did you listen to me? Noooo! Of course, that's not anything new. No one around here ever listens to poor old Zack. All nuns know is praying, nothing else. As I see it, unless she whips around her rosary beads like a magic wand, you ain't likely to eat nothing but my beans until she leaves." Zack uttered a raspy chuckle. "Your grandpa must be rolling over in his grave right now." He waved his hand toward his tin. "Go ahead, help yourselves. I can use the company."

Ten minutes later Zack sat on the rock wall beside Ben and Lefty. He pushed a wad of beans onto his fork with his knife and took a bite. "Taste damn fine, if I do say so myself."

"I'll say this," Ben said around a mouthful, "you make the best beans. Unfortunately, I had my heart set on beef stew."

Zack shrugged, took another bite and pointed his fork at Ben. "I spent the last few hours repairing the fences in the north pasture."

"We just strung new barbed wire there last week."

"Doesn't matter how old the wire is when

someone hacks it through in a half dozen places."

"That confirms our suspicions. Someone's messing around."

Lefty frowned. "I try to keep a watchful eye, but I can't be in more than one place at once."

Zack shifted his behind against the hard rock wall. "What we need is armed men scouting the perimeters of this property."

Lefty nodded his agreement. "But men take money, and there's little enough of that to go around."

Masking his concern, Ben smiled calmly at his two companions. "Don't worry about a thing. I'm going to Butte in a few days. I hope to persuade the Federal Bank to give me another loan."

Lefty took a swallow of black coffee. "You think you'll get it?"

"I hope so. We Rickers have always made good on our debts. All I need is time to get back on my feet." Ben didn't let on that he expected to be turned down. At least, that was what had happened the last time. He remembered his granddaddy's words of wisdom. When a bird craps in one eye, look down before it craps in your other eye, too.

As a little kid, he'd laughed at the expression, not understanding what it meant. But now, he knew the meaning too well. The last time Ben had asked the Federal for a loan, it had taken less than one minute for Ward Metcalf to answer with an emphatic No.

Against his better judgment but having no other choice, Ben had decided to give the banker one last try, although he expected to be crapped on again.

Shortly before dawn, a stocky figure studied the longhorns grazing peacefully. He pulled the dynamite from his saddlebags. As the rising sun brought a blush to the dawn sky, he touched the lit end of his cheroot to the fuse, hurled the explosives several feet from the steer and waited for the blast. The quaking ground beneath his stallion's hooves heralded a job well done.

CHAPTER 5

Elizabeth heard the low rumble of thunder, yet when she looked out the kitchen window, she saw a clear, rosy sky. Before she could investigate, Ben Ricker tore through the kitchen with his boots tucked under his arm, buttoning his pants. An instant later he disappeared out the door. Whatever was wrong had given her a much-needed reprieve.

As she scrubbed the gooey oatmeal from her hands, her stepfather's words haunted her. *Elizabeth, you're worthless.* Though Robert T. Hines's degrading comments rarely dented her upbeat disposition, Elizabeth's miserable attempts at cooking had left her feeling down. Everything she'd made so far had erupted over the sides of the pot. First the stew, and this morning she'd left the kitchen to fetch a bucket of water. When she returned, the last of the oatmeal was flowing over the rim like lava from a volcano. Submerging her hands in a bucket of water, she freed her fingers of the sticky mess before cleaning the stove again.

A few minutes later, Cecelia's alarmed cry sent Elizabeth running to the bedroom, where she found Clyde tearing the room apart.

"No," Elizabeth said in a commanding voice that had no effect on the child. She grabbed his arm to prevent him from emptying another box of their possessions. Clyde struggled to free himself from her grasp.

"What's wrong, honey?" Elizabeth asked, forcing him to look at her.

He grunted, his terror-filled eyes brimming with tears. Elizabeth released her hold and watched him scramble across the room where he rolled up in a tight ball and whimpered.

Realizing this was the first time she'd seen Clyde without his toy, she threw her brother a stern look. "Did you hide Clyde's stocking doll?"

Joshua shook his head. "How come you always blame me?"

As Elizabeth glanced around the room, she saw guilt on Cecelia's face.

"Do you know where Clyde's toy is?" she asked her sister.

With thumb in mouth and head bent, Cecelia managed to mumble, "That old thing stunk."

"PeeUuuuu," Joshua interrupted, wrinkling his nose. "It smelled like poop."

Elizabeth leveled him a stern look. "What have I told you about saying bad words?"

"But you said to tell the truth, and it did smell like . . ."

"Joshua Hines, you say that disgusting word again, and you'll be tasting soap." Allowing a few seconds for her words to penetrate, she hugged Cecelia. "You're a big help, Pumpkin. Where is Clyde's toy now?"

"After he fell asleep, I washed it and hung it out back to dry."

Elizabeth patted Cecelia's arm. "Don't be upset, Pumpkin, you didn't do anything wrong." Smiling, she pulled Clyde to his feet and gathered him against her chest. "Shhhh, don't cry, honey."

They found the crude doll hanging from the clothesline behind the house. Clyde grabbed the toy. As he hid it beneath his shirt, Elizabeth felt the muscles in the tiny body relax.

"If only we understood each other," she whispered, then set him down and watched him scurry back into the house. Somehow, she'd find a way to help the boy.

Later that day, while Elizabeth diced vegetables, Cecelia kneaded the biscuit dough.

"It's hotter than hel . . . you-know-where in here," Elizabeth said, slipping a finger under her chin to loosen her white wimple.

"You could change out of those clothes for a while. Mr. Ricker isn't around."

"It's tempting. But if he comes back and catches me wearing anything but black, we'll find ourselves thrown out of here in a hurry." Elizabeth pondered Cecelia's woebegone expression. "Stop what you're doing this instant. It's time we had some fun. Get your brother and Clyde and meet me back here in five minutes."

Cecelia rushed to their bedroom. Elizabeth covered the bowls of cut vegetables and dough with clean towels, then headed to Granny's room, where she hesitated a moment before knocking and looking inside.

"What do you want?" Granny asked, her face pinched in anger.

Elizabeth stepped into the bedroom. "I wanted to thank you for your help this morning."

Granny waved away the comment. "Weren't nothin'."

"If you hadn't shown me how to build a

68

slow fire in the stove, I'd be ruining supper again for sure."

"That it?" Granny asked, dismissing her.

"I was wondering if you had a pair of scissors and some thread I could borrow."

"What you be needin' them for?"

"I want to make Clyde a new shirt."

"My sewing basket on the dresser should have whatever you need. Be sure to bring it back when you're done, you hear?" Granny pointed a bony finger at Elizabeth. "And don't you be wastin'. I ain't made of money, you know."

Elizabeth glanced at Granny hunched forward in her chair. How difficult it must be to know you're losing your eyesight. Before Elizabeth knew what she was doing, she walked across the room. "The children and I are going to the stream. I thought you might like to come along."

"What for?"

"It's too nice a day to stay inside."

Granny pursed her lips. "No matter what Ben told you, I can take care of myself. You needn't be watching me every minute." She set her chin at a stubborn angle and stared straight ahead, then reached over the side of the rocking chair and stroked Bernie's back.

"I was hoping you could help me."

Granny's eyes narrowed. "You pullin' my leg?"

"I have three children to take to the stream for baths and maybe a bit of fun. I'm sure you know what a job that can be. I could use some assistance. I'd be grateful, if you'd come along."

For a moment Granny peered at Elizabeth without saying a word. "Well . . . maybe I can give you a hand. This time — but don't go makin' a habit of this." Her crotchety voice hinted of displeasure, but her faint smile told the real story.

Some time later Granny stepped off the porch, tucked a shotgun under her arm, and tripped over a branch. Elizabeth grabbed her elbow.

Granny yanked her arm away. "I can walk!"

Josh snatched the branch from the ground, tucked it between his legs, shouted "Giddy up," and galloped off.

Clyde grunted and ran after Josh. Cecelia stayed by Elizabeth's side.

Granny dug a corncob pipe from the pocket of her overalls. "Do you smoke?"

"No, I don't."

"You don't know what you're missin'." Granny lit her pipe and puffed several times.

"Why does my grandson call you Sister?"

"I'm a nun," she replied, feeling uneasy.

"You're here alone?"

"Yes."

"That's strange. I didn't think nuns went anywhere alone. How is it you come clear 'cross country by yourself?"

"I was given a special dispensation."

Granny shook her head. "Back in Butte, a nun ain't allowed to cross the street without another Sister by her side, and you're tellin' me you came clear from Boston. Don't rightly make sense. If it's all the same, I'll call you Lizabeth."

Before Elizabeth could reply, Josh raced toward them and slowed his imaginary horse to a canter. "Whoaaaa." He stopped and eyed Granny. "Women don't smoke pipes," he said with the conviction of a six-year-old.

"Looks like you're wrong, now don't it?"

Joshua shrugged.

"Do you know what kind of pipe this is, young man?"

"No, ma'am."

"It's made from a corncob. Tobacco always tastes better in a corncob pipe."

"Can I touch it?"

Granny lowered the pipe.

He ran his fingers along the outside and

sniffed. "Smell's really good."

"That's why I brung it along. I like the smell, but the dern pesky black flies don't. This'll help keep 'em away."

"Can I puff on it?"

"When you're older, you can."

"Why'd you bring a gun?"

"In case a grizzly happens along." Granny turned to Elizabeth. "Since my eyes started going bad, I keep my shotgun by the dresser in my bedroom. I feel safer having it close."

Josh interrupted. "A real bear! Montana has real bears with fur and really sharp teeth?"

" 'Fraid so."

"Boy, I'd really like to see one." Josh's eyes widened. "We gots no bears in Boston, isn't that right, Betts?"

Elizabeth cringed inwardly. "That's right."

Granny puffed on her pipe. "The lad's a mite confused too. Seems he thinks of you as Betts."

Elizabeth shooed Josh away, lowered her voice, and changing the subject, asked, "How large are the bears around here?"

"Ben killed a grizzly last winter that weighed near nine hundred pounds. But you needn't worry. Grizzlies usually stay away. Just make sure you don't leave any food outside. Always burn uneaten meat scraps in the barrel out back. Most critters have powerful noses."

Nine hundred pounds. Elizabeth's heart thumped. "I'll remember that, count on it."

When they reached the stream, Granny edged close to the bank, removed her shoes, rolled up her pant legs, and wiggled her toes in the frigid water. "I've always loved it here," she said, a haunting smile lifting the corners of her mouth.

Setting the sewing basket on a nearby rock, Elizabeth grabbed hold of Clyde's shoulder when he scampered by. "Bath time." She noted Clyde didn't flinch at the tone of her voice. "Bath time," she repeated when he glanced up at her, pointing to the bar of soap and towel she'd brought along.

Within seconds, Josh stripped to his underwear, charged toward the chilly water and dove in, splashing everyone on shore.

Granny shook the water from her overalls. "You little whippersnapper, when I get hold of you, you'll be sorry."

Josh laughed and slapped his palm in the water, sending a heavy spray over Granny.

At a speed that belied her age, Granny scrambled off the rocks, landed beside Josh and dunked him head first into the icy stream. He resurfaced, looking dumbstruck.

Granny gripped his shoulder. "If you've a

mind to splash me again, let me know now so I can give you another dunking. Are you gonna behave yourself, boy?"

Shivering, Josh nodded. "Yes, ma'am."

"Figured as much." Wet from the knees down, she climbed out of the water and sat on a boulder. She turned her back to Josh and chuckled.

Elizabeth unbuttoned Clyde's shirt. He grunted helplessly when she tried to persuade him to put down his toy. Without warning, Clyde undid the buttons on his pants and stripped naked before jumping like a madman next to Josh, who hooted with delight. "Josh," she hollered over the roar of voices. "Lather up and see to it that Clyde does, too."

After Elizabeth cajoled Clyde to put his pants back on, she talked Cecelia into going in the water with her chemise. Soon, all three children were clean.

While they played, Elizabeth tore open the seams of her red silk skirt she'd brought along. It wasn't the most practical material for a boy's shirt, but it would have to do.

Worn clear through, no amount of mending could save Clyde's old shirt. With nimble fingers she stitched the fabric, and as she watched the material take shape, Elizabeth felt a deep sense of pride.

With a weary sigh, Ben wiped the sweat from his brow before dipping the Stetson low on his forehead. "How many longhorns you figure we lost, Lefty?"

"Zack counted thirty. I found twenty or so."

Ben gave a discouraged sigh. "Another fifteen trampled themselves to death at Narrows Ridge."

"What do you think set them off?"

"Someone spooked the herd. I saw fresh hoof prints, along with a cigar butt and matches. I have no way of knowing who was there."

"You want me to ride out and get the sheriff?" Lefty asked.

"No hurry. What's he going to do?"

Lefty gave a tired smile. "He'll scratch his big belly and drawl, 'I need evi-daaance. I can't go running round half cocked on account of wild suspicions. I need proof, boys, or I can't do a gol-darn thing.' "

"I'd end up in jail for kicking his sorry ass off my property." Ben stopped mid-stride. "Smell that?"

Lefty dismounted. "No, I can't smell a thing."

Ben smiled confidently. "It's a good sign. Sister hasn't burnt supper yet. Maybe you and I will be eating something besides beans tonight."

"I hope so."

Ben clenched his jaw. "We better, or the good Sister packs her bags."

Some time later, Ben and Lefty sat at the table. Ben looked around in astonishment. Wild flowers in a glass pitcher decorated the table, which was covered with a lacy cloth he didn't recognize. Folded next to each plate were linen napkins, all prim and proper, adding to his aggravation. What the hell for, he didn't have a clue. If the Sister thought he and his ranch hands were going to eat with napkins over their knees or tucked into the necks of their shirts, she had another think coming. Before long, she'd want them drinking tea from dainty cups with raised pinkie fingers. He threw his napkin across the room, where it landed on three corners like an Indian teepee.

"Never seen so many forks and spoons in my lifetime," Lefty said, mirroring Ben's thoughts. "Sister Elizabeth must know we're starving because she gave us enough utensils for both hands."

Ben frowned. "You're just looking at typical Boston waste. After supper, I'll remind

Sister Elizabeth she's now in Montana." He shook his head in disgust and swore under his breath. "That beef stew sure as hell better be terrific, or she goes."

Before Ben could cuss again, he was surprised to see Granny walking across the kitchen. She looked as though she'd gotten some sun. Her pale cheeks glowed a healthy pink.

"What have you been up to?" he asked, expecting the usual lengthy recitation of aches and pains.

"Went to the stream with Lizabeth and the young 'uns. I got that boy of hers real good, too."

He noticed the twinkle in her eye and felt warmth in his chest. "You didn't?"

"Bet your boots, I did. That little whippersnapper had it coming to him. Surprised him, too. You shoulda seen him." For the first time in weeks, Granny laughed.

The door swung open and the children paraded out single file. Joshua first, wearing a heavily starched shirt. It was a wonder he could bend his arms. Cecelia, trussed up in a fancy silk dress, crossed the room with the lady-like grace of a grown woman, not a nine-year-old. At first, he didn't recognize the boy holding onto Sister Elizabeth's hand. Hair trimmed and slicked back, wearing a red silk shirt, Clyde grunted and looked at Ben with a touch of pride in his dark pupils.

Ben glanced at his own dusty shirt and concluded the Sister looked worse than he did. Flour dusted her black habit; her white wimple was stained. A fire-red tendril curled across her forehead and reminded him of her wild mane cascading over her naked body. To drive away the insanity clouding his mind, he concentrated on the forks to his left. He gathered all the utensils on both sides of his plate, kept one fork, one spoon and one knife, and while making deliberate eye contact with Sister Elizabeth, dropped the unnecessary implements in the center of the table with a clang.

As if she didn't give a damn what he thought, she swung around and stirred the stew in the large kettle on the stove. Taking a worn towel from the cupboard, she opened the oven and removed biscuits that didn't have a fleck of black on them.

Ben's stomach galloped like a wild bronco. His mouth watered in anticipation. To his right, Lefty wrapped long fingers around the knife by his plate.

Not one to believe in miracles, Ben eyed the biscuits skeptically. They looked too good to be true, yet as Sister Elizabeth approached the table, their delectable smell filled the air. Biscuits clunked into the bowl on the table, nearly cracking the ceramic container. Ben knew the biscuits would be tough, but expecting they'd at least be edible, he took one, bit down and nearly broke a tooth. The crumbs held together like marble pellets. Across from him the children chewed patiently, except for Clyde, who spit out the baked granite. For the first time since he'd entered the kitchen, Ben regretted heaving his napkin across the room.

Next came the stew. What surprised Ben were the miniature dumplings in the thin gravy. He forgave Sister for the terrible biscuits. Dumplings were his favorite. When he bit into one, he choked on a lump of uncooked flour. He washed it down with coffee that tasted like dishwater. Next, he sampled the potatoes and carrots. Raw, everything undercooked. Too hungry to complain, he crunched his way through the meal.

Undaunted, Clyde tackled the stew with bare hands. Sister Elizabeth pulled his fingers from the dish, dried them with her fancy linen napkin, and insisted he use a spoon. Clyde threw the utensil to the floor and grabbed another carrot with his fingers.

After several failed attempts, Sister Elizabeth squeezed his shoulder. "That's enough for now, Clyde. We'll try again tomorrow."

Ben was impressed with her patience. While everyone around him attempted to eat the crisp vegetables, he mistakenly tried the beef, which resembled rawhide laces and tasted no better. No amount of chewing dented the tough meat. If he hadn't looked up and seen the rosy glow on Granny's face, he'd have fired Sister Elizabeth. But he couldn't fire the woman responsible for Granny's smile.

The biscuits were rock hard, the coffee bland, and the stew inedible. Nothing could make this meal any worse, Ben thought, until he glanced down and spotted the tiny spider floating in the bottom of his bowl.

CHAPTER 6

The next morning, Josh circled the table several times before tying his imaginary horse to the back of his chair.

Cecelia kept her eyes downcast and a thumb in her mouth. "What are we having for breakfast?"

"Don't tell. Let me guess." Josh clapped his hands with excitement.

Elizabeth nodded. "Sure, go ahead."

Josh smacked his lips. "Mmmm mmmm, bet we're having my favorite. Bacon and eggs. Right?"

After last night's fiasco, Elizabeth had decided to keep the meals simple. She wasn't ready for bacon and eggs yet. "No."

His eyes widened. "Pancakes?"

"No."

"We must be having pig slop again."

"Where'd you hear such a thing?"

"Granny Ricker was talking to Bernie last night after supper. She said that was what you cooked. Pig slop," he repeated with a wild grin.

Elizabeth tapped her shoe against the kitchen floor. "My cooking isn't any such thing. You say that again, and I'll blister your bottom."

Josh folded his small arms over his chest. "What are we having?"

"Oatmeal and leftover biscuits."

He stuck out his tongue. "Yuck, not those hard things."

"I've soaked the biscuits in milk and added a little sugar. They're not bad."

"I don't want no yucky biscuits." He scrunched his face.

"Joshua Hines, sit down and be quiet."

Grudgingly, he climbed onto the chair but grumbled, "I ain't eating no yucky biscuits."

"I know for a fact cowboys eat biscuits and milk for breakfast."

A spark of interest flickered in his eyes.

Elizabeth glanced around the room. "Where's Clyde?"

"Still asleep," the children answered in unison.

When she went into the bedroom, she found the boy curled in a ball at the foot of her bed with his toy against his temple. Elizabeth studied the child's innocent expression. The boy was alone in the world with

82

no one to love him. Her heart tightened. What would become of him after she and the children left?

"Clyde," she whispered, not wanting to startle him. Then louder, "Clyde." When the child didn't stir, she suspected he might be deaf. To prove her theory, she clapped both hands above his head. Still, he slept. When she nudged his shoulder, he coiled into a tight ball and hugged his toy to his chest.

When she tilted his head and forced him to look at her, she felt a ray of hope. Maybe there was nothing wrong with the child's mind. She needed to figure out a way to communicate with him.

She patted her stomach and, making chewing motions, pointed to the kitchen.

Clyde leaped out of bed and scampered from the room. Without bothering to wash his hands and face, he climbed onto a chair and grabbed the bowl of biscuits and milk from Cecelia.

Elizabeth rushed across the kitchen and pushed the dish away. Once she had his attention, she wagged a finger in front of his face. "No."

Unbidden, he grunted his disapproval and dove into the bowl of milk and biscuits bare-handed.

"He can have mine," Cecelia said, reaching for another bowl.

"Clyde has to learn to follow rules."

Cecelia looked concerned. "He can't help it. He doesn't understand."

Elizabeth wrestled the biscuit from Clyde's hand. "I know that, sweetie, but he never will if we allow him to do whatever he wants."

Elizabeth waved her finger in Clyde's face. When he stopped grunting, she thought she was getting through to him until he lunged for the bowl and dumped its contents in her lap.

Elizabeth sprang to her feet, jumped back and slipped on the wet floor. As she fought to regain her balance, strong arms circled her waist, and she came face to face with Ben Ricker. The heat from his hands penetrated Elizabeth's habit. She stared helplessly at his warm amber eyes, his masculine jaw, and his nicely ridged upper lip.

Mr. Ricker steadied her, then dropped his hands to his sides and stepped away as though he couldn't wait to escape. Elizabeth's body still tingled where his fingers had lingered. Had Ben Ricker felt the same powerful jolt? Was his body humming as hers was? The smell of burnt oatmeal broke through the haze clouding her mind.

She spun around, lifted the lid on the pot and eyed the blackening mess. She heard Ben Ricker's warning before he slammed the door.

"Sister, you're trying my patience."

As Ben approached the bunkhouse, he heard the strains of "Oh My Darling, Clementine" coming from Zack's harmonica. Won in a card game two years back, the harmonica against Zachariah's lips could split eardrums. Unfortunately, or maybe for the best, Zack had mastered only one other song, "Little Brown Jug." Most mornings and every evening, sure as the sun rose and set, the harmonica found its way to the old man's mouth, where it remained until nightfall.

Some time later, Ben washed the last bite of beans down with a swig of strong brew. Whereas Sister Elizabeth's coffee was colorless and tasteless, Zack's was rich, dark, and could probably dissolve metal if given the chance. Ben rubbed a hand over his tired eyes and gazed at his old friend.

"You're a damn fool," Zack said.

"You may be right. I never expected to be eating beans for breakfast," Ben said.

"Nothing wrong with beans any time of day. They stick to your ribs and give you energy," Zack pointed out.

"I could use some of that."

"You can't continue busting your behind in a mine that hasn't produced a plugged nickel in years."

"You're right. Which is why if I get the loan, I've decided to buy the sawmill I told you about the other day."

"We're ranchers, not lumbermen," Zack said, disgust curling his lip.

"If I can sell some of the timber around here, I'll be able to get out of debt and increase our stock."

"It don't seem right." Zack spooned the leftover beans into the metal tin before sitting opposite Ben. "Sister's breakfast scare you off this morning?"

"I just don't know what to do about her."

Zack rubbed his whiskered chin. "Seems simple to me. The Sister can't cook. Tell her to leave."

Ignoring the comment, Ben heaved a quiet sigh. "You should have seen her with Clyde. No one has ever tried to teach that boy anything."

"Maybe if Sister Elizabeth quit wasting time on Clyde, she might figure out which end of a spoon is which and use it to rustle up some grub."

■ ■ ■ ■

Elizabeth was running out of chances. The next time Ben Ricker sat at her table, she needed something really special. She was willing to try to cook anything that wasn't beef stew. But she needed help from a real expert.

She saw Zack outside the bunkhouse and hurried to speak to him. "Granny mentioned you make the best baked beans around."

"That's a fact."

"Does Ben like your beans?"

He cast her an incredulous look. "He must. He even eats them for breakfast."

Elizabeth noticed a torn pocket and a missing button on Zack's shirt. "I'd like to make a deal with you, Zachariah."

"What kind of deal?"

"You show me how to cook your wonderful beans, and I'll sew you a new shirt."

He ran a leathery palm over his whiskered chin. "Sure could use a new shirt, but . . ." His gaze narrowed. "For all I know, you sew like you cook. I could end up with a shirt that's missing a sleeve."

"I may not be much of a cook, but there's nothing I can't sew."

■ ■ ■ ■

Ben couldn't hear the jangle of his spurs over the blood rushing in his ears when he strode into the Federal Bank in Butte, Montana. Everything that mattered to him was at stake. If he didn't persuade Ward Metcalf to grant him the loan, he could lose the Gold Nugget Ranch. The muscles along his shoulders and neck ached from the tension.

With wire-rimmed glasses perched low on his nose, Ward sat at his desk writing on a pad of paper. Ward was a fair man, Ben told himself for the hundredth time since leaving Welcome. From way back, the two men had hated each other, but this was business and business shouldn't conflict with personal feelings. Even as boys in Miss Riley's third grade class, they had tormented each other with names and hidden punches. Ben was taller and stronger, but Ward had beaten Ben academically.

As Ben crossed the room with a confident gait, Ward glanced up at him. His trim mustache twitched over a phony smile. He extended a manicured hand. "Good to see you, Ben." He waved for Ben to sit in the chair opposite the desk. "It'll take me just a minute to finish up here." He jotted several more notes and figures. After slipping the sheets of paper in a folder, he tucked the file in his desk drawer. Locking his fingers together, he turned his attention to Ben. "What can I do for you?"

Ben saw the gleam in Ward's eyes and knew his rival was enjoying this moment. He had rehearsed his speech on the ride over, but now words escaped him. He felt as if he were back in grade school and had just lost the spelling bee. "I need to borrow three thousand dollars."

Ward swiveled around in his chair and reached into the cabinet behind him where he withdrew a file. "Says here you already have a loan with an outstanding balance."

"I know I owe the bank a considerable sum, but we Rickers have always made good on our debts. Once I get back on my feet, I'll pay you back in full."

Ward's grin widened. "What will you do with the money?"

The vise around Ben's chest tightened. The barn and house needed repairs, and he couldn't manage his herd with a skeleton crew. "Jacob Farley from Anaconda is selling his sawmill for a fair price. Virginia City and Butte are growing communities. I've already drummed up orders from a few merchants."

"What do you know about sawmills?"

"I know it's a thriving business. I spent the better part of a week at Jacob's mill, learning how to operate the equipment. I'm convinced the sawmill will solve the Gold Nugget's financial problems." Ben could have said more, but he knew by the look on Ward's face that he should save his breath.

Ward drummed his pencil along the oak surface of his desk. "You and me go way back, Ben, but I can't let our friendship sway my decision."

Ben cleared his throat. "If the weather co-operates, I'll be able to pay you back with interest in a year."

The staccato tap of the pencil intensified. "We can't count on the weather, now can we? And I can't run a bank on maybes. If the money were mine, I'd say sure, but the people who make deposits count on my good judgment. You understand, don't you, Ben?"

Ben withdrew a piece of paper from his pocket. "I've written down the figures for my projected income over the next five years. With the additional money from the mill, I can't lose. The gang saw can cut a thousand feet of timber in ten hours. Depending on the grade, that amount of wood will fetch between forty and fifty dollars."

Ward pushed away from the desk and rested one booted foot over his knee. "I can't gamble with other people's money."

Ben's stomach twisted. He'd failed Granny. And himself.

"The bank can't issue you the loan." Ward paused and gave Ben the familiar, superior look he'd seen back in grade school. It took every bit of Ben's restraint not to walk out.

"Tell you what I'm going to do." Another dramatic pause ensued, followed by a wide flash of teeth below a twitching mustache. "I've made investments and turned a tidy profit. Because we go way back, I'll let you have the money you need."

Ben's natural distrust of the man grew.

Ward lowered his voice. "According to your figures, you stand to make a lot of money."

"So."

"It's my money making it happen. I should benefit, too. I'll make out the paperwork right now. You can have the three thousand dollars if you pay the full amount plus an additional five hundred dollars within three months. Otherwise, you sign your ranch over to me."

"That's insane."

"Take it or leave it."

"The paper I handed you shows I need at least six months to turn a profit."

"Looks like you'll have to move a bit faster."

"If my ranch is worth so much, why can't I get a regular loan from the bank?"

Ward heaved a long sigh. "According to the bank records, you haven't made a payment on your existing loan in some time. I know you've had some bad breaks. I'm doing this out of friendship. If you don't pay me back, it'll pain me to take your ranch."

Ben figured his options. None. He hesitated a few seconds before agreeing.

Ben was on his way out of the bank when he noticed the *Wanted* posters tacked to the bulletin board. One of an attractive woman caught his eye. Long hair swept up and dressed in a white frilly blouse, the woman looked out of place next to the bearded outlaws.

A five-hundred-dollar reward was being offered for information leading to the capture of Elizabeth O'Hara, a thief, who had kidnapped two children. Ben studied the photograph. Tendrils of hair curled around the woman's delicate face. He felt drawn to her eyes.

It took him a moment to realize the woman in the picture was Sister Elizabeth.

CHAPTER 7

Sitting astride his horse and peering through binoculars, he stayed downwind so the animal wouldn't detect his scent. When the grizzly left, he seized her frightened cub, dug in his heels and steered his horse toward Ben Ricker's ranch.

Searching for her sister, Elizabeth was about to knock on Granny's door when she heard voices inside the room.

"Speak up, I can't read your mind, and I sure don't understand one word you're sayin'."

"Bernie . . ." Cecelia mumbled, her sad tone tearing at Elizabeth's heart.

"Humph, what about Bernie?"

Elizabeth was ready to rescue her sister when Granny murmured, "Child, I won't hurt you."

Cecelia whispered, "I came to see Bernie. I miss her. But Betts . . . er, Sister Elizabeth said I was to leave you alone so Ben wouldn't send us away."

Elizabeth wasn't the sort of woman to eavesdrop, but she wouldn't leave until she was certain Cecelia was all right.

"It ain't like I'm so old I need to nap. Besides, it's only fair you come to visit your dog."

"Mean it?"

" 'Course I mean it. I said so, didn't I? What are you waitin' for? Stop standin' there stiff as a fence post and get down on your hands and knees."

Cecelia mumbled something Elizabeth didn't understand. She assumed her sister was speaking with her fingers wedged in her mouth.

"Seeing we're gonna be spending time together, you might as well tell me your name."

"Cecelia." She paused. "Can I touch the puppies?"

"I ain't never seen a more timid child," Granny said softly. "Go ahead, that's what you're here for. Would you like to hold the pups?"

"I mustn't soil my dress. Papa says little ladies shouldn't look like ragamuffins."

"When my Ben was a boy, he had enough dirt behind his ears to plant the spring crop.

And when I was your age, I wasn't much better. You're too goldarn young to be worried 'bout messing up a dress. Why don't you put on your britches?"

Cecelia mumbled again.

"Gotta take those fingers out of your mouth and speak up. Otherwise, you're gonna have me thinkin' I'm goin' deaf. You wouldn't want to cause me any more grief, would you?"

"No, ma'am."

"That's much better. You're too pretty to be hiding your face behind your hand."

"Yes, ma'am."

"Call me Granny."

"Granny, I don't have britches."

"What do you wear when you make mud pies?"

"I've never made mud pies."

"Land sakes, it's time you did. How old are you, anyway?"

"Nine," she replied clearly.

"When you speak up, you have a very pretty voice, Cecelia."

"I sing," she volunteered with a hint of pride.

"I think we can help each other. I got my *Harper's Bazaar* magazines by my chair. I used to enjoy looking at the pictures of the ladies all gussied up in silk and lace. I can't make 'em out anymore. I'd like you to tell me what you see."

Elizabeth heard the creak of a rocking chair.

"But the magazines are ten years old or older," Cecelia pointed out.

"So?"

"But the clothes aren't in fashion."

"Never mind that. They're still pretty. Tell me 'bout the dress on page sixteen."

Elizabeth heard the rustle of paper.

"Says here the dress comes in red or blue . . ." Cecelia stated.

"My dress is blue, its color rich as a late summer sky."

"With long sleeves . . ."

"And tiny pearl buttons at the wrists," Granny added.

"You know this by heart."

"Yes, but I want you to tell me 'bout the collar with ruffles and the gathers at the waist."

Zack finished the last notes of "Little Brown Jug" and slipped his harmonica in his pants pocket. "It's a fact. Good beans take time," he stated with authority.

Elizabeth pushed aside her growing panic. "Time's something I don't have."

"You can't hurry good beans."

Elizabeth protested, "Surely they don't need to soak all night."

"You can harness a swelling river in springtime easier than you can rush good beans."

"That may be true, but what am I going to do about supper?"

Zachariah's whiskered chin rose. "Ain't no concern of mine."

"But supper . . ." Her voice trailed off.

"You'd best listen up, or you won't have nothing for tomorrow night's supper either."

Elizabeth followed Zack to the well, where he filled a large earthenware pot with water that he strained through thin cotton.

He added the beans, unfolded the white material, and pointed to several tiny bugs. "You won't find any critters in my cooking. I suggest you use salt pork and leave out the ants and spiders."

Elizabeth bristled for an instant. She was sick of being the brunt of cruel jokes. But something about Zack's mischievous eyes settled her Irish temper before it had a chance to flare. Instead, she discovered she liked Zack. She broke out in an unladylike laugh, joined by the old man's raspy chuckle.

In a cloud of dust, Josh arrived. "Whooooaa." He yanked at imaginary reins.

"Mister, what's that in your pocket?"

"It's a mouth organ." Zack pulled the harmonica out for the boy to inspect.

"That's no organ. Organs have white keys and lots of pedals. They're big," he concluded.

"I'm an expert 'bout two things, beans and mouth organs."

Josh gazed at Elizabeth. When she nodded, he looked back at Zack. "Jeez, I never saw such a tiny organ. Can you play some music on it for me?"

"Sure can." Zachariah lifted the harmonica to his mouth.

After several renditions of "Oh My Darling, Clementine" and "Little Brown Jug," Zack tucked the musical instrument back in his pocket.

"Wow, that's great! Can I blow in it, huh?"

Elizabeth knew she'd been right to leave Boston when she saw the enthusiasm on her brother's face. She also noticed the mud ringing his mouth.

"Er, maybe some other time. Right now, I got work to do. The Sister and me are making beans."

"Beans, yuck." Josh wrinkled his nose.

Zack pointed at the child. "Won't have you talking that way about beans. Downright sinful, wouldn't you say, Sister?"

"You're absolutely right."

Elizabeth wondered what Zack was up to when he lifted the shovel from the nail outside the bunkhouse. Figuring her cooking class was done, she'd started for the house when she heard Zack call out.

"Sister, you giving up already?"

The very words stirred her blood. Ready for battle, she turned. "I never give up. I assumed we were through."

"We've only just begun." Zack push the tip of the shovel into the ground.

A short while later, Josh galloped over and leaped into the growing mound of dirt.

Zack looked aggravated, but instead of yelling at Josh, he tapped his shoulder. "I got a deal to make with you."

"What?"

"If you help me with this pit, I'll let you try my mouth organ later."

"Really?"

"Can you collect rocks for me?"

"What for?"

"Never you mind. You'll see soon enough." Josh scampered off.

Elizabeth found her thoughts wandering back to Boston with all its conveniences.

Zack cleared his throat. "The hole should be around thirty inches deep. Not twenty, not forty."

"Thirty inches," she repeated as if this all made sense.

"It's important you line the hole with rocks. They'll help retain the heat."

She was getting more confused with each passing minute. Rather than admit her ignorance, she pasted a knowing look on her face and dropped several more stones into the pit.

"That about does it for now," Zack said, clapping the dirt from his knees. "Tomorrow, after the beans have soaked twenty hours, we'll collect hard wood and get us a fire going. When we have a good bed of coals, we'll lower the bean pot into the hole and cover it with a few inches of dirt."

Elizabeth couldn't hide her amazement. "You mean we're cooking the beans in that hole?"

"Best beans on earth are cooked in the ground."

"Wouldn't it be easier to use the oven?"

"Might be easier, but not better."

Elizabeth's growing anxiety peaked. She'd taken another major step backwards in civilization. She hadn't yet mastered the iron monstrosity in the kitchen, yet she was going to cook beans in a dirt hole. "Surely you're joking."

"Never been more serious in my life."

"What if the fire goes out?"

"Then the beans will be hard as rocks."

Elizabeth's despair must have shown on her face because Zack reached for her hand.

"If you have a good bed of coals, the beans will be perrrrfect." He stressed the last word and squeezed her fingers. "These here beans will be the best you ever tasted. Don't you worry none. Trust me."

Elizabeth didn't trust men, but she saw the sincerity in Zack's eyes.

"Yes," she replied after a moment, almost daring to believe in the old man.

On her way back to the house, Elizabeth encountered a surprising sight. She stared disbelievingly at Granny sitting beside the well, stirring a large mud puddle with a long stick. Elizabeth had never seen a grown woman molding mud into shapes, but what astonished her most was her sister sitting in the dirt beside Granny.

Cecelia wore oversized overalls cut at the knees, with a length of rope around her waist. She was busy sculpting intricate shapes, her fingers coated with mud. "Look what I've made," Cecelia said, pointing to a wet mound in front of her.

"What is it?"

"It's a mud pie."

"Best mud pie I ever saw," Granny added with a dirt-smudged grin.

"Granny says she'd never know by looking at me that I've never done this before." Elizabeth's heart lightened as she kissed her sister's forehead. "Pumpkin, you're the best."

Later that day, Elizabeth was peeling vegetables in the kitchen when Cecelia entered. "Where's Granny?"

"She's using the privy."

Elizabeth glanced out the window. As Granny entered the outhouse, a brown dog scampered from the small wooden structure. At first glance, Elizabeth thought it was Bernie, but dismissed the notion because the creature was too plump. Who would trap an animal in an outhouse? She made a note to speak to Josh later. She looked away and inspected Cecelia's mud-streaked face. The child's smile radiated warmth and happiness.

In Boston, Elizabeth had deliberately disregarded Robert T. Hines's never-ending rules about lady-like behavior. But Cecelia had diligently obeyed and had suffered for her devotion to the cold-hearted man. "Go wash up, sweetie."

"What are you making for supper?" Cecelia asked in a clear voice.

"I don't know yet. I figured I'd throw myself on Granny's mercy and ask for her help."

"Good idea, Betts." Cecelia giggled, music to Elizabeth's ears.

Then Granny let out a blood-curdling scream.

CHAPTER 8

Several feet from the outhouse, a huge bear pushed itself onto its hind legs and swatted the air. Elizabeth's mind spun. Where were Josh and Clyde? She ran into the bedroom. Tears of relief stung her eyes when she saw the boys safely inside.

"Ssss . . . stay here," she shouted.

She wrenched the kitchen door open and watched the bear tear a board from the privy.

Granny peeked through the opening. "Get the shotgun outta my room."

Elizabeth tripped going up the stairs and hurried into Granny's bedroom. She wrapped trembling fingers around the gun barrel and flew down the stairs. On her way outside, she slammed her hand in the door. Pain shot up her arm.

Behind her, she heard Josh crying. "Betts, come back, I'm scared."

She turned around and saw Cecelia pulling him inside.

The bear ripped another board off the outhouse.

Granny hollered, "Lizabeth, shoot!"

Blood pulsed through Elizabeth's veins as she raised the shotgun and fired. The impact threw her to the ground.

The bear pierced her with rage-filled eyes. As Elizabeth scrambled to her feet, the animal bolted toward her. She stared into its feral eyes, its breath hot and putrid. With a deep growl, the bear rose to its full height; its mouth opened wide.

Terrified, Elizabeth slammed the shotgun against its chest. The bear whacked the weapon from her hands and knocked her down.

Ben rode atop his mare, growing angrier by the minute. Miss O'Hara was about to vacate his property.

If he had a lick of sense, he'd turn her in and collect the reward. Maybe he still would. Five hundred dollars was a lot of money. She was a thief. A kidnapper.

He pressed his horse forward. When the ranch came into view, he spotted a grizzly tearing apart the privy. From inside came Granny's terrified screams. Twenty feet away lay Elizabeth's lifeless body.

He grabbed his shotgun and sighted down the barrel. Fearing he might harm Granny, he fired a shot in the air. The grizzly dropped onto all fours and lumbered off with her cub.

Ben kneed his horse to a gallop. Granny ran from the outhouse toward Elizabeth as he slowed his mare and hit the ground running. The children dashed outside and grabbed him.

"Don't let Elizabeth die," Cecelia pleaded.

"I'll do my best. Stay here."

Josh tightened his arms around Ben's leg. "I love Betts. I want to go with you." Clyde looked frightened, and Cecelia whimpered.

Ben rested a hand on the boy's shoulder and nodded at Cecelia. "You kids have to be brave. Let go of me, Josh, so I can check Elizabeth and Granny. You hold onto Cecelia's hand and let me see what I can do."

Granny shouted, "Get over here, Ben! I need your help."

He ran the remaining few yards and dropped to his knees.

Granny pressed two fingers to the underside of Elizabeth's wrist. "She's still alive."

With great care, Ben pulled off the black veil and white cloth covering her head. She moaned softly.

His heart turned over with relief.

Granny grabbed his arm. "Will she be all right?"

"I don't know." Had a rib punctured her lung? Done irreparable damage? A grizzly could crush a grown man. Elizabeth didn't weigh more than a hundred pounds.

"Saved my life," Granny said, her voice shaking. "Ain't never seen nothin' so brave. I'm alive 'cause of her."

As Ben lifted Elizabeth into his arms, he saw a widening patch of blood ooze through the black fabric.

As he rushed into the house, Granny gathered the children to her side. "Get those chins off your chests. Won't do to have Lizabeth open her eyes and see long faces."

Ben dashed up the stairs, kicked his bedroom door open, and gently lowered Elizabeth onto his bed. Reaching behind her, he undid the tiny row of buttons down her back and leaned her against the pillow before slipping her dress off her shoulders. When he saw the deep gashes on her right upper arm and shoulder, his stomach clenched.

In the hall, he heard children's voices. The door opened, and Granny rushed toward the bed. "How's she doing?"

"I don't know. Did the bear hurt you, Gran?"

Granny dabbed her handkerchief at the corners of her eyes. "I'm all right, thanks to Lizabeth." She squinted up at him. "That grizzly attacked 'cause her cub was trapped in our privy."

"Are you sure?"

Doubt crept into her face. "I saw a brown blur."

Every muscle in Ben's body tensed. "Until I figure out what's going on, you and the children stay close to the house."

Granny ran gentle fingers along the side of Elizabeth's face. "She's gotta make it. Those children need her."

Ben wanted to take care of Elizabeth, to protect her and cherish her. The thought startled him.

"Lefty should be working the lower pasture. I'll send him after Doc Cartwright. I'll be back as soon as I can."

"Don't worry 'bout me. Tell Lefty to hurry. While you're gone, I'll clean up her wounds as best I can."

Ben kissed Granny's forehead before glancing down at Elizabeth's pale face. She was the prettiest woman he'd ever seen.

She was also a thief and a liar.

Disoriented, Elizabeth came to with a start.

"Don't fret, Lizabeth. Ben's gone for

help," Granny said.

Elizabeth's head throbbed. She inhaled a small gulp of air; pain knifed through her chest. When she squeezed her eyes shut, the nightmare returned. She saw the massive bear, felt its claws tearing, ripping. Fear paralyzed her. Would she be crushed to death? Who'd take care of Josh and Cecelia?

The door opened and footsteps sounded across the wooden floor. "How's she doing?" Ben asked.

"She's awake," Granny said.

Elizabeth glanced around the masculine bedroom. "Where am I?"

"This is my room. I thought you'd rest better in here," Ben said.

"The children . . ." she started to ask.

Ben placed gentle fingers on her hand. "They're worried. Are you up to seeing them?"

Elizabeth nodded. Pain knifed through her body.

Granny opened the door. Josh bounded into the room and would have leaped on the bed had Ben not caught him in mid-air. "Whoa, partner, you have to be careful."

"Betts, you were just like Davy Crockett, fighting a grizzly with your bare hands."

Elizabeth forced a weak smile. "From now on, I'll wear my coonskin cap."

"Can I get one, too?"

Elizabeth winced as another jab of pain shot through her.

Ben tugged at Josh's hand. "Let's go outside and watch for the doctor."

After Ben left, she noticed Cecelia looking forlorn and chewing her thumbnail. "Pumpkin, I'm all right."

Frightened eyes glanced up. "Honest?"

"Come here and see for yourself."

Tears streamed down Cecelia's face. "Please don't die."

"Lizabeth's a tough gal, like me," Granny added, smiling lovingly at Elizabeth.

A deep sense of belonging filled her.

Granny spoke again. "She's the only one I know who's danced with a grizzly and lived to tell 'bout it."

"Wouldn't that news cause a stir back in Boston." Cecelia managed a tremulous smile, then covered her face with trembling hands and sobbed.

Granny held Cecelia in her arms and patted her back. "Nothin' wrong with a good cry once in a while." Then, glancing at Elizabeth, she added, "I owe you my life. I'm gonna take good care of you. Count on it."

Warmth stirred deep inside Elizabeth's heart. It had been a long time since someone had looked out for her. Although every muscle ached from her head right down to her toes, she felt curiously happy. The strangest thought entered her mind.

Thank goodness she'd read the newspaper article that led her to Welcome, Montana.

Elizabeth wasn't sure how long she'd dozed, but she was aware of people talking in the room. When she opened her eyes, she saw Ben and Granny speaking to a man.

Granny rushed to her side. "We've been tellin' the Doc 'bout your adventure."

The doctor raised bushy eyebrows. "According to Granny, you're a heroine. According to that young lad downstairs, they should write a song about you."

He didn't resemble the doctors back home. His striped shirt was tucked into farmer pants splattered with dark spots. He looked more like someone ready to slaughter hogs than a full-fledged doctor. Not that Elizabeth ever had the displeasure of viewing such a dreadful sight.

He rubbed his pant leg. "Don't let the blood frighten you, ma'am."

What respectable doctor made house calls with someone's blood on his clothing? Did her concerns show on her face?

"I'm Doc Cartwright. At least, that's what my friends call me when I do house calls.

The rest of the time, they call me Pete."

The name rang a bell. He looked familiar.

"You're Pete, the bartender?" she asked, waiting for him to refute the ridiculous statement.

He smiled at her — the same friendly smile she'd seen at the Golden Harp Saloon. "I wondered when you'd notice."

CHAPTER 9

"How's your roof coming?" Ben asked Pete.

"Finally got her covered and tar papered. Good thing too, 'cause my rheumatism's been acting up lately. I expect torrential rain any day."

Pete was a man of many talents: bartender, doctor, and weather forecaster. Elizabeth bit her lower lip and managed to keep quiet.

As the doctor spoke to Granny, Elizabeth noticed his shoes, encrusted with what she assumed was manure. Several pieces of straw stuck out of his pants pocket. He was uncombed and unshaved. The distinct odor of alcohol reached her nose. Had Doc Cartwright spilled the liquor while serving his drunken friends, or had he imbibed?

Real doctors wore suits and starched white shirts. They carried small black bags, and most definitely did not have chicken dung on their shoes. Another horrid thought lodged in her mind, and she couldn't shake it loose. Was she Doc Cartwright's first and only patient?

Elizabeth was about to ask him that very question when Ben piped up, "How's Millie doing?"

"It was a difficult birth, but she and the twins are doing fine." Pete's confident tone set Elizabeth's mind at ease.

He turned and fastened his gaze on her as he withdrew a stethoscope from his pocket. She gave him credit for wiping the instrument with a clean white handkerchief. "A gal your age should know better than to arm wrestle a griz."

Elizabeth gritted her teeth against the onslaught of pain. "I'll not ask for a rematch, you can count on that."

Pete snorted with delight. "I like your spunk, Sister."

Ben frowned and left the room, slamming the door on his way out.

Granny helped her to sit, which hurt like the dickens, but Elizabeth didn't so much as moan. When she finally lay back against the pillow, she was drenched in sweat.

With a gentleness she hadn't expected, Doc examined her wounds. "That bear sure messed up your arm, but I doubt you broke any ribs. You should be good as new in a week or so. I'm going to have Granny make a poultice to draw out any infection. And you're in for a treat. I'm prescribing Granny's apple brandy for the pain."

Liquor would not pass her lips, but Elizabeth saw no point in discussing the issue.

Pete grinned down at her. "If you don't have any questions, I'll be on my way. I have a bar to tend."

"The twins you delivered, are they boys or girls?" Elizabeth asked.

"Girls, and a darn good thing, too. Millie's getting on in age, and the Browns sure didn't need another bull."

Before Elizabeth digested this information, Doc grabbed hold of Granny's arm and escorted her across the room. "I'll take my fee out in trade."

Granny swatted his arm. "You always were crazy 'bout my apple brandy."

"You got that right."

Elizabeth saw the look of anticipation on Pete's face as he went out the door. She'd seen men go crazy for liquor. If she had a say, she would not allow the children to be exposed to more drinking.

A few minutes later, Ben Ricker arrived carrying a glass of amber liquid. "I've got something that'll help you rest. Doc Cartwright wants you to take a few swallows now and a few more when you wake up."

All the fear, all the confusion that brewed inside Elizabeth burst free. "You think I'm blind? I know a real doctor when I see one. Pete's a bartender, for heaven's sakes. He came here with Millie's blood on his pants. Millie, a cow," she finished in a huff.

A cold look crossed Ben's face before he flashed his white teeth. "Let me assure you, Pete is a doctor. You've had quite the day, and I can't blame you for showing stress." He focused on a spot above Elizabeth's shoulder. "I'll forever be indebted to you for saving Granny."

When he finally glanced down, his grin seemed strained. "Let me help you take a sip of this."

"If it's alcohol, I'll not touch a drop."

"It's medicine so you'll rest," came his impatient reply.

"Pete said he was prescribing Granny's apple brandy. And I'll not imbibe liquor like a common drunk."

"I'm not asking you to go on a bender. Just take a few sips of brandy to numb your pain."

She pressed her lips shut.

He set the glass down with a loud clunk. "Suit yourself."

Until now, Elizabeth hadn't had a chance to consider how she was dressed. "Where's my wimple and veil?"

He turned away and inhaled a ragged breath. As the silence in the room stretched between them, Elizabeth's nerves tightened.

"I burned them with the other rubbish." Ben swung around. His cold eyes pierced through her. "The jig is up, Elizabeth O'Hara."

Three days later, Ben tiptoed into Elizabeth's bedroom and saw Granny sleeping in the rocker by the bed. "Granny," he whispered and bent to kiss her cheek.

Her eyelids fluttered open. "Lizabeth's no better."

When Ben rested his hand on Elizabeth's brow, the heat almost branded his palm. She moaned softly. The sound wrenched his insides as he studied her flushed face and her shallow breathing.

"We gotta do something, Ben."

"We're doing all we can."

Granny pushed herself up from the rocker and ran gentle fingers along Elizabeth's face. "Cecelia helped me put cold compresses on Lizabeth's forehead all day. Nothin's helped. She's burnin' up. I'm worried sick."

Ben pulled Granny against his side. "Me, too."

"If the fever doesn't break soon, we could lose her. What'll become of those poor children downstairs?"

Ben figured they'd go live with their father in Boston. But he didn't say a word.

"Did the doc come out today?"

"Yes, he said to try and keep her cool. Cecelia and me wore a path up them stairs, bringing ice cold water from the well. Nothin' made a lick of difference."

Ben hugged his grandmother. "You've had a long day. Go to bed."

"You're dead on your feet. Let me stay the night. You need your rest more than I do," Granny said, looking exhausted.

"I'll be fine. If Elizabeth wakes up, I'll come get you."

He walked his grandmother to the bedroom door and kissed her wrinkled cheek. "Goodnight, Gran."

"You take care of that girl, you hear?"

"I'll do my best."

"I'm countin' on you." Granny shut the door.

Ben yanked the chair closer to the bed, settled his lanky frame in the rocker and reached for Elizabeth's limp palm by her side.

"You're going to get better, I promise you that," he said, doubting his own words.

Could she hear his voice? She gave no indication, but he continued for his sake as much as hers. "I'm much obliged to you for saving Granny's life. It was a foolhardy thing to do, and I suspect it means you have more spunk than sense." He paused and cleared his throat. "About the other day when I called you Elizabeth O'Hara. I should have waited until you were back on your feet."

He examined her small, graceful fingers. He held on tight, willing her to draw strength from him. "If you can hear me, Elizabeth, I want you to know, you needn't worry about a place to stay. I don't care what you've done." That thought stopped him cold. She was a thief and a liar. His stomach knotted. He hated what she represented, but he owed her.

Ben Ricker always paid his debts.

He issued a frustrated sigh and examined her long hair flowing over the patchwork quilt. He crushed one silken strand between his fingers. As his eyelids grew heavy, thoughts of Elizabeth lulled him to sleep. He saw her again at the stream with droplets of water clinging to each curve, one nipple barely visible beneath the cloak of fiery red hair. The old guilt of spying on a nun haunted him until he remembered the truth.

His heart leaped with anticipation as he gave his subconscious free rein.

Ben jolted awake and heaved a disgusted sigh. As Elizabeth lay unconscious, he'd imagined her naked beneath him. He cursed his attraction to the red-haired beauty and reminded himself that she stood for everything he despised.

She moaned softly.

He jumped to his feet and leaned over her. She looked worse, her face red and blotchy, her breathing labored. Fever could kill.

She mumbled incoherently.

He brought his ear to her lips. "Talk to me, Elizabeth. You have to come out of this."

She didn't stir.

He slapped her hand. "Come on, Elizabeth, wake up and talk to me."

After a minute, he allowed her limp palm to slip from his grasp. He ran from the room and took the stairs two at a time, grabbed the bucket from the kitchen counter and flew out the door. He returned with icy well water that sloshed over the bedroom floor and splattered against his pants. Elizabeth would die if the fever didn't break. He wouldn't let that happen.

Elizabeth groaned weakly.

With only a moment's hesitation, he

pulled the blankets off the bed and fumbled with the tiny buttons at the neck of her nightgown. As he attempted to unfasten them, he swore liberally, finally yanking the material apart. He was about to place a cold wet cloth against her neck when he spotted a wedge of her chest crimson with fever. He ripped the nightgown down the middle, dunked a sheet into the icy water, and draped the sopping material over Elizabeth's burning flesh.

He wrapped wet towels around her head and face, leaving only her eyes and nose exposed. He tucked her fingers under the wet sheet and waited for signs of improvement.

Pacing back and forth, he crossed the room and flung open the windows and then went back to stand by Elizabeth's side. Running a finger along the slope of her nose, he was disappointed to find it hot to the touch. For the next hour, he covered her with wet sheets. Each time she moaned, Ben's heart twisted with fear.

He collapsed in the chair, cupped his hands together. Fingers drumming the arm of the chair, he watched Elizabeth growing weaker. His attempts to lower her temperature had failed. The wet sheets and towels didn't remain cool long enough. He needed colder water and much more of it.

A thought struck.

Galvanized into action, he bolted from the room and ran to saddle up his horse.

With his arms wrapped around Elizabeth, Ben kneed his horse forward. He felt the heat of her fevered body through the thin fabric of her nightgown.

As the moon slipped behind a cloud, Ben peered into the darkness until he made out the path to the stream. A low-lying branch whipped his cheek and scraped his ear. He swore under his breath.

A moment later he slid from the horse with Elizabeth in his arms. Slowly, in the pitch darkness, he inched over the rough terrain and climbed into the stream. His legs soon went numb.

He lowered Elizabeth into the icy water and waited for her to react. But she stayed limp. He shifted her body from side to side. As the water rippled around them, he shivered from the cold. Reaching into the stream, he scooped water over her face.

She stirred, and his breath hitched. "Elizabeth."

When the moon slid from behind the clouds, he studied her features. Was it hopeful thinking, or did she look better? His teeth clattered as he jostled Elizabeth up and down.

He thought she said something. "Come on, we had a deal, you said you'd cook for me. Where's your pride?"

Slowly, her eyes opened. She whispered something he didn't catch.

He lowered his head to her lips. "What did you say, Elizabeth?"

Her weak voice was music to his ears. "Mr. Ricker, have you taken leave of your senses?"

CHAPTER 10

Elizabeth awoke and waited for the musical chimes signaling breakfast, always an elaborate affair with more choices than there were days in the week. She was debating whether to eat pancakes, crepes, or eggs when the flapping wings of birds overhead startled her. She opened her eyes to find, not the ornate ceiling in her bedroom, but a leafy canopy. The worn blanket beneath her smelled of horse and did nothing to cushion her bottom from the twigs and pebbles on the ground.

When she tried to sit, she grew dizzy. What was she doing here? A light breeze reminded Elizabeth she was wearing only a nightgown. She brought her hand to her chest and discovered her nightgown torn.

Some distance away she heard the rustle of branches. She remembered the grizzly attack. Her heart thudded as she wrapped her fingers around a large stone.

She lifted her head and spotted Ben squatting by the stream, splashing water on his face. His scowl reminded her of the outlaws pictured in magazines. A warm feeling settled deep inside as she studied his strong, unshaven jaw and dark hair curling over his collar. He stood and started toward her. His wide stride and deeply shadowed face gave him a menacing appearance.

"Why am I here?" she asked him.

"Your wounds got infected. I dunked you in the water to bring down your fever."

She gazed into his cold eyes. "You don't like me very much, do you?"

When he hesitated, she knew it was true.

He planted a fake-looking grin on his handsome face. "Why wouldn't I like you?"

"You didn't answer my question. I won't have you dancing around the issue."

"I'm much obliged to you for saving Granny." He plunked his Stetson on his head. His hard gaze warned her to drop the subject.

"Who ripped my nightgown?" she asked, clenching the material together with both hands.

"I did what needed to be done," he said before turning his back to her.

As he walked toward his horse, Elizabeth realized he'd saved her life. "Thank you," she said, not sure if he'd heard.

Elizabeth spent three days in bed, recovering her strength. Ben kept his distance. How had he discovered her identity, and would he tell anyone? She ventured downstairs, determined to question him.

Though still weak and somewhat light-headed, she followed the wonderful smells into the kitchen and saw Ben pouring batter into a large iron skillet. He turned as she entered and smiled affably.

"Up and about, I see. That must mean you'll be taking over your kitchen duties soon."

She breathed a sigh of relief. He wasn't sending her away. He must have seen the surprise on her face because he put the spatula down.

"Something wrong?"

"I wasn't sure if I still had a job."

"Why wouldn't you?"

Before she could change her mind, she plunged ahead, "You called me Elizabeth O'Hara the other night."

He turned back to the stove. "That's your name."

"I need to know what you're planning to do with the information."

"I figured we'd let the others at the ranch

know you aren't really a nun. You used the disguise as a prank to get me to hire you. Relax, the rest of your secret's safe with me."

She wondered how much he knew. "What secret?"

"That you're a common thief, that you took off with a small fortune from your stepfather's safe, that you kidnapped his children. If I hadn't seen for myself how good you are to those kids, I'd have turned you in. There's no denying you love the children, and they love you."

"There's nothing I wouldn't do for those two."

He studied her for a moment. "I can't figure out why you'd do such a thing."

"I did what I had to do."

"Care to elaborate?"

"No."

"You're really something, standing there with pride bursting from every inch of your stubborn hide. Humph, Elizabeth O'Hara. Your name matches your disposition. Uppity, pure Easterner through and through."

"The name Benjamin Ricker conjures the image of a slack-jawed, hayseed farm boy."

"I'd rather be a hayseed farm boy than a city slicker any day. At least I don't have my mug posted alongside other outlaws inside every bank and post office from here to kingdom come."

"What are you talking about?"

"I saw your picture on a *Wanted* poster coming out of the bank the other day. Your old man must be loaded. Five hundred dollars is a lot of money."

"Don't call him that. He's not my father." Ben shrugged.

"My picture's in the bank, and there's a reward?"

"Yup, a lot of guys would do most anything for that kind of money. You had better watch your back, Miss O'Hara."

"You won't turn me in?"

"Nope, not that I don't want to."

"Then what's stopping you?"

"Granny would never forgive me if I did. And she means as much to me as those children in the other room do to you."

"Thanks."

"Let's get this straight. I'm not doing you the favor. I don't like thieves, and I especially don't like liars. No good ever came of the two. You haven't spoken one word of truth since you met me. You've made a fool of me, and I don't like it one damn bit."

What could she say? He was right, but she'd done it to survive. "You don't understand."

"No, and I don't want to. Chances are

you'd give me a crock of bull, so save your breath."

Elizabeth wanted to light into him, give him a snappy reply, dent that tough exterior of his, but she couldn't come up with one single word.

Four days later, Elizabeth saw a blonde woman walking toward the house. "Queenie?" she asked.

"Sweetie, men don't recognize me either with my breasts covered up." Her deep, sultry laugh ended any doubt.

Elizabeth grabbed Queenie's hand and led her inside. "Am I glad to see you again."

"The last time I got this kind of reception, I was twenty years old and the only hooker in Virginia City."

Elizabeth felt better than she had in days. "You're too much. But that's what I like about you."

The older woman sat at the kitchen table and eyed Elizabeth. "I heard about the bear. Lucky for you it was just an itty-bitty one."

"Little! It was huge."

Queenie roared with laughter. "Honey, I was just pulling your leg."

Elizabeth poured them both a cup of tea and sat down at the kitchen table opposite her friend.

"Anything exciting happen besides tangling with a bear?" Queenie asked.

"That's enough excitement to last me a long time."

"I almost envy you. Can you imagine what wrestling a bear would do to my career? Queenie, whore extraordinaire, the bigger they are, the harder they fall."

Still laughing, Queenie reached into the sewing basket in the center of the table and pulled out the shirt Elizabeth was making for Zachariah. "Did you sew this?"

"Yes, but it still needs a good ironing and buttons at the cuffs."

She fingered the material. "Fine work."

Pride bubbled inside. "Thanks."

"Have you made anything else?"

"Well, yes." Elizabeth went into the bedroom and came back with a box she'd hidden in the corner. "This is a surprise for Josh." She'd made him a stuffed white horse with a long brown mane and tail. Unable to contain her excitement, she pulled out another. "I made one for Clyde, too, only his is gray and black."

Queenie examined the handiwork. "This is fine stitching. What do you charge, honey? These large breasts of mine don't fit into regular clothes without a lot of alterations. You're a talented lady, and I wouldn't mind paying for your services."

"You mean it?"

"Of course. If word gets around, I bet lots of men will order shirts. Make an extra one, and I'll display it at the Golden Harp Saloon."

A weight lifted from Elizabeth's shoulders. With a means of support, she and the children could leave sooner. She could never return to Boston, but California appealed to her.

"What kind of doctor is Pete?"

Queenie scrunched her forehead. "Boy, you better not let him hear you call him Pete when he's doctoring."

"What do you mean?"

"At the bar, he's Pete, but when he's taking care of patients, he insists people call him Doc Cartwright. He'll rant and rave if you don't. This small peculiarity takes some adjusting to, but he's a great guy."

"But is he a great doctor?"

"You're alive, aren't you?"

"But he takes care of cows."

"Doc is the most goodhearted man I know. He'd take care of a rattler if it needed his help. He opened the bar because he likes being with people, and until the town grows, he needs the added income. When he does sell, I'm fixing to buy the place. I've been stocking my money away for the last two years."

"Does that mean you'll retire as a . . ." Elizabeth was at a loss for words. She could feel her face growing hot.

"Whore, go ahead and say it. It's what I am, and there's no sense pretending I'm not. And to answer your question, yes. I plan to retire and lead a respectable life." She paused and glanced out the window. As she spoke about the bar, her faced glowed with excitement. "I want to give the place some class. Dress it up some. Maybe even set the gold harp in the center of the room with flowers around it."

"There really is a harp?"

"Of course, I was the one who named the saloon. I bought the harp figuring I'd learn to play some day. That's a real kicker, don't you think? Aren't only angels supposed to play harps? It's probably written somewhere in the Bible."

"I wouldn't know."

Queenie patted Elizabeth's hand. "I heard you weren't a nun."

Elizabeth's heart slammed against her ribcage. "Who told you?"

"A gentleman from Boston came nosing around the bar yesterday, asking a lot of questions."

133

Elizabeth's stomach clenched. "What did he want to know?"

"He asked if anyone had seen Elizabeth O'Hara. That's you isn't it?"

"Yes," she said, her heart fluttering.

"That's what I figured. When I first saw the poster, I wasn't sure, but then he took out pictures of the children and I knew. He's offering five hundred dollars, cash, for information leading to you and the children. Someone wants you found real bad, sweetie."

"Did you tell him anything?"

"Sure did."

Elizabeth's breath caught in her throat.

Queenie laughed. "I told him if I ever spotted such a pretty lady, I'd give him five hundred dollars to take her away from my territory."

Elizabeth squeezed Queenie's hand. "Thanks. I owe you."

Queenie waved the comment away. "It's nothing."

"Did he show the pictures to anyone else in the bar?"

"No one that mattered. Before he left, he hung a poster, but I tore it down as soon as he walked out the door."

Elizabeth smiled gratefully. "You're a real friend."

"Now tell me something. Who's Robert T. Hines?"

Elizabeth handed Zack his new shirt and waited for a reply. He stood in his discolored union suit and trousers, examining each seam.

"Ma'am. I never expected to own a shirt like this one." He stuck one arm, then the other into the sleeves. "Fits right nice."

"I wasn't sure whether you'd like the monogrammed pocket."

He secured the buttons and glanced down. "I never had such a fancy shirt. Every cowpoke around will want to borrow it, but the Z on the pocket says it was made especially for me." He beamed a crooked smile.

Elizabeth had never seen a man so excited about a shirt.

Once Zack buttoned the front, he turned, undid his fly, and tucked the shirttails into his pants. When he faced her again, he looked confused. "Only thing I don't understand is this thin pocket, next to the other." He stuck a finger in the narrow opening.

"It's for your harmonica."

His smile widened. "You're some smart lady, Elizabeth." He removed his shirt, folded it carefully and tucked it under his

135

mattress.

"Aren't you going to wear it?"

"I certainly will, but it's too fine for everyday use. I'm keeping it for special occasions."

"You should enjoy it," Elizabeth urged him.

"It's only Tuesday. No man in his right mind would wear a shirt like this one to do ranch work. No sir, I got myself a Sunday shirt. Never had one until now. I sure am getting fancy in my old age."

Elizabeth inspected his threadbare old shirt. "Did you know there's a button missing?"

He shrugged. "Never cared much for mending."

"Give it to me, and I'll put one on for you," she volunteered.

His brows rose skeptically. "Is it gonna cost me?"

"Nothing. I'll do it because we're friends."

"In that case . . ." He turned and sauntered across the room, returning a moment later with three other shirts. "Consider me a real good friend and fix these, too."

"Well . . ."

"I knew it. It's gonna cost me, right?"

"I need a favor."

When she told him what she wanted, he

replied, "Like I said, you're one smart lady."

After sawing lumber all day, Ben stepped onto the porch and nodded at Granny and the three children. Cecelia, dressed in a pair of baggy overalls with a rope around her thin waist, cradled a puppy in her arms. The stark-looking eyes he'd seen when she'd first arrived had softened. Bernie stretched alongside a wooden rocker with her other puppy while Granny rubbed its belly.

The scene made him realize how much Granny relied on Elizabeth's ready-made family. He dreaded to think what would happen when they left. Would Granny's depression return? He hadn't missed the gloomy conversations they'd had about her meeting her Maker or how her husband Tom was calling her to join him. If he had a nickel for every time she'd mentioned being a useless old lady, he wouldn't have needed to borrow money.

When he glanced at Josh and Clyde, he noticed they were playing with two stuffed horses. He wondered where they'd gotten the toys.

As he sat in the chair beside Granny and removed his hat, Cecelia marched up to him. "You can't go in the kitchen," she said, her bossy tone similar to Elizabeth's.

"Why not?"

"Just because."

Josh leaped onto Ben's lap, almost tipping the rocker over. "Betts says we're having something real special for supper. It's a surprise." His childish voice nearly pierced Ben's eardrums.

"That's good news. I'm so hungry, I could eat a bear."

Josh shook his head. "Don't mention bears around Betts."

"Why not?"

The child's eyes widened, and he cupped his hand over his mouth. "The last time I talked about that great big grizzly almost biting her head right off she said if I mentioned that bear again, she'll lower my britches and swat my behind."

Ben smiled down at him. "Is that right?"

"So you better be careful, Mr. Ricker."

He chuckled. "I'll keep that in mind. Thanks for warning me."

When Josh hopped down, Ben reached for the shoe polish and brush he kept in a wooden box behind the rocker. As he shined his boots, Bernie stood, sniffed loudly, stretched, and then meandered in his direction. Within seconds the dog's wet nose landed on the polished leather.

"Shoo." Ben shoved the dog away and

buffed the dog drool from his boot.

"You'll rub the leather right off if you keep that up," came Zack's raspy voice.

Ben was shocked when Zachariah strutted onto the porch like a proud rooster. "Why are you all duded up this evening?"

"Can't a man dress for dinner without everyone fussing?"

"You're eating here with us tonight?"

"Sure am. I hear Elizabeth made something special for supper."

"I heard that, too." Ben couldn't remember the last time Zack had eaten in the main house. Something didn't figure. And the man was dressed as if he were going to church. "Where did you get the shirt?"

"Elizabeth stitched it for me."

Because she couldn't cook, Ben had assumed she couldn't sew, either. Apparently, he'd been wrong. "It's nice."

Zack lifted his brow in disdain. "Nice? Are you crazy? It's the best shirt I ever owned and better than any you own, too. I think you're jealous. Looky here." He withdrew his harmonica from a narrow pocket. "It fits perfect. No chances of it falling out. This shirt's really something."

"Yes, it's the best shirt I've ever seen. There, are you satisfied? Now put that thing away," Ben said, jerking his head toward the harmonica.

Zack scowled at Ben, then winked at Josh and Clyde. "You boys are in for a real treat." He put his harmonica against his lips and played several refrains of "Oh My Darling, Clementine."

Ben wasn't certain when Elizabeth came out, but he noticed the song turned mighty pretty when her voice joined in.

"Supper's nearly ready," Elizabeth said a moment later, without so much as a glance in Ben's direction.

When she looped an arm through Zack's and escorted the old man into the house, Ben felt a moment's jealousy. The strange feeling surprised him.

Lefty arrived a few seconds later. "What's for supper?"

"Damned if I know. It's supposed to be a surprise. Elizabeth's cooking, so far, has been nothing but surprises." Ben roared with laughter at his own joke, trying desperately to push thoughts of Elizabeth from his mind.

Everyone sat at the table while Elizabeth scurried around the kitchen making last-minute preparations. She wore a deep blue dress of fine silk that hugged her body. Her hair, pulled back behind her ears, cascaded in thick strands down to her waist. For a while, Elizabeth had masqueraded as a nun, but tonight she looked like an angel.

Ben figured he could cup both his hands around her tiny waist and his fingers would touch. He shook the nonsense from his mind as he stood, walked across the room and returned with an opened bottle of Granny's apple brandy.

"Anyone care for a glass?" he asked, looking around the table.

"I do," Josh shouted.

Ben ruffled his hair. "You're too young, kiddo. But I'll let you have a sip of mine if it's all right with your sister."

Elizabeth bolted across the kitchen as if he'd suggested the kid drink arsenic. "I'll not have you poison this poor child with liquor."

Ben grinned. "To look at your face, you'd think I had him swigging from the bottle. I was going to let him have one small sip. Gran let me when I was his age, and it didn't harm me none."

She huffed. "That is a matter of opinion."

After she turned around, he winked at Josh. "Sorry."

"Are you gonna get soused, Mr. Ricker?" Josh asked in his high-pitched voice.

Ben didn't have to ask him where he'd learned that word. Anxiety clouded Cecelia's eyes. He wondered about the children's lives back in Boston. Neither child mentioned their father or talked about returning back East.

"Course not," he whispered for the children's sakes and saw the relief on Cecelia's face. But when he caught Elizabeth glancing his way, he brought the bottle to his mouth and took several large gulps then wiped his mouth on his shirt sleeve, all the while staring her down.

"Ah, you don't know what you're missing, Elizabeth," he said, certain this was the worst brandy he'd tasted.

She cast an if-looks-could-kill glance his way, then marched right out the door.

Lefty elbowed Zack. "Where'd you get the fancy shirt?"

Zack beamed. "Elizabeth made it for me."

"Look at the horses she made for me and Clyde," Josh said, swinging his stuffed animal over the table and knocking a glass of water onto Ben's lap.

Ben leaped to his feet, grabbed the linen napkin by his plate and dabbed the darkening stain on his pants.

Josh pushed himself against the straight-back chair and raised his hand over his face as though fending off a blow. "I'm sorry. I didn't mean it. Honest."

"It was an accident. Don't worry about it," Ben said, patting the boy's shoulder.

Elizabeth entered with a large pot. Ben couldn't figure out why she'd gone outside to fetch their supper, but right now, he didn't care. "I'm so hungry, I could eat a bear," he said with a low chuckle.

Ignoring him, she set the pot on the cook stove.

Ben nudged Lefty. "The last time Elizabeth cooked biscuits, she saved me money."

"How's that, boss?"

"When I ran out of shoes for my horses, I used her leftover biscuits. They've lasted longer than the real thing."

The men and children erupted into fits of laughter. From the corner of his eye, he saw the stricken look on Elizabeth's face before she bolted outside.

Granny pounded her fists on the table. "What's gotten into you, Ben? I never knew you to be so cruel."

With Granny's words echoing after him, Ben went to find Elizabeth. He needed to undo the harm he'd done.

CHAPTER 11

The full moon illuminated the barn, the corral, and the nearby fields, but Ben saw no trace of Elizabeth. He hoped she hadn't darted into the woods. After checking the porch and searching the grounds, he was beginning to consider that possibility. He stood at the back of the barn and listened. Except for the crickets chirping and the occasional horse whinny, he heard nothing that would indicate where Elizabeth had gone.

"Foolish women," he muttered under his breath, including Granny in his assessment. They didn't know a joke when they heard one. It riled him to remember the looks on everyone's faces when Granny accused him of being cruel. Even Zack and Lefty sat with saintly expressions, acting as if he'd committed a crime when not seconds earlier they had laughed at his witty comment. Anyone with a lick of sense would have seen the humor in what he'd said, though his words held more truth than fiction.

Ben had almost decided to search the path leading to the stream when he heard sniffing. He froze, craned his head toward the sound, and was ready to change direction when Bernie rounded the corner. The mutt shoved its snout against every twig and plant along its path. Its long tail whipped Ben's jean-clad leg when he stepped over the animal, but before Ben could move away, Bernie licked his boot. He nudged the hound away and continued around the barn with the dog at his heels.

As he circled the front of the barn, he noticed someone had left the door ajar. He eased into the wooden structure, stared into the pitch-black interior, and listened. Except for Bernie's constant sniffing, Ben heard nothing out of the ordinary.

Bernie woofed and disappeared into the darkness. Thinking the dog might have located Elizabeth, Ben lifted the lantern from the peg by the door and struck a match. The wavering light cast long shadows along the straw-covered dirt floor as Ben headed in the same direction as the dog. He spotted Elizabeth deep in the shadows, standing with her back to him. As he stepped closer, he saw her shoulders trembling. The sight tore at his insides because he'd hurt her feelings. He hung the lantern on a nearby nail and stepped forward.

"Elizabeth," he whispered, cupping her shoulder with his right hand. "I didn't mean to upset you. I was joking and expected you to laugh along with the others."

She turned around and dashed a tear away with the back of her hand. "I'm not upset."

"Then why are you crying?"

She speared him with a look of disgust. "I prepared a meal, your favorite, and you didn't give me a chance to serve it."

Her voice had started out meek, but she continued in a roar. "Cry? Ha, that'll be the day when I shed tears for the likes of you."

"What's wrong with me?" he taunted, not wanting the moment to end.

"It would take from now till dawn to begin to list your faults."

"You have a few faults of your own, Miss O'Hara."

She folded her arms across her chest in that stubborn stance he'd come to recognize. "I don't suppose your good manners will prevent you from listing a few."

"You got that right." He rested his forefinger against his temple and pretended to contemplate his answer. "Let me think a minute, I'm sure I can list several."

146

She glared up at him.

He laughed and stepped closer. As her warm breath fanned his face, he caught the heady fragrance of lilacs. He had the overwhelming urge to brush his lips against hers. Would she kiss him back? Would her lips part under his gentle probing?

For one insane moment, he considered making a move. Fortunately, he came to his senses. This was dangerous territory, and he had enough to worry about without adding a Bostonian to his troubles.

He tweaked her nose. "You're stubborn as a mule but twice as cute."

A corner of her mouth lifted. "And you, Mr. Ricker, look no better than a horse's hind end."

"I expect that means you find me attractive."

She huffed aloud. "That's ridiculous."

He didn't reply, but instead studied the arch of her brows, her dainty nose, and plump lower lip.

He couldn't look away.

Worse yet, he didn't want to.

She blew an errant strand of hair from her forehead. Her chest rose and fell.

His throat constricted. Run like hell, he told himself, but found his feet rooted to the spot. When her tongue darted over her mouth, he was a goner.

Without a word he ran anxious fingers through her silken hair. He brushed his mouth against hers. Her lips were soft, full, and more intoxicating than Granny's apple brandy. He wrapped his arms around her small frame and drew her to him. Her spine stiffened under his touch, but she didn't pull away as he'd feared.

He angled his mouth over hers and traced his tongue along the seam of her lips. Her eyes opened in surprise but closed as she moaned softly. When she leaned into him and her lips parted, a bolt of lightning shot through him.

Elizabeth's legs turned to mush as hot embers flared in the pit of her stomach. Much to her horror, she grabbed hold of Ben Ricker's broad shoulders. Without a thought for impropriety, she stroked his face and marveled at the rough texture. Her questing fingers threaded through his hair and came to rest along the back of his neck. On impulse, she darted her tongue against his lower lip.

"Oh, Lizzy," he groaned.

Startled by her boldness, she tried to pull away but found herself imprisoned in his embrace — a prison of her choosing.

Not one second too soon, Bernie lunged

at Ben's leather boot. The dog's heavy frame rested against Elizabeth's legs. As Ben tried to shove the dog away, the fog lifted from Elizabeth's brain. Once she was able to think clearly again, she was mortified. Ben's kisses had knocked her senseless.

She was relieved when he dropped to his knee and rubbed Bernie's head. "You foolish mutt." He spent considerable time patting the dog.

Bernie's stiff tail tapped the hard-packed dirt floor.

Elizabeth wondered if Ben was trying to collect himself. As she glanced down at him, she remembered the feel of his arms around her. Heat rushed to her face and flooded her body. Never in her twenty-two years had she felt such excitement, such yearning.

Finally, Ben rose. When their eyes met, she laughed nervously. "Bernie loves the smell of shoe polish."

"I already figured that out."

"Mr. Ricker, that dog's always getting into trouble," she added, talking about anything but what was on her mind.

"I don't doubt that for a minute." His Adam's apple bobbed up and down. "Lizzy, I want you to call me Ben."

"All right," she said when she'd found her voice. *Lizzy,* she repeated silently to herself, liking the sound of her name on his lips.

It seemed natural when he reached for her hand and escorted her outside. "What's a man have to do to get supper around here?"

"Wait till you see what I've prepared."

"Give me a hint."

She smiled at him, her heart skipping a beat. "Oh . . . why not. I made your favorite. Baked beans."

Ben opened his mouth and without saying a word shut it again.

Elizabeth was delighted. Not only had her good news surprised Ben, it had rendered him speechless.

Elizabeth tossed and turned all night. When she finally fell asleep, she dreamed of Ben Ricker holding her tight, his kisses hot and demanding, driving her to heights she'd never thought possible. In her dream, he moaned, and his hand closed over her breast. When she awoke and remembered her wayward thoughts, her face grew hot.

She was relieved that Ben wasn't around when she entered the kitchen some time later. She served the children lumpy oatmeal and, sitting beside Clyde, forced a spoon into his hand.

He grunted disapprovingly as she wrapped his fingers around the utensil.

She lifted his chin so he'd see her smile. "That's a good boy."

Clyde took several bites using the spoon.

"Guess what, Betts?" Josh asked, oatmeal spraying from his mouth.

"What have I told you about talking with your mouth full?"

"Sorry. Granny's birthday is next week. Can we have a party, huh?"

Elizabeth didn't hesitate. "I think a party is a fine idea."

"I know what Granny would like to have most of all," Cecelia said. She left the room and returned a few minutes later with an old issue of *Harper's Bazaar,* pointing to a picture of a pretty dress. "Granny likes blue."

Elizabeth took the magazine from her sister. "Let me keep this for a while."

When Lefty entered the room a moment later, Elizabeth greeted him with a smile. "Can I get you something to eat?"

"Thank you, ma'am, but I've already eaten." He paused, then continued, "I do have a favor to ask." He dug into the cloth bag tucked under his arm. "I was wondering what you charge for mending. Between overseeing the steers and helping out with the lumber operation, I don't have much spare time."

Elizabeth examined the denim-colored shirt he'd handed her. One sleeve was ripped along the seam, and three buttons were missing. "This won't take but a few minutes. I'll mend your shirt this afternoon."

"That would be great, ma'am."

"Please call me Elizabeth. When you call me ma'am, I feel like an old lady."

Lefty smiled shyly. "I'll remember that, Elizabeth. I sure didn't intend to make you feel old. Heck, I think you're younger than I am."

Elizabeth compared Lefty to Ben, a gentleman who would never inform a lady she looked slightly better than a donkey.

"I'll be going into town tomorrow for supplies. Do you need anything?" Lefty asked.

"I'd like you to pick up several yards of fabric at the mercantile."

"Sure thing. Will you be making more shirts?"

"I hope to. Queenie thinks I can make a living with my sewing."

"I know I'd buy a shirt."

"Would you really?"

"Yes, the shirt you made Zack is the envy of every man."

Elizabeth smiled at the compliment. "One more thing. I'm going to give Granny a surprise birthday party."

"The Rickers never make much of a fuss over birthdays," Lefty said, reaching for the doorknob.

Elizabeth waved away his concerns. "Then it's about time someone did. I'd like you to buy some colored paper for decorations. Maybe some peppermint candy."

"I want to give Granny a new pipe," Josh shouted from his chair.

Cecelia added in a gentle voice, "I'd like a length of blue satin ribbon for Granny and pins to curl her hair."

Lefty lifted a hand. "Whoa, you ladies better make a list."

When Lefty shut the door a few minutes later with his list in hand, Elizabeth spotted Clyde tipping the cereal bowl to his mouth. She pretended not to notice. Clyde's table manners had improved, and she was willing to overlook an occasional transgression. He no longer grabbed food from everyone else's plate, and he now washed his hands before and after each meal. She was certain there was nothing wrong with Clyde's mind.

After breakfast, Elizabeth washed and dried the dishes. Making sure no one was watching, she removed two bottles of Granny's apple brandy from the corner cupboard, pried off the cork from the bottles, and poured out half the fermented liquid. Then, using a funnel, she filled the bottles with water strained though a clean handkerchief. The bloated cork wouldn't go back in the bottle, but she knew what to do because she'd done this before. Slowly, she whittled the sides of the cork with a sharp knife until it slid easily into the narrow glass neck.

CHAPTER 12

In the three days since Ben had kissed Elizabeth, he'd kept his distance, and except for a quick good-morning nod, he hadn't said one word until this morning when he entered the kitchen shortly after dawn. She hadn't been able to rid her mind of his embrace, and seeing him standing before her brought a flush to her face.

"How are you doing, Elizabeth?"

Against her will, her heart swelled with joy. She hated that his presence affected her so much.

"Fine," she replied, noting the flutter in her stomach.

He looked at her, seemingly lost for words. She saw the longing in his eyes and hoped it wasn't reflected in hers.

He cleared his throat and took a step back. "Then you're up to doing a few extra chores. I'll pay you, of course."

When she squared her shoulders, she felt

a slight twinge of pain along her chest. "Yes, I'm certainly well enough to do whatever needs to be done. The more money I make, the sooner I can leave." She hadn't meant to say that, but now that she had, she held her breath. Would he ask her to stay? Why did it matter? She couldn't stay. Wouldn't stay. Would not allow any man to claim her as his own.

"Good," he said, his voice gruff. "Eggs need to be collected from the twelve chickens in the coop. They're Granny's chickens, but she hasn't shown interest in them since her eyes went bad. Zack and Lefty have been taking turns with them, but they can no longer spare the time."

He paused and took a breath. "Since you're in such a doggoned hurry to get out of here, milk the cows while you're at it. I'll pay you for that, too."

"No problem. I'll take care of everything."

He gave her a long, hard look and took the liberty of glancing down.

She'd worn her yellow taffeta dress with scooped neckline, and the way he examined her made her feel as if she were naked. She took a calming breath and counted to ten but knew she was fighting a losing battle. "Mr. Ricker, I'll not have you eyeing me like a thick slab of beef." She cursed her inadequate wardrobe.

Her words penetrated his daze. "Don't you have something more appropriate to wear?"

"You didn't seem to mind what I had on the other night."

He stepped closer. "Consider the other night a lapse of good judgment. You'd best forget about what happened. I know I have."

She was spitting mad. "I don't even know what you're talking about."

"Good."

Elizabeth grabbed the basket from the counter. "Now that that's settled, I have work to do. Good day, Mr. Ricker." This she punctuated with the slam of the door.

Hoping to accomplish the chore while the chickens slept, Elizabeth tiptoed into the hen house to collect the eggs but was greeted by twelve squawking birds with cocked heads and red, beady eyes. Their frenzied clucking and flapping wings stirred up an ungodly stench. She covered her nose with her handkerchief, but it did little to stifle the atrocious odor.

The first hen Elizabeth approached pecked her fingers, drawing blood. Elizabeth jumped back and gave the matter some thought. Back in Boston, the cook bought their eggs from the store near their house.

Elizabeth had never had reason to touch an uncooked egg, much less steal one from beneath a chicken. She caught a glimpse of Zack outside and considered throwing herself on his mercy, but quickly dismissed the idea. She couldn't take the chance word would get back to Ben.

With a little ingenuity she'd collect the eggs. There was nothing she'd like better right now than to break an egg over Ben Ricker's head.

She set the basket down and clasped her hands together. Chickens were dumb, she'd read that somewhere. Although, the ones eyeing her didn't look too stupid. Twelve killer chickens glared at her. She was clearly outnumbered.

She found feed in a bin in the corner of the hen house. "Good chicken," she cooed. The bird's head darted side to side.

Elizabeth put several pieces of grain slightly out of its reach. The bird gawked around, and as it lunged for the feed, she grabbed the warm egg from its nest. When she glanced down at the egg in her hand and saw it was smeared with chicken poop, the egg slipped from her grasp and splattered on the hen house floor.

The next egg she stole was messier than the first, but she was prepared and though her stomach rolled over, she managed to set the egg in her basket without breaking it. Goosebumps covered her arms, and she was gagging by the time she'd collected the egg from under the last chicken.

The yellow taffeta dress sported several stains by the time she left the hen house. Though the spots were undoubtedly one hundred percent chicken dung, to Elizabeth they represented courage. The chore was revolting, but there was satisfaction in having accomplished the unpleasant task.

Fearing she'd lose her courage if she waited, she marched straight to the barn. She set the basket of eggs on the dirt floor and grabbed the milk bucket hanging by the stall. She'd never seen a cow up close before today, and it was not a sight she enjoyed.

The animal was huge, and when it opened its mouth, the barn nearly shook with its fierce sound. Or was it merely her quaking in her shoes? Where the chickens could have maimed her, this animal could kill. Terror consumed her. She could not do this. The animal looked mean, and the large nose ring in its nostrils oozed with . . . well, she tried not to think about that. Her stomach churned. Sweat beaded her brow.

She heard footsteps approaching, turned,

and saw Ben. Trying to look calm, she nodded toward the basket. "I've just finished
collecting the eggs."

"I can see that."

"I'm going to milk the cow." She lifted the
bucket, which rattled in her trembling hand.

"Do you need help?"

She almost blurted out no, but caught
herself in time. "Maybe."

"Would you like me to give you a hand?"

Dizzy with relief, Elizabeth nodded. "I'd
appreciate that." Determined to get the
milking over with, she reached for the latch
that led to the animal's stall.

"Stay away from Brutus, he's one mean
bull."

She covered her mistake with a smile. "I
just wanted to make friends with the other
animals while I was here."

"Brutus isn't interested in making friends.
His one mission in life is keeping the ladies
happy."

When Elizabeth figured out his meaning,
she blushed. "Oh."

At the sawmill later that day, Ben's thoughts
kept drifting back to Elizabeth. He felt
guilty about the way he'd shot off his mouth
that morning. He'd been rough on her and
certainly hadn't meant to say what he had.

But it was better this way, better that she knew where they stood.

He'd told her the truth. The first kiss had been a momentary lapse of judgment. The second and third had been insanity. Ben had no intention of letting that happen again.

But that didn't give him an excuse to be mean. He knew she'd have a devil of a time collecting the eggs from the brooders. He'd taken a perverse joy in giving her the task, but he'd never expected her to succeed.

He knew by the marks on her hands and arms that she'd fought for each egg she'd gathered. Remembering her delicate fingers nicked by the sharp beaks brought on another rush of guilt. He promised himself he was through thinking of the red-haired beauty, hair that felt like silk and smelled of lilacs.

Determined to change his direction of thought, he grabbed paper and pencil and calculated how many feet of lumber they'd cut. "We've had a good day."

Zack rolled his eyes. "We're cattlemen, not lumberjacks. Your granddaddy's turning over in his grave each time that blade saws another log."

"Granddaddy doesn't have to pay the bills anymore."

"It ain't right, I tell you."

"If you have a better idea, let me know because I could sure use the extra cash."

The old man clamped his lips together and threw another plank on the growing pile. "Sonofabitch," he muttered under his breath.

Ben thought Zack was still grumbling about the sawmill until he spotted Ward Metcalf sauntering in their direction. He pulled his Stetson from his head and wiped his forehead against his shirtsleeve. "What brings you here, Ward?"

The stiff mustache that hid Ward's upper lip twitched. "Just checking up on my investment." He craned his neck and admired the land that stretched as far as the eye could see. "You've got yourself a mighty fine spread here."

The man reminded Ben of a vulture coming in for the kill. "I expect to have your money in plenty of time."

"I hope you do. It would pain me to have to take your farm."

"Men like you get their kicks preying off the desperate." Zack cussed, spat on the ground and marched off.

Ward leered at his retreating back. "Crazy old coot thinks he knows everything."

Ben's jaw clenched. "While you're on my property, I won't have you speaking about

Zachariah that way."

Ward still wore a smile, but his eyes were filled with contempt. "As long as it's your property, I'll try to remember that."

"See that you do."

As Ben and Ward walked back to the farmhouse, Ben spotted Josh and Clyde galloping around the yard. Ben ruffled Clyde's hair. "How's it going, sport?"

Clyde responded with a loud laugh.

"Me and Clyde are chasing the bank robbers," Josh shouted, pulling a bent stick from his pocket. "Pow, pow. I just killed one dead over by the barn. Giddy up," he hollered, slapping the horse's imaginary haunch and waving for Clyde to follow.

Ben couldn't believe the change in Clyde since Elizabeth's arrival. He'd developed some manners and acted like a regular kid. As the two boys disappeared from sight, Ben offered Ward a seat on the porch. Much to his chagrin, Ward accepted his offer.

"Care for something to drink?"

Ward tipped the rocker back and rested a booted foot on the porch railing. "Don't mind if I do."

"Beer or apple brandy?"

"No one in their right mind has beer when they can have Granny's apple brandy."

Ben sauntered into the kitchen where Elizabeth was mixing batter. She'd tried to wash the spots out of her yellow dress. Even stained, it was the prettiest thing Ben had ever seen. But he wasn't about to tell her that.

"Will you be having supper with us?" she asked.

"Haven't decided yet." For the last three days Ben had stayed away, figuring he needed a cooling-off period. So far, it hadn't worked.

He took two glasses from the cupboard and grabbed a bottle of brandy before going back out the door.

Ward pulled a knife from his pocket. "Let me do the honors. I have a corkscrew on this contraption." He took the bottle from Ben, removed the cork with ease and filled the glasses.

Elizabeth arrived with a dish. "Would you gentlemen like to sample my oatmeal cookies?"

Ward jumped to his feet and removed his hat so fast it made Ben sick. His mustache lifted in a phony smile. "Why thank you, ma'am. Oatmeal cookies are my favorite." He took a bite, lifted his eyes skyward. "Deli-cious," he said, dragging out the word, making Ben's stomach roll over with disgust.

Elizabeth blushed. Her eyes lit with pleasure.

"One will never do me. If you don't mind, I'll take two."

Elizabeth fussed with her hair. "Certainly. I have another batch in the oven. If you'd like, I can wrap some up for you to take home with you."

Ward's grin stretched clear across his face.

Couldn't Elizabeth see through his deceiving, conniving ways?

"I thank you. I'll eat but two a day to extend the pleasure."

When Ben grabbed three cookies off the plate, Elizabeth didn't seem to notice. He took a bite and despite the fact they were hard as rock, he forced himself to say, "These are good."

Elizabeth glanced his way and started to smile, but Ward ruined Ben's compliment when he took a bite and stirred the crumbs around his mouth. "Ambrosia, my dear. I've never tasted better."

Elizabeth's cheeks turned pink before she disappeared into the house a moment later. Ward snapped the cookies in two and after glancing toward the door, shoved them in his pocket. "Where'd you find such a vision?"

Ben could have spit nails. "She's the cook."

Ward's right eyebrow rose. "The cook, humph. Does that mean you aren't involved with her?"

"She's the cook, and not a very good one at that," he repeated, growing more irritated with each passing minute.

"When a lady's that gorgeous, who cares whether she can cook." Ward's shifty eyes met Ben's. "Then you wouldn't mind if I asked her out?"

Ben caught his breath and gave a nonchalant shrug. "It's nothing to me." He stewed for several minutes. Ward Metcalf was the last man on this earth he wanted within a mile of Elizabeth. As he gave the matter more thought, he realized he didn't want any man near Elizabeth.

Ward took a swallow of brandy. "Has your grandmother changed her recipe?"

Ben swallowed several gulps. "Tastes the same to me." It didn't, but Ben wasn't about to give Ward the satisfaction. He drank a little more just to prove his point.

Granny had definitely lost her touch.

CHAPTER 13

The next day Ben was on his way across the yard when he spotted Elizabeth clad in pink, streaking into the kitchen. As he approached the house, he could hear Queenie's boisterous laughter coming from inside. He swung the door open, and took a closer look, and damn near dropped in his tracks.

When he'd suggested that Elizabeth wear something more appropriate, he hadn't meant pink floral britches with an embroidered heart on the back pocket. As that heart drew his eyes to her shapely rear, he forced a ragged breath past his parched throat.

Queenie slapped the tabletop. "What d'you think, Ben?" She rose and gave him full view of wide hips covered in bright green pants about to burst at the seams. When she twirled around, he spotted a purple flower on the back pocket.

It took a moment before he could speak.

"I hope you two aren't planning to wear those outside."

"What's wrong with them?" they asked in unison.

He took a gander at Elizabeth's outfit. Her britches were loose-fitting, gathered and cuffed at her ankles. She looked too damn sexy for her own good.

Elizabeth's gaze sliced right through him. "Granny wears pants all the time."

"Yes, overalls, not . . ." He couldn't think of a suitable word for the fancy britches.

"Queenie says it's about time women stopped wearing men's overalls. She says I may be able to start up my own business selling fashionable clothing to the ladies in the area."

"I don't think the men are going to like it much."

Queenie chuckled. "Sweetie, you may be wrong about that."

Lefty, decked out in a new shirt, picked that moment to enter the kitchen. The appreciative look he swept over the two women about said it all, and though Ben saw no need for words, Lefty didn't keep his big mouth shut.

"Wow, you ladies look . . ."

Ben interrupted. "Better leave it at that."

Lefty's face flushed. "You may be right,

boss." He turned his attention back to Elizabeth. "How's the big surprise party going?"

Elizabeth looked around and lowered her voice. "Great. I don't think Granny suspects a thing. I made the cake last night after she went upstairs, and the children helped wrap the presents. I still have to frost the cake and hang decorations."

Queenie gave a chuckle and eyed Ben. "I told Elizabeth to make Granny a pair of these britches in yellow, but she had other ideas."

"Humph, thank goodness."

Ben had voiced his opinion several times. This party was a fool-hearted thing. Granny would never go along with such nonsense. The surprise would be on Elizabeth when Granny set everyone straight.

Elizabeth called the children into the room. Cecelia, poor little thing, had a blue pair of coveralls with a butterfly on the rear. Ben tried to hide his chagrin, but he exchanged bewildered looks with Lefty.

Josh scurried to Ben's side and lifted his package for inspection. The brown paper was decorated with pencil drawings of guns and horses. "I wrapped this all by myself."

Ben tapped the boy's head. At least the kid wasn't wearing a pair of the ridiculous pants. "What's inside?"

"It's a surprise. I'm not supposed to tell."

"Can you give me a hint?"

Josh's expression grew thoughtful. "Granny puts tobacco in it."

Ben ruffled the boy's hair and laughed aloud. "I wonder what that could be?"

Josh twisted an imaginary key over his mouth. "I won't tell."

Ben had become attached to the boy. He was as bright as they came and a real charmer. He'd better give the kid a few pointers about the way a western man was suppose to dress, or the boy could end up with embroidered horses across his backside. "I'm glad you aren't wearing pants like your sister's."

Josh made a face and stuck out his tongue. "I wouldn't be caught in those for nothin'."

"I'm glad to hear that." Ben had at least one male on his side. "I've been thinking. If you're going to stay here a while, shouldn't you have a real pair of cowboy boots?"

"I told Betts that, but she said to pretend these were cowboy boots." Josh lifted a scuffed black dress shoe for Ben to examine.

Ben whispered in Josh's ear. "Girls don't understand about such things."

The boy gave an exaggerated nod. "That's what I figured. If I had real boots, then I'd need only one more thing to be a real cowboy."

"Yeah, what's that?"

"A horse." His crisp voice radiated through the kitchen.

Elizabeth spun around and carried the cake to the table. She lifted the pan over the serving dish and tapped the bottom. Ben watched her frown. He bit back a comment.

She gazed at Queenie. "It's not coming out."

"I can see that, sweetie."

"Why not?"

"Honey, cooking isn't part of my job."

Ben couldn't remain quiet another second. "Did you grease and flour the pan?"

When Elizabeth's startled eyes met his, Ben had his answer. He fully expected her to crumble on the spot, maybe shed a few tears.

Instead, she smiled innocently. "Children, I have another surprise. I made a pan-cake for Granny's birthday. After Granny blows out the candles, each of you can spoon out a serving and decorate it yourselves."

A chorus of cheers ensued.

Elizabeth never ceased to amaze him. She'd made a mistake and come out a hero.

Josh, bless his soul, was the only one to question the new confection. "How come we never had pan-cake in Boston?"

"Because I just now invented the recipe."

He looked at his sister with awe. "Geez, maybe I can invent something, too."

Ben laid a hand over his small shoulder. "If you stick around Elizabeth long enough, I'm sure you'll come up with a real doozie."

As Elizabeth stuck candles on the unfrosted cake, Queenie set her gift on the table. Gazing at Ben, she gave a raucous laugh. "You better hire a guard for Granny. One drop of 'Eau De Paris' behind each ear and every man over fifty from here to Timbuktu will be drooling at her bedroom door."

It was a visual Ben didn't want to think about.

Elizabeth exchanged conspiratorial looks with Cecelia. "It'll go perfectly with our gifts."

That worried Ben. "What did you two get Granny?"

Elizabeth rushed over to where he stood. "Cecelia and I have been working long hours, and I can hardly wait to see Granny's face. I just hope it fits."

Her enthusiasm was contagious. Without thinking, he reached out and touched her arm. His heartbeat grew rapid. "Slow down, you still haven't told me what you bought."

"Oh." She giggled like a schoolgirl.

She was by far the prettiest woman he'd ever seen. A man could get lost in her eyes, eyes that twinkled with excitement and made his pulse thunder in his ears.

"We made Granny a dress."

"And I bought a matching ribbon for her hair," Cecelia volunteered.

Granny never wore dresses. Ben hated to think of their disappointment when Granny turned down their gifts. Granny didn't mince words, and there were times when her comments hurt, but you always knew where you stood. He'd tried to discourage them about this party, but not a soul had listened.

"If it doesn't fit, I'm sure you can fix it."

"Of course." Elizabeth brought a hand to her mouth. "Now why didn't I think of that?" As she marched back to the table, Ben studied the heart on her pocket. It wasn't until Lefty cleared his throat that Ben realized where he'd been staring.

Elizabeth clapped her hands. "All right, put your presents on the table." The children set their packages near the cake, except for Clyde, who hid his behind his back.

"Put the mints up here," Elizabeth said, tapping the tabletop. The boy stared down at his shoes, his lowered lip quivering.

Elizabeth knelt down and gathered the

boy in her arms. "What's wrong, sweetie?"

Ben knew Clyde couldn't hear her voice, but it didn't take ears to understand that she cared. Ever so slowly, Clyde lifted an empty can of mints for Elizabeth to see.

Ben's heart broke for the unfortunate child. As thoughts of his own childhood ran through his mind, he held his breath. How would Elizabeth solve this problem? Even she couldn't make peppermints materialize from nothing. He watched her kiss Clyde's brow and smile down at him. "It's a pretty tin." She nodded her approval. "Put it right here, along with the other presents. I'm sure Granny will love it."

Ben didn't know how much Clyde understood, but the child was smiling as he set his gift beside the others. If only Ben's own mother had cared half as much. He brushed away the wayward thought. That was a long time ago. He no longer cared.

As Ben set the tobacco he'd brought for Granny alongside Josh's pipe, he hoped the party wouldn't end in disaster.

One thought kept going through his mind. Elizabeth's gift further emphasized their differences.

He'd been right to keep his distance.

Half an hour later, the women were decked

out in fancy dresses. Zack and Lefty wore their personalized shirts with initials on the pockets. Hair slicked, Josh and Clyde both resembled drowned rats as they sat in straight-back chairs waiting for Granny's arrival. Ben, however, wore the same shirt and jeans he'd slipped on that morning. The total extent of his preparations was brushing sawdust from his shoulders.

As he saw it, once Granny figured out what the fuss was about, there would be no party. Ben planned to dig a piece of cake from the pan, apply a liberal amount of frosting, and get back to work.

It surprised him when a few minutes later Granny arrived with a bandana over her eyes, being led by Elizabeth and Cecelia. Even without the blindfold, he doubted Granny could see the table six feet away. Her face flushed with anticipation, Elizabeth looked like a child herself.

Granny took a faltering step. "If I break my neck, you're to blame."

Elizabeth laughed. "Don't worry, I have ahold of you. Just a few more steps."

Ben assumed the party would end any second. As he looked around, he saw the smiles on everyone's faces. The children, especially Josh, seemed frozen to their chairs. Ben had never seen the child so still.

Elizabeth led Granny to the table and helped her sit in a chair decorated with large paper flowers.

As Cecelia removed the bandana, she kissed Granny's cheek. "Happy Birthday, Gran."

Granny looked confused. "Hogwash. Is this what all the commotion's about?"

Cecelia gave Granny's hand an affectionate squeeze. "I love you, Granny."

Granny's eyes misted with tears. "You do?"

As Cecelia hugged the older woman, Josh leaped from his chair. "I bought you something really, really special for your birthday. And except for putting it in my mouth a few times, it's new. And you know what? Clyde ate your present, but he's really, really sorry. But don't worry about it, 'cause Elizabeth says the box is nice even if it has Clyde's teeth marks on it."

Granny burst out laughing. "You little whippersnapper, you're too much."

Ben couldn't believe his eyes, or his ears. Maybe he should have changed his shirt after all.

Cecelia led the group in song. As strains of "Happy Birthday" filled the kitchen, Ben wondered how he could have been so wrong about this party.

Granny was delighted with the pipe. Next, she ran her fingers against the smooth surface of the empty tin. "Thank you, Clyde. It feels like a beautiful container."

Clyde grinned when Granny wrapped him in her arms.

After the child scrambled away, Queenie elbowed Granny. "Wait till the men get a whiff of this. You'll have to fight them off with a stick."

Without waiting, Queenie opened the cologne and waved the glass applicator under Granny's nose.

Granny sucked in a deep breath. "Mmmmm, that sure smells pretty."

Queenie dabbed the perfume behind Granny's ears.

"But who's gonna smell it back there?" Granny grabbed the applicator and splashed a generous amount on both wrists, then inhaled deeply.

Zack swaggered over to Granny. "Sweetheart, let me test that stuff." He took a sniff and let out a hoarse growl that had the women hooting with delight.

Granny slapped him away. "Get out of here, you crazy old fool."

"Not till I get a kiss from the birthday gal." Zack nuzzled Granny's neck, then plastered a wet noisy smack on her cheek.

Granny shoved him away. "Have you gone daft?" The blush on her pale cheeks made her look years younger.

Ben couldn't believe it. Granny was enjoying the attention.

When it came time for her to open the bag with the tobacco, Ben was feeling down. He wished he'd made more of an effort to get Granny something truly special. Though he couldn't figure what that might have been. Since she'd stopped working the farm, her interests had waned. And even if he had wanted to buy her an expensive gift, money was tight. But he could have at least wrapped his present.

As Granny lifted the tobacco pouch, she inhaled. "Mmmm, nothin' like a good smoke."

Ben sauntered across the room and kissed her. "Happy birthday, Gran."

"Was this shenanigan your idea?"

He heaved a deep sigh and was about to tell her he'd had no part whatsoever in the preparations when Elizabeth walked to his side. "Let's just say it was a group venture."

What happened next was a whirlwind. Granny was whisked into Elizabeth's bedroom. Before shutting the door, Cecelia announced, "No men or boys allowed."

Josh stuck his tongue out at his sister. But

the smirk she bestowed on him made it clear she was on the inside looking out. The door slammed with a resounding whack, leaving the men to contemplate what to do next.

From the kitchen, they could hear Granny's raspy voice commenting on the mental stability of those in the room. "Have you girls gone plumb crazy?"

This was followed by Queenie's rowdy laugh and shushed whispers. Several minutes went by before the door opened and the ladies made a grand entrance.

It took a moment before Ben even recognized his grandmother. She swept into the room, decked out in a deep blue satin gown fit for royalty, accenting the womanly figure normally hidden beneath men's overalls.

Soft tendrils of silver hair curled over her forehead and cheeks. The rest was tucked in a bun and held in place with a matching ribbon that curled down to her neckline. A small cameo rested on her chest, which rapidly rose and fell. Just the right touch of makeup accented her gray eyes and pink lips, but the rosy glow of Granny's cheeks was her own.

Ben blinked twice as he crossed the room to take her arm. His grandmother was truly beautiful. His throat thickened as he escorted her across the kitchen. He'd been dead wrong about this birthday party.

Had he been wrong about other things?

When Zachariah whipped out his harmonica and started tapping his toes to "Oh My Darling, Clementine," Ben whirled the belle-of-the-ball around the kitchen.

As the music died, Ben twirled Granny around twice more. Flushed and looking happier than he'd ever seen her, Granny took a breath and gestured to the onlookers. "I never had myself such a fine birthday, and I want to thank every one of you."

She ran trembling hands over the satin creation. Then she did something totally out of character. She started to cry.

Concerned, Ben wrapped a comforting arm around his grandmother's waist and escorted her to the chair decked out with paper decorations. He dropped to his knee. "What's the matter?"

"Don't mind me. I'm just acting like a sentimental old fool." She made a visible effort to control herself. Inhaling a shaky breath, she traced the ruffled edges of a flower taped to her chair.

After ushering everyone from the room, Elizabeth knelt in front of Granny. "Are you all right?"

"I'm just so doggoned happy." Granny

sniffed one of the paper flowers, which Queenie had sprinkled with cologne. "These smell prettier than the real thing."

"I wasn't sure whether you'd want a birthday party," Elizabeth said as Granny dashed another tear from her cheek.

Granny brushed her handkerchief against her eyes. "This is darn embarrassin'. Of course, I wanted a shindig for my birthday. Men don't understand 'bout such things, but we womenfolk know better."

Elizabeth sighed. "Men don't even try to understand."

"Some do and some don't, but I wouldn't change a thing even if I could."

Elizabeth had made lots of changes in her life, and she hoped to make more, but she had no intention of changing her opinion about men.

"I love the way the material swishes when I walk." Granny ran trembling hands over her soft satin skirt. "It don't take no eighth-grade diploma to know you're the one who put on this here party. I'm much obliged, Lizabeth."

Elizabeth rested her hand on Granny's fingers. "I'm glad you like the dress."

"This is just like the dress in my *Harper's Bazaar*. I've had more than my share of birthday presents. But I've been surrounded by men, and they don't have a lick of sense when it comes to buying gifts. One year I got a broom, another time, a new rolling pin and baby chicks. Once I even got a shovel, and I didn't complain, but I'll tell you this, I ain't ever got anythin' near as nice as this here dress."

Granny's voice faltered. "I ain't been this happy in years. All gussied up like this, I feel like a high-falutin' lady."

Elizabeth kissed Granny's forehead.

Josh dashed into the kitchen.

"Granny, can I fix your pan-cake for you, huh?"

"Pancakes? Lizabeth, you're one smart woman, but pancakes are meant for breakfast. You sure do get lost around the kitchen." She blinked away tears. "But you know what? I don't care a lick, 'cause you have a heart of pure gold. You and the children have filled this old house with love. You've brought new meaning into my life. And I aim to keep you 'round for a good long time."

CHAPTER 14

Between overseeing the herd and helping at the mill, Ben hadn't set eyes on Elizabeth for three long days. That hadn't stopped him from thinking about her. Each time he entered the barn, he remembered the kisses they'd shared, how her body had molded to his, and the soft feel of her warm flesh beneath his fingertips.

As long as he lived, he'd never forget the smell of her hair or the way she'd clung to him. Whenever he closed his eyes, he could feel her gentle fingers on the back of his neck. Unable to push the thoughts from his mind, he'd dwelled on every aspect of the infuriating woman until he thought he'd go crazy if he didn't at least catch a glimpse of her sparkling blue eyes. Whenever he got the hankering to mosey on down to the ranch, he reminded himself that Elizabeth was an Easterner sure to leave Montana behind without a backward glance — just as his mother had done.

But it was getting damn hard to concentrate on her shortcomings. Whatever faults the woman possessed evaporated the instant he thought of how well she cared for Cecelia and Josh. And Granny. She'd worked for hours taking apart her own clothing and then stitched until dawn, just so Granny would own a dress like the one in the magazine. The cameo around Granny's neck had been Elizabeth's, too. No matter what Ben might think of Elizabeth, the woman was generous, kind, and certainly smarter than he was concerning his own grandmother. He hadn't even realized that Granny had wanted such things. Never in a hundred years would he have believed it.

He couldn't keep his heart from turning over whenever he remembered how patient Elizabeth was with Clyde and how she'd turned the boy's life around. She wasn't even responsible for the child, yet she continued to care for him as if she were. Ben's mother, his own flesh and blood, hadn't had enough patience or love to stick around. Yet Elizabeth protected and cared for her brother and sister and Clyde, a child she barely knew, and she seemed to do it without regret. His admiration for her grew with each passing day.

Adding to his dilemma, those foolish pink pants of hers were engraved in his subconscious, and he couldn't shake the image no matter how hard he tried. But he did his damnedest to do just that as he grabbed hold of the saddle-horn and leaned forward, scanning his fields for signs of the missing steers.

Lefty halted his mare a few feet from Ben. "Whoa, Bessey; easy, girl." His expression grew serious. "What's on your mind?"

Ben stared at the landscape before him. "The ranch, everything." He forced air into his lungs. "I wish I knew who's cutting our fences."

"You can't keep pushing yourself or the men like this."

Ben rolled his shoulders, trying to ease the ache in his tired muscles. "I've been thinking the same thing. It's time I hired someone to work at the mill."

Ben saw concern in Lefty's eyes. "Can you afford to do that?"

"I can't afford not to. As I see it, I have two choices: either go on as we have been and try to do everything ourselves, or hire someone to run the mill so we can concentrate on the steer. I figure if we sleep during the day, we can take turns keeping an eye on the longhorns and the fences at night."

Ben pointed at Lefty. "And I'll tell you this, if I catch the bastard responsible, I intend to shoot to kill."

"I see two down there, boss."

Ben glanced down the embankment and saw a couple of steers grazing beneath a large ponderosa pine. He slapped his horse's rump and galloped down the hill with Lefty not far behind him. As the two men approached, the docile animals lifted their heads for a moment before turning their attention back to the rich grass at their feet.

Ben hopped down from his mount and looped a rope around the nearest longhorn's neck when he heard the loud baying of another animal in pain. He hurried toward the distressful cry and found its source several feet away. Rage consumed him. The animal had broken its leg. He could feel the beast's fear, see it in its brown eyes. The animal struggled to stand, but fell back with a helpless wail. Ben didn't have the stomach for this senseless death. Bile rose in his throat. His gut clenched as he withdrew his Colt .45 from his holster and fired one shot into the animal's skull.

The sound of the bullet tearing through flesh and bone punctuated the thoughts running through Ben's mind. If things didn't turn around real soon, he'd lose his ranch and everything else that mattered to him.

A dozen longhorns were still missing six hours later when Ben returned to the ranch. Every muscle ached as he swung down from his horse and gazed at Zack. "I was thinking we should take a break and have supper at the house tonight. What d'you think?"

"It's a good idea only if you aren't going to harass Miss Elizabeth about her cooking."

Ben couldn't believe his ears. Zack had turned on him, too. "I was just kidding around the other night, and you know it."

Grim-faced, Zack gave an exasperated huff. "Only it hurt her, and it's not right. She's doing her best."

Ben gave a derisive snort. "Whatever happened to, 'You hired a cook. She don't know squat, so tell her to take a hike'."

"I can't believe I said that."

"Believe it."

"Well, if I did, I was wrong. She's coming along nicely."

"Tell me how you jumped to that conclusion."

Zack scowled. "Birthday cake wasn't so bad."

"It wasn't so good either. As I recall, it

was burnt and stuck to the bottom of the pan."

"Kids loved it. And once you cut off the lower third, the rest tasted fine."

"The top of that cake was dry as sawdust and you know it. Old man, you've sold out because of that fancy shirt she made you."

"I'm telling you, that woman's a gem."

"She may be a gem, but she's no cook."

"Who cares? The woman's worth her weight in gold. If I was ten years younger, I'd go after her myself."

"You old goat, you'd need to be forty years younger to court Elizabeth. And even then, you wouldn't stand a chance with an Easterner."

Zack's whiskered chin rose in defiance. "And why not?"

"Easterners are too soft, and when the going gets rough, they turn tail and run."

"Are you talking about Elizabeth or your mother?"

A chill raced up Ben's spine. He bit his lower lip to keep from saying something he'd regret.

"Open your eyes, boy. Elizabeth's got gumption. She ain't likely to run because things get rough. If she was a man, I'd say her balls were larger than the ones on Buck Sander's bull."

Ben glared straight ahead.

"Let go of the past. Stop comparing every woman to —"

Every inch of Ben's body tightened as he pierced the old man with a warning look. He knew his mother hadn't loved him enough, but he didn't need to be reminded.

Zack took a breath and cut the sentence short. Then he poked Ben's chest. "Just 'cause Elizabeth comes from Boston don't mean she's the same. I've seen you moon over that little gal. You better make a move now before it's too late."

The old man's gall never ceased to amaze him. Ben was good and angry, but he couldn't let that last comment pass. "What are you yakking about now?"

"Ward Metcalf came sniffing around this afternoon. He arrived with fancy chocolates, that stiff mustache of his twitching up a storm. Damn near made me sick. But I'll tell you this," Zack stuck a gnarled finger in Ben's face, "Elizabeth was eating up his compliments, and he was laying it on real thick. That lady's starving for attention, and Metcalf's willing to provide it."

Ben pretended the news was nothing to him.

"So if you have a mind to lay claim to that little gal, you'd better get it done real soon."

Ward Metcalf. The mere sound of the name turned Ben's stomach. He suspected Metcalf was behind his trouble, but he couldn't be certain. Who else would benefit if his ranch didn't turn a profit?

He turned to Zack and saw him staring at him as if he expected a reply to his ridiculous banter. Ben was about to tell him to mind his own business when he spotted Lefty atop his palomino, galloping toward them.

Lefty pulled hard on the reins as he reached them. "A man's been shot. I found the body about six hundred feet from here on the path behind the outhouse."

"Anyone we know?"

"Don't think so."

The two men followed Lefty and found the body lying faceup. Ben knelt beside the corpse, which was already growing cold. The man had been shot through the head with what he suspected was a small caliber bullet. He glanced up at Lefty. "Were you the one who turned his pockets inside out?"

"He was like this when I found him."

When Ben lifted the dead man's shirt, he spotted an empty money belt cinched tight over his belly.

Zack's shaggy eyebrows rose. "If the stiff was loaded, he ain't now."

While Zack went in search of the dead man's horse, Ben grabbed the body's shoulders and Lefty took the feet. They lugged him into the barn, planning to lay the corpse on the wagon bed where it would remain until morning, when someone could make the trip into town. As they neared the wagon, Ben saw Elizabeth walk by with a pail of milk in her hand.

She saw the corpse and went white as chalk. "Donald."

"You know this man?" Ben hadn't meant to sound so gruff.

She reminded him of a cornered animal as she shook her head, tears welling in her eyes. Horror twisted her face, transforming her lovely features into a mask of pain.

Had Ben not been holding onto to the dead man, he'd have rushed to her side. A thousand questions popped into his mind. Helplessly, he watched the bucket handle slip from her fingers. Her hands rose to cover her mouth. Milk splattered her britches and shoes. She didn't seem to notice the guttural sound that escaped from deep in her throat.

Shivers raced up Ben's spine. He motioned Lefty to set the body down, so he could comfort Elizabeth. As they lowered the dead man to the ground, she ran from the barn.

Ben found Elizabeth behind the house, sitting on an old stump with her back to him. She didn't even glance up when he hunkered down beside her. In her hands she held a bunch of pine needles that she pulled apart one by one.

"Elizabeth, it's time you told me what's going on."

She didn't even pause, just kept shredding the pine needles as if it mattered a darn.

"Elizabeth, tell me what that man was doing on my land."

After a moment she lifted her head and gazed at him with bleak blue eyes that tore at his heart. "I'll take care of it. It's my problem."

"Not any more. When your problems spill over onto my property, they become mine. You know who that dead man was, and I need to know, too."

When she didn't answer, he continued, "Does he usually travel alone? I've got Granny to consider."

His words jolted her. "Of course, you're right." She took a deep breath and lifted her obstinate chin. "I wouldn't want to put anyone in danger, especially Granny. If you'll help me pack my belongings, I can be on my way first thing tomorrow morning."

He cursed long and hard, but he didn't even get a rise out of her. "You aren't going anywhere till I get to the bottom of this. So if you think you can sashay out of here without a word of explanation, you can think again."

Her pupils narrowed. He noticed how her back stiffened. Foolish woman.

A gentle breeze ruffled her hair; the scent of lilacs stirred his senses, leaving him reeling with desire. With every fiber of his being, he wanted to protect her. "When are you going to tell me what's going on around here?"

She heaved a ragged sigh, and he brushed the pine needles from her palm, tucking her hand into his. "Elizabeth," he said, in a gentle tone. "You're no longer in this mess by yourself. Let me help you."

She gazed at him as if she couldn't believe his words.

"I want to help," he repeated, remembering how her lips had felt against his. He needed to touch her. Before he knew what he was doing, he reached up and traced the left side of her face with one finger. Her hair, like silk, brushed his hand.

She glanced down at her knees and smoothed out the material over her legs.

He squeezed her hand tight. "Tell me. You and I are staying here all night if that's what it takes."

"I don't even know his last name. Donald worked for my stepfather, which means he isn't a nice man. No one connected to Robert T. Hines is."

"Does Donald work alone?"

"I think so, but I can't be sure."

"Now, tell me what's going on." Ben waited patiently for her to continue.

When she looked up, her eyes implored him to understand. "You saw Cecelia when I first arrived. The poor child was scared to speak. She's a prime example of what Robert T. Hines does to people." Her lips twisted in a sneer. "Robert T. Hines is a clever man. To the outside world, he comes across as a doting father, but he doesn't give a damn about anyone but himself. He picked on Cecelia and Josh, belittled every attempt they made to please him. Nothing was ever good enough. And as terrible as he was sober, he was worse drunk. I knew if I didn't get those children out of Boston, away from that evil man's influence, they'd be permanently scarred. Though he never struck either one of them, I never doubted it would come to that."

Ben noticed Elizabeth was trembling. He

pulled her to her feet and hugged her tight. "Did he ever strike you?"

She gulped a breath of air. "Once, after he'd been drinking."

Ben's body went rigid. He pulled away and tilted Elizabeth's chin. "Did he hurt you?"

She gave him a gentle smile. "Not bad, but that's when I vowed to escape."

Ben pulled her head to his chest. He could feel her heart pounding against him. "The poster says you left with a small fortune from his safe."

"I had planned to do just that. Unfortunately, he invested in some big business deal the day before. The money I took was barely enough for train fare out here. I used every last nickel we had to purchase the wagon and horse that brought us to Welcome."

"Of all places, why choose Welcome?"

"When I escaped, there wasn't time to plan an itinerary. As bad luck would have it, we were already on the train bound for nowhere in particular when I read about Welcome in the newspaper."

Her stroke of bad luck had been Ben's good fortune. He almost told her that, but instead he said, "Welcome's not so bad."

"It's fine for a cowboy."

"You got that right."

"There's nothing for a woman here."

"Oh, there's plenty for a woman to do. Look at Granny."

"Look at Queenie," she countered.

"Sure, there aren't many opportunities right now, but there will be in time."

"I feel as if time is passing me by."

"You have plenty of time."

"I'm twenty-two, You know what that means, Ben Ricker?"

He didn't have a clue. "Beats me."

"Most women my age have a husband and babies by now. I'm an old maid."

"You're kidding, right?"

"Do I look like I'm kidding?"

"You don't look a day over twenty-one and a half," he said with a broad grin.

"This isn't at all funny."

"You're damn pretty for a little old lady."

"You, Ben Ricker, are the most aggravating man I've ever met."

"Does that mean you like me?"

She laughed. "No, it does not."

The musical sound warmed his chest.

"How long are you aiming to stay?"

"I'll be leaving as soon as I save up enough money to head to California. I hope to open a dress shop with my own creations."

"Why not do that in Montana?"

"California is more open to change."

"And Welcome isn't?"

"Even you said the people around here would have trouble accepting my designs."

"Can you imagine the women gathering eggs in one of your creations?"

"There's nothing to keep me here." Her imploring eyes settled on his, as if she was waiting for him to say something to the contrary.

He remembered his talk with Zack, but he still couldn't find the right words to ask her to stay. He wanted to tell her he was damn happy she was on his ranch. He wanted to tell her how he dreamed about her both day and night. He wanted to hug her to him and never let her go. But he didn't say any of that because a distant memory came back to haunt him.

He remembered a little boy and the ruckus he'd caused the day he found his mother packing, his small hands grabbing hold of her skirts, begging her not to leave. Sobbing uncontrollably, the child promised he'd act better. If she stayed, he'd even clean the house and learn to cook. But nothing he'd said had changed a thing.

When his mother climbed aboard the wagon and sat beside some strange man, she'd turned and waved to him one last time. His father had held him as he shrieked for her to come back. And all the tears, all the pleading, had gotten him nowhere. His heartache was fresh in his mind. He could never chance being hurt like that again.

She inhaled slowly. "Besides, I need to earn my own way. I'm going to prove to Cecelia that a woman can succeed without a man. I never intend to marry."

There it was again — the tone that spoke volumes. The words saying she'd eventually leave him. Just as his mother had so many years ago.

He cleared his throat. "It looks like we have something in common. I'm never getting married either."

Chapter 15

Around sundown the next day, Zack eased the empty buckboard into the barn.

Ben strode over to help unhitch the horses. "Did the sheriff have any words of wisdom for us?"

Zack gave a disgusted grunt. "You know him, more belly than brains. Figured out it was a small caliber bullet only after Pete dug it from the dead man's head. So the sheriff scratches hisself and after working on it a while, finally says, 'Looks like it's a small bullet.'" He shook his head. "Pete says the bullet most likely comes from a two-shot Derringer, like the ones some of the ladies carry around."

Ben yanked the bridle from the horse and started to brush the sweat from the animal. "What did our fine law enforcement official have to say about that?"

"After considerable time, he picks the bullet up with his thick sausage fingers, examines it 'bout two inches from his eyes, and finally says, 'As I see it, this here comes from a two-shot Derringer.' "

"Anything else?"

"No. I left, or I'd have puked." Zack made a rude noise. "Next time we got business with the sheriff, send Lefty. I don't have it in me to talk to that fool again anytime soon."

"Did anyone ask who the dead man might be?"

"Yup, but I did as you said. I burnt the posters of Elizabeth we found in his saddlebags before going to town. I told everyone we didn't have any idea who he was." Zack stopped talking a minute, then continued. "Who do you think shot him and took his money?"

"I don't know."

After looking around the barn, Zack covered his mouth with his hand. "Might it be Miss Elizabeth?"

"If I hadn't seen the shock on her face when she saw the body, I'd have suspected her. There's no way she did it."

"Who, then?"

"Maybe someone was trailing him. This guy was no saint. Most likely, he had his share of enemies. The person who killed him took the money and ran. We might never know who's responsible."

Several minutes later, the two men left the barn and started across the yard. "Are you having supper with us tonight?"

"Nah, my mouth's been salivating the whole way home just thinking of my beans. Care to join me?"

Ben waved his offer away. "Another time. I figure I'll take my chances with Elizabeth's cooking."

Zack's face hardened. "You better not pull any of that crazy stuff."

"Don't worry. I'll behave myself. Even if the biscuits are too hard to chew, I'll bring mine out to the barn, use a sledge to bust it up, and eat every hard crumb, and I'll smile the entire time."

Zack scowled and shoved his finger into Ben's chest. "That's just what I was talking 'bout. Keep that wise mouth of yours shut tight."

Just thinking about the foul expression on the old man's face had Ben grinning ear to ear when he entered the kitchen. His smile vanished the instant he spotted Ward Metcalf sitting at the supper table with Josh on his lap.

"Look what Mr. Metcalf brought," Josh shouted in his ear-splitting voice while digging two chocolates from a fancy box.

Ward's mouth curved in a brazen grin that sent his mustache twitching upward. "Care to try a bonbon, Ben?"

"No thanks, I don't want to ruin my appetite." Truth was, his appetite had soured the instant he first saw this man in his kitchen.

When Granny entered the room, decked out in her fancy dress, Ward slid Josh from his knee and crossed the kitchen at a brisk clip. With more ceremony than seemed fitting, he escorted Granny to her seat and before letting go of her palm, he lifted her hand to his mouth for an honest-to-goodness kiss. "It's been a pleasure, Madame."

If Zack were here, he'd have puked for sure. Watching the foolish spectacle turned Ben's stomach.

Granny, bless her soul, slapped him away. "Get away, you damn fool."

Josh smacked his chocolate-covered lips. "These bonbons are really, really good."

Ben rested a hand on the boy's head. "Cowboys don't use words like bonbon. It's chocolate, plain and simple."

Ward's mustache dropped a notch.

Ben felt a moment's satisfaction.

Josh popped another piece of candy in his

mouth. "These chocolates taste really, really good." A mischievous grin lit his face.

Proud of the kid, Ben ruffled his hair. "That's much better."

Just then, Elizabeth, dressed to the hilt, entered the kitchen. If Ben thought Ward's performance had been something before, he soon realized the man was just warming up.

Ward gushed his approval. His eyes damn near fell out of their sockets as he strode across the room and kissed Elizabeth's palm.

Elizabeth giggled like a schoolgirl.

Ben was tempted to shove a bonbon up each of Ward Metcalf's nostrils.

Determined to appear calm, he scraped his chair back and took a load off. He allowed Ward to perform his circus act, and he'd have laughed aloud had Elizabeth not seemed to be enjoying herself.

Every time Elizabeth came near the table, Ward jumped up like a jackrabbit. He'd smile down at her and insist on taking the dish from her hands.

Ben didn't think he could take much more of this. He'd have gladly eaten beans with Zack, but he needed to keep an eye on things. Finally, the meal was ready: beef, potatoes, and carrots.

Ward helped Elizabeth sit, then pushed

her chair in as if she were an invalid.

"Thank you, Ward." She smiled politely, her eyes twinkling their approval.

As Ward sat down, he slid his chair a few inches closer to Elizabeth. "Now, promise me you won't go getting up for anything. If there's something you need, tell me, and I'll get it for you. Someone like you shouldn't be carrying dishes around anyway."

"She's the cook," Ben reminded Ward, in case he'd forgotten. "I'm paying her to work."

"Someone like Elizabeth should have people waiting on her."

The tiny hairs on Ben's neck stood up straight. "Since you're doing a fine job, maybe I should let her go and hire you."

Ward brushed off the comment like the true gentleman that he was.

Ben cleared his throat. "We've been having trouble around here lately."

"What kind of trouble?" Granny asked, clearly upset.

Ward scowled. "Now look what you've done. Men with good manners never discuss their problems at the table in front of such fine ladies."

"I'm sure they don't." Ben blew a breath between clenched teeth. "As I started to say earlier, someone's been cutting our fences."

Granny grabbed a bun from the basket. "You have any idea who?"

"Can't say for sure." He studied Ward's face, but the weasel's expression never changed. Ben wasn't even sure he'd heard him because his attention was riveted on Elizabeth and the children.

"I've heard some wonderful things about you, Cecelia," Ward said.

The young girl's cheeks blushed bright crimson.

"Elizabeth's been telling me what a help you are in the kitchen." Ward then turned his comments to Josh. "And I hear you're a real smart kid. Elizabeth says you know your numbers and can already read some words."

Josh buttered his bun and shrugged.

Ward patted the boy's shoulder. "You study hard. When you grow up, I can always use another smart person in my bank."

Josh made a face. "I don't wanna be a banker. I wanna be a cowboy, like Ben."

When Elizabeth laughed, Ward made a feeble effort, but Ben roared louder than anyone else.

Clyde, sitting on Ward's other side, slurped up his potatoes at a rate that suggested he hadn't eaten in weeks. Ben noticed the flash of irritation that crossed Ward's face when he glanced at the child. But Ward's phony smile was back in place when he looked at Elizabeth. "I can't believe what a good job you've done with Clyde."

Again, Elizabeth's face lit with pleasure. "I think he's a smart boy. Who knows, he might be the one who ends up working at your bank."

No one but Ben saw the disbelief in Ward's eyes.

Ben speared Ward with a look of disgust. "It's never going to happen. The boy's too valuable. I plan to keep him on at the ranch."

In his excitement, Josh slammed his hand against Clyde's arm, almost pushing him off the chair. "Hear that. Me and you are gonna be cowboys."

Ward went on and on about how good the meal was. Even Ben admitted it wasn't bad. The meat was fairly bland, but it was edible, much better than he'd expected. The potatoes had lumps, and the carrots were undercooked, but now wasn't the time to point out such things. "Yes, you've done a good job, Lizzy."

She rewarded him with a warm smile.

Ward reached for another bun and grinned helplessly. "These have to be the best I've ever tasted. I don't want you to think me a glutton, but I just can't help myself."

Elizabeth lapped up his compliment like a starving kitten. "Thank you."

Ben felt he should say something, too. "These are real good." He didn't think he could take another bite, but he grabbed a bun, broke it in half, and shoved it in his mouth.

She didn't seem to notice.

After supper, Ward insisted on helping Elizabeth clear the table. He even offered to do the dishes. Elizabeth had to refuse several times before he would take no for an answer. Meanwhile, Ben sat on the porch stewing. When Ward finally took a seat beside him, he seemed relieved to escape.

"Phew, that was a close one. For a minute I was afraid I'd be doing woman's work."

Ben couldn't even look at the man. Instead, he concentrated on his initials carved on the arm of the old rocker. "Laying it on quite thick in there, don't you think?"

Ward laughed. "Let me give you some free advice about the ladies. Give a woman enough compliments, and she'll be eating out of your hand."

"Elizabeth isn't the type."

Ward seemed damn sure of himself when he thrust his chin forward. "Trust me, that little filly isn't immune to the Metcalf charm."

Later that evening, Ben saw a guilty look on Josh's face as the boy peeked around the corner of the house. When Ben pretended to glance away, Josh and Clyde darted across the yard and disappeared inside the barn. Certain they were up to no good, Ben decided to investigate.

He followed them into barn and craned his head, listening for the boys' voices.

"You mustn't tell anyone I found Granny's old pipe in the trash bin," Josh said, his voice hushed.

Ben tiptoed closer. Clyde grunted.

"It's not as if I stole it, 'cause Granny didn't want the pipe anymore. She has the spanking new one I gave her for her birthday."

From this distance Ben could make out the boys' heads. He watched Josh motion for Clyde to crouch down beside him. Bringing the pipe to his nose, Josh inhaled a deep breath. "It smells really good. Here, you want to take a whiff?" he asked, sticking the corncob pipe in Clyde's face. Then he pointed to the dry hay scattered about. Clyde immediately scurried around and gathered large handfuls mixed with pebbles.

Ben watched Josh brush dirt off a few choice hay blades, and with a knife cut the straw into tiny pieces while Clyde looked on in awe. Josh gave Clyde a conspiratorial grin. "Looks just like real tobacco."

Clyde nodded.

"I sure don't see any difference."

Josh was ready to strike a match when Ben cleared his throat. "What are you two boys up to?"

Josh jumped, hiding the match in his pocket and the pipe behind his back. "Nothing."

Ben stepped toward the boys. "Don't hand me that. I saw the matches and the pipe."

Josh studied his shoe a moment. Slowly, he looked up. "Are you gonna tell Betts?"

"It depends."

" 'Cause Betts is gonna tan my hide if she finds out."

"Are you playing with matches?"

Josh shook his head.

"Are you telling me the truth?"

Tears sprang to the boy's eyes. He dug in his pocket and removed the match. "I didn't light it."

"But you were going to."

Josh nodded.

Ben ruffled his hair. "Look, if you give me the matches, I'll let you keep the pipe, and I won't say a word to Elizabeth. But I need your word that you won't light any more matches. Fire and hay don't mix. You understand?"

"Yes . . . you aren't gonna tell Betts?"

"Only if you give me your word that I can trust you."

Reluctantly, Josh dropped three matches into Ben's upturned palm. "When I'm bigger, I plan to have my very own pipe and matches."

Ben bit back a grin. "Just make sure you're a lot older."

"You won't tell Betts?"

"This is our secret," Ben replied, taking the small hand in his.

Two weeks later, Ward Metcalf had become a permanent fixture on Ben's ranch, and Ben was having a rough time dealing with the constant compliments and the wide phony smile. Looking at that twitching mustache, honed to sharp points and curling up at the ends, was more than Ben could stomach.

Josh came up beside him. "Why're you spying on Betts?"

"I'm just admiring the ranch house from here. Nothing wrong with that, is there?"

"Guess not. But did you notice we can

see Betts and Mr. Metcalf really good from here?"

Ben pretended to be surprised. "Golly, you're right." The light from the kitchen door spilled onto the porch, illuminating Ward, dressed in a dark suit, bearing gifts again, probably some for the kids and Granny too. When Ward did his buttering up, he did it on a grand scale. His carriage, with fancy gold scrollwork and heavy brass fittings, was parked out front.

"Can I stand here with you so we can admire the ranch together?"

"Sure thing." When Ben glanced down at Josh, he noticed the boy was leaning against the barn door in a nonchalant pose with legs crossed. A good dose of pride hit him when he realized the boy was mimicking his every move. To test his theory, Ben uncrossed his legs and folded his arms over his chest. Sure enough, Josh did the same. Ben doubted he'd ever have a son, but if he did, he'd want the boy to be just like this one. Come to think of it, he'd want a daughter like Cecelia, too. Even Clyde, thanks to Elizabeth's tireless efforts, had potential. Ben figured he'd grow into a productive adult. He might never be capable of working at Metcalf's bank, but that was in the boy's favor.

"Betts is going on a real date."

That was the first Ben had heard of it. "So?"

"She's got on the new dress she made, and Cecelia helped her put her hair up in big curls. I even seen her pinch her cheeks. I asked her what she did that for, and you know what?"

"What?"

"It's to color them." Josh grunted in disgust. "Isn't that dumb?"

"A date, you say. Where's Ward taking her?" Ben's stomach knotted. He didn't like pumping Josh for information, but right now, the boy was his only source. Besides, according to local gossip, Ward had only two hands but more moves than a chessboard. Ben needed to know the score.

Josh shrugged. "Betts says Mr. Metcalf is treating her to dinner. Are we 'bout done admiring yet? This is getting boring."

"You're right. Let's us two cowboys hit the trail. Besides, you and I have something important to do."

The youngster's eyes grew wide. "What?"

"When I was in Butte this afternoon, I picked up a surprise for you and Clyde. If you get him, I'll meet you two in my room lickety-split."

Josh took off at a trot. Ben lingered a moment longer. He told himself he didn't care. It was Elizabeth's life. It was no business of his whom she went out with. She could take care of herself. But he wasn't so sure. She didn't know Ward the way he did. Ward was shrewd and underhanded. When Ben saw Ward with his hand on Elizabeth's elbow, leading her to his carriage, Ben decided Ward was also the luckiest man in the world.

Chin dragging, Ben entered his room a few minutes later to find Josh and Clyde jumping on his bed. "Hey, get down from there. If you bust up my bed, I'll have to share yours."

"Yippee!"

"Forget it. I had enough of that when Elizabeth was hurt. My ribs are still bruised from the battering I took."

Josh took a flying leap and landed with a loud thump. His shadow, Clyde, did the same. "What you got for us, huh?"

Clyde looked as excited as Josh, though Ben suspected he didn't know what was going on.

"Look under the bed," he replied with a deep laugh. The boys' antics were good for his mood.

When Josh found the boxes and flung them out, he nicked Clyde's forehead. Ben ran to check on the child but figured he'd live when he didn't bat an eye.

Josh opened a box. "Real cowboy boots. Look Clyde, real boots, just like Ben's." He beamed and whipped off his old shoes, throwing them across the room. "I'm never gonna take these off," he said, with such admiration in his eyes that Ben felt an overwhelming surge of love for the child.

Once the boots were on, Josh yanked Clyde across the room and stood beside Ben. "Now we're the same. Me and you and Clyde are cowboys, right, Ben?"

"Looks that way."

After the boys left, Ben went down to the kitchen for some apple brandy. He headed to the porch with a bottle and decided to sit in his favorite rocker for a spell. As he gazed at the moon, a light breeze stirred the lilac bushes at the corner of the house, filling the air with their sweet smell. It was a truly a beautiful spring night, and that worried him.

Ward would use that in his favor. If he laid it on thick in public, Ben didn't want to think how the man must act in private. He made a disgusted sound as he pulled the stopper from the bottle. The cap came off far too easily, and one swallow confirmed his suspicions.

He set the bottle down and leaned against

the chair. He pushed himself back and propped his boots on the porch railing, closing his eyes for just a few minutes. He heaved a tired sigh. In another four hours, he'd need to relieve Lefty. Luckily, no one had tampered with the herd since the two of them had started doing their rounds at night.

One minute Ben was calculating the money he needed to save his ranch, the next he was awakened by voices at the other end of the porch.

"I hope you weren't disappointed with the meal. I only wish I could have brought you somewhere special to eat."

"The meal was fine."

Ward reached for Elizabeth's hand, gave it a squeeze.

Ben's heart fell.

"Then you didn't mind eating at my house?"

Elizabeth laughed softly.

A feeling that came damn close to jealousy churned in the pit of Ben's stomach.

"You have a lovely home, Ward." She paused and covered her mouth in a gesture Ben considered totally feminine. "I must admit, when I learned we were dining in, I was a little concerned until I found out your housekeeper was going to be there. You're a true gentleman, Ward Metcalf."

Ward actually bowed from the waist.

Ben gagged at the sight.

"You've enriched my life, Elizabeth."

She looked into Ward's face.

Ben knew he should leave, but he couldn't do that without being noticed, and it was clear to him they wouldn't be happy to find him hidden in the shadows.

Ward took Elizabeth's hands in his. "I know you haven't known me long, but I feel as if we've been together much longer." He looked down at his shoes and shuffled nervously.

Ben recognized an act when he saw one.

"I don't want to do anything improper, but . . . will you allow me to kiss you?"

Ben held his breath, and when Elizabeth nodded, he had to stop himself from charging across the porch. Ward's mouth lowered. It seemed like forever, but Ben knew it couldn't have taken but a few seconds. Helplessly, he watched the stiff mustache connect with Elizabeth's cheek. It took a moment for that fact to register. When it did, he could have hooted with joy.

"You taste sweeter than dessert."

Another soft laugh from Elizabeth.

Another gag from Ben.

"Elizabeth, I have something to say of a

serious nature, and I want you to listen. I'm the kind of man who makes important decisions every day. It's what I do for a living. When I find something I want or something I know will be a good investment, I don't sit around for weeks and think about it. I move on it right away."

"But what does that have to do with me?"

Ward lifted Elizabeth's hand to his lips and allowed his mouth to linger there a moment. "Elizabeth, I'm asking you to marry me."

CHAPTER 16

Elizabeth couldn't believe her ears.

Marriage. To Ward?

The shock must have registered on her face because she detected a frown beneath his groomed mustache.

"Don't answer now. Give yourself a chance to get used to the idea."

Though Ward had much to offer, there was no sense holding back the truth. "But I don't love you."

"What's that have to do with anything? In the Orient, parents arrange marriages for their children at the time of their birth. They grow to love each other. Besides, I'm very fond of you, and I think you like me, too."

"Yes, of course I like you."

"Do you enjoy my company?"

"Of course." Elizabeth let go of Ward's hands and clutched her chest. When he'd first proposed, her heart had stopped, but now it was thumping so hard she could barely catch her breath. "I think it's only fair to tell you I've no intention of . . ." She'd meant to tell him she wasn't going to marry anyone, but he pressed a finger to her lips.

"Shhhh, not now. Give yourself a chance to think. Handle our possible marriage the same way I do business. Take a piece of paper, draw a line down the middle, and write the pros and cons in each column."

Elizabeth couldn't believe any of what he was saying. Bitterness crept up the back of her throat. If she were to divide a piece of paper in half, the cons would far outnumber the pros. "Don't you find making a list a bit cold?"

"Not really. Here, let me give you a head start. On the plus side, I'm a reasonably good catch." He raised a hand in protest. "Now don't go looking at me like that. I'm simply stating a fact. I own the bank. I have a nice home and more money than most men in Montana. I don't see how I could honestly consider that a flaw. It should be obvious that I'm smitten with your beauty."

Warmth rose to her cheeks. Yes, she'd seen the admiration in his eyes. "Ward, if you don't mind my asking, have you made a list about me?"

His mustache twitched upward. "Not on

paper, but there's one in my mind. First, you're a beautiful woman. You're far prettier than any other female in these parts. Any man would be proud to be seen with such a gorgeous lady on his arm."

She mulled over what he'd said. "You keep mentioning my appearance as if it's what matters most to you."

"Oh, my dearest lady, though your appearance is what I first noticed, it didn't take me long to see the warmth deep in your soul. You are a good, kind, and absolutely wonderful person. But I'd have to be blind not to know that you're beautiful. You aren't going to hold that against me, are you?"

Ward Metcalf was a smooth talker, no doubt about that. She laughed in spite of herself. "No, I certainly am not faulting you for that."

"Consider this, though it might not be my place to mention anything. Your brother and sister can be a handful. You could use my help raising them." Ward cleared his throat and loosened his collar a notch. "Frankly, it's obvious that Josh could use a firm hand once in a while. He runs around the house like a wild savage most of the time. The child needs a father, someone he can look up to, someone to set some limits."

"He's just a spirited boy."

"Yes, but without a man's influence, who knows what he'll become."

On several occasions, Robert T. Hines had referred to Josh as an ill-mannered child. Spirited boy sounded so much better, but she wondered whether the two terms might carry the same meaning.

Ward must have seen her hesitation because he continued, "I hate to tread on delicate ground, but most women your age are already married. There can't be many suitors willing to take on a ready-made family. I'm offering you a home and escape from your financial responsibilities. A woman like you should have servants at your beck and call, not the way it is here." He waved his hand to indicate Ben's ranch. "You deserve better than this. If you marry me, you'll never have to work a day in your life."

Her stepfather had servants, and he'd admired her mother's appearance. But he'd been controlling. And her mother had been unable to leave the house without her husband's permission. Elizabeth would never settle for that type of life.

"But I was thinking of opening a dress shop . . ."

Before she could finish, he broke in and patted the top of her head, the way one did a small child. "Don't you worry your pretty head about earning a living. If you marry me, you won't have to toil even one hour. Besides, it wouldn't be fitting for a man of my standing to have a wife working outside the house." A wide grin spread across his face. "My dear, if we wed, your only job will be keeping me happy."

Elizabeth blinked twice. For a moment she thought Robert T. Hines was standing on the porch in front of her. She searched his features and concluded there was no resemblance, but the words were the same. This man was narrow-minded and egotistical.

In that instant, she knew she would never marry the likes of him. But then again, she would not marry any man. She wasn't sure how to break the news to him without hurting his feelings. When she looked up, he mistook her silence for something else.

"I'm leaving first thing tomorrow morning on business. Give me your answer when I return in about a week. I'll have something wonderful to think about while I'm gone." He brushed his mouth against her forehead, turned, hopped into his carriage, and drove away.

After working half the night, Ben entered

the kitchen at sunup without so much as a hello. In his peripheral vision, he caught the confusion on Lizzy's face. *Damn woman,* he thought to himself again as he stalked out of the room. During the long hours before dawn, he'd muttered the familiar phrase whenever he thought of her on the porch with that weasel. And he'd thought of nothing else.

Ben awoke after noontime, barely able to keep his eyes open. His head pounded relentlessly. No doubt his lack of sleep was responsible for his deteriorating condition. Before he could stop himself, he was thinking about Lizzy again. Why couldn't she see through Ward Metcalf's bullshit? He fully expected her to tell everyone she was leaving to marry Ward.

Though she'd told Ben she never intended to get married, he knew women changed their minds. His mother had. One day she was swearing to love and honor; the next she'd hightailed it back to Boston, never to return, never to claim the son who'd waited years to see her face.

Ben stared at the overhead ceiling, figuring Elizabeth might already have made her announcement over breakfast. Well, he was damn glad he'd missed that.

He tumbled from bed and after washing

up, headed to the kitchen for a cup of dark coffee and something to eat. He was itching for a fight when he stormed into the room. He figured he'd gladly wrench the neck of any person who got in his way.

Elizabeth stood at the stove with her back to him, her fiery hair clasped loosely at her nape. He knew the warm flesh behind her ear would smell of lilacs. More than anything in the world, he wanted to test his theory. What would she do if he pulled her against him and kissed that very spot? A few minutes earlier he'd been dragging his butt, but any remaining fatigue evaporated as his mind conjured up sizzling images.

He was grinning when she turned.

"Good morning, Ben."

The way she said his name gave him hope. What kind of logic was that? He called himself a jackass. Of course, she called him Ben. What did he expect? Though surely, he hadn't mistaken the warmth in her eyes.

His heart gave a sudden jolt.

"When Josh threw back the covers this morning, he showed me his boot-clad feet," Elizabeth said.

"You telling me he wore them to bed?"

She nodded. "He claims he's never taking them off."

Ben felt good inside. The laugh that burst

from him was totally unexpected. "That little guy's a pistol."

Her eyebrows wrinkled. "I had planned to buy him boots with my sewing money. You certainly can't be expected to pay for my brother's shoes."

"You're right, of course. And I'd have never bought him shoes. He's a cowboy. He needed boots. I took care of the problem because I wanted to. You most definitely are not going to repay me."

She grew thoughtful, but when she glanced back at him, her blue eyes sparkled with joy. "Thank you. You've made Josh very happy."

"It was no big deal."

"It was to him."

Ben really liked Josh. It surprised him to discover how strongly he felt about the boy. He'd never had children around, and up until now, he'd thought he liked it that way. But he'd been wrong. The ranch wouldn't be the same when the children left.

His very existence would be dismal without Elizabeth.

Unexpectedly, the idea came to him. He wasn't about to let her leave without a fight. He had at least a week before the weasel returned. During that time he planned to do everything in his power to persuade Elizabeth that she and the children belonged on his ranch.

He'd show her she didn't need Ward Metcalf's money. If he could convince Elizabeth she could make a decent living on her own, then maybe she'd see how absurd Metcalf's proposal was. She didn't love the man. When she'd said so, he'd given a silent cheer.

"I have a little business venture to discuss with you."

"What's that?"

"I've hired two new men to work at the mill. I want you to make lunch for them and bring it over to them around noon each day. I'll pay you, of course."

"How much?"

"Effective immediately, I'm upping your salary to twelve dollars."

He'd expected her to express her gratitude, but instead she dared to remind him, "That's more like it. No decent cook gets paid two dollars a week."

He agreed with her wholeheartedly. Pointing out she was not a decent cook would be counterproductive, so he merely nodded and smiled. She seemed content with that. On a roll, he figured he'd sweeten the pot. "Also, midday, I want you to bake oatmeal cookies or a cake for me and my men. I'll give you another dollar a week for that."

Her eyebrows rose in distrust. "I didn't think you liked my baking."

He did his best to look hurt. "You've got to be kidding. I love your cookies, and the cake you made for Granny's birthday was really good."

Elizabeth's oatmeal cookies were hard and so sticky they could pull teeth, but he was beyond caring. He'd seen the way Ward had praised them, shoving them in his pocket when Elizabeth was out of sight. If Ward could lie about Elizabeth's cooking and get away with it, Ben could certainly stretch the truth a little. This was war, and he aimed to use any weapon at his disposal.

"Would you like me to bake something today?"

"Tomorrow will be soon enough."

She looked disappointed.

"I was hoping you'd take the rest of the day off and go horseback riding with me."

"What about the children?"

"I'd like them to come, too."

She clenched her hands in front of her. "Hot damn, that sounds like fun. Oops . . ." She covered her mouth. "I'll have to stop saying things like that. There's no longer any need. But they just seem to slip out."

It was a shame Metcalf wasn't around to

hear her choice of words. His mustache would have hit his chest for sure.

Ben shrugged and was going to let it pass, but he couldn't control his curiosity. "Why is that?"

Sadness clouded her eyes. "Robert T. Hines wanted his women to dress like ladies, to act like ladies, and to speak like ladies at all times. At first, I tried to obey his stringent rules, but he was always disappointed with my efforts. Finally, I gave him reason to be unhappy. Unfortunately, I no longer have to use colorful language, but the words still spew from my mouth of their own volition."

Cecelia and Clyde decided to stay with Granny, but nothing could have stopped Josh from going. As Ben saddled up the horses, Josh was running in circles around the yard. "Yippee!"

Ben stopped what he was doing to look at the boy, who was leaping over a low fence. He could see the limitless energy in Josh's small body. His new boots were already scuffed, and the shirt Elizabeth had tucked into his pants a moment earlier had come undone. "Hey, partner, get over here. If you're not too busy, I want to explain a few things about the horse you'll be riding."

The boy streaked across the yard, arms and legs a blur. Ben had never seen a child move so fast.

"This is Jethro," Ben said, patting the animal's neck.

"Is this really, really big horse mine?" Josh craned his neck and eyed the large beast.

"For this afternoon, he is." Jethro looked impressive, but he was easygoing. Extremely lazy was more like it. Chances were they'd have to stop several times to prod the animal along.

"Pick me up. I wanna sit in the saddle."

Ben shook his head. "What kind of talk is that? A real cowboy would do that by himself." He stacked boxes alongside Jethro and made sure the boy didn't fall when he climbed up.

The wide grin Josh bestowed on him was priceless. Josh reached out and took Ben's hand. "I love you, Ben. I really, really love you."

Ben was flabbergasted by the sincerity of the boy's tone. He was all choked up. "That means a lot to me."

Then, without warning, Josh slammed his palm against Jethro's haunch and hollered, "Giddy up!" at the top of his lungs.

Another horse would have been spooked, but not Jethro. The horse gave the boy a slow glance before taking a bite from the feed bucket at its feet.

"You mustn't ever do that."

"I wanna go really, really fast."

Ben's expression grew stern. "Listen up good, or you'll be off that horse before you can blink an eye. Never raise your voice around your horse, or any animal for that matter. You want them to trust you. Always keep your tone even. Don't ever sneak up on a horse either. Make sure it sees you, then reach up and give the horse a light pat on the neck so he can get used to you. It's not a bad idea to bring the animal a cube of sugar or a bite of apple. A horse is a cowboy's best friend. Josh, do you understand? Because you could get hurt if you don't listen."

"I understand. I won't ever talk loud around Jethro." The boy's small arms reached around the horse's neck. "I'm really, really sorry."

"When you want Jethro to go faster, nudge his ribs with the heels of your boots. Not hard, just a little." Jethro only went two speeds, slow and slower, but Ben wanted Josh to believe he was in control. "Another thing you need to do is hold the reins and when you want him to turn, you tug the rein in the direction you want him to go.

When you want him to stop . . ."

"I know, I know, I say whoa and pull back the reins."

"You're a smart boy."

With an ear-to-ear grin, Josh nodded enthusiastically. "Can I ride him now?"

Ben wondered what was keeping Elizabeth. While they waited, he saw no harm in letting the boy go for short ride. "Sure, but just lead him to the porch, then stop by the berry bush."

"I can go all by myself?"

"You're a cowboy now. It's your job to ride Jethro to the blackberry bush."

Jethro had a thing for berries, and he wouldn't budge once he reached them, anyway. Once the horse picked up the scent, he'd trot in that direction on his own.

Josh's chest seemed to expand with pride. "Geez, wait till Betts sees me on Jethro. She'll faint for sure."

As Ben broke into a laugh, in an even tone Josh gave the command, "Giddy up."

Jethro had taken two steps when his nostrils twitched. Ben could see that Josh had forgotten which rein to pull, but it didn't matter. Nothing was about to change Jethro's course now that he had gotten a whiff of fresh blackberries. Ben was still chuckling to himself when Elizabeth

231

bounded from the house and took a flying leap toward her brother.

"Stop that horse this instant, Josh."

Josh was beyond listening. "I'm a real cowboy!" His high-pitched voice indicated he'd already forgotten the rule about keeping an even tone.

When the horse wouldn't stop, Elizabeth blocked Jethro's path. The animal nudged her aside and gave a loud snort. She grabbed the reins and pulled with all her might, but Jethro kept plodding slowly toward his goal, dragging her alongside.

Ben meandered toward the porch and waited for Jethro to arrive. As Elizabeth's flailing arms wrenched the reins from Josh, she kept shouting, "Whoa, whoa, you damn beast."

Meanwhile, Josh dug his boots into the Jethro's ribs. "Giddy up."

If looks could kill, Ben would have drawn his last breath when Elizabeth ran to him a moment later. "Don't stand there with that stupid grin on your face. Get Josh down from that woolly mammoth." With a trembling hand, she pointed to the horse that was munching away without a care.

"Lizzy, Josh is safe." He hauled her out of earshot. "Do you honestly think I'd take foolish chances with your brother's life?

Give me more credit than that."

The rough sound of his voice penetrated her thick skull.

"But the horse is so big."

"Big and slow. Josh thinks he's in charge, but he's not. Jethro will follow my horse and he won't deviate from the course I set. So relax."

She took a moment to digest what he'd said. "I owe you an apology. When I saw Josh atop that giant beast, I was frightened for his safety. I've been responsible for both him and Cecelia for so long that I guess I overreacted."

Ben took her hand. "You sure did. But I don't blame you. I was wrong, too. I should have explained what I was going to do."

She looked at him then, really looked at him. The temperature outside rose several degrees as Ben lost himself in those deep blue eyes. For a moment no one else existed. He took a breath and filled his senses. Her hair, highlighted by the sun, took on the color of rose gold. Never before had he noticed the green flecks in her irises. He inhaled the fragrance that was totally hers, a rare mixture of lilacs and soap with a hint of cinnamon. "Lizzy," he whispered.

Her eyes lit with passion and set his blood

on fire. She licked her lips. His throat grew dry.

He wanted to yank her against his chest, kiss her senseless, plunge his tongue beyond her dampened lips and let her know the wild thoughts running through his mind.

But he couldn't with Josh close by.

Instead, he entwined his fingers with hers and felt their warmth clear to his heart. "I just hope Jethro has had his fill of berries, or it'll take both of us to pry him away from that berry bush."

CHAPTER 17

Since arriving in Montana, this was the first time Elizabeth was free to enjoy the day. After she'd climbed aboard the furry beast Ben had assigned to her, she took a refreshing breath of mountain air. At least that's what she tried to do, but the scent of the animal beneath her was hard to ignore. Farm smells took some getting used to, but when Ben flashed his white teeth, she forgot all about the pungent odors. The memory of his lips on hers tumbled through her mind.

"How's it feel? Are the stirrups the right height?"

She hadn't heard a word he'd said. "Huh?"

"Are the stirrups okay, or as you Bostonians probably call them, foot rests?"

"I know what stirrups are." Only because he'd used the term a few minutes earlier. "And yes, they feel splendid."

"You're comfortable, then?"

The bulky animal almost split her in two. Comfortable? He had to be kidding. "I'm doing quite well."

"Would you like to go real slow or run like the wind?"

She had a sneaky suspicion her horse belonged to the same category as Josh's. Ben had had to bribe Hector with two apples before the smelly beast would take a step.

"I'm feeling wild today. Let's see how fast we can go."

"Yippee," came the cheer from behind her. "I was hoping you'd say that. 'Cause I want Jethro to run really, really fast," her brother said.

Ben led the way, and though Hector slowly ambled along, she almost fell off. She wrapped her arms around the horse's neck and regained her balance. She was glad Ben hadn't seen her ungraceful maneuver.

Unfortunately, before she could straighten, big-mouthed Josh shouted, "Betts, that's not how to sit. Mr. Ricker, isn't that right?"

Ben studied her with concern. "I thought you said you'd ridden before."

Despite the animal causing her behind to bounce up and down, she managed to sit up and smile. "I have ridden, but it was some time back."

Ben shook his head. "Yeah, I bet."

"Wipe that know-it-all look from your face," she replied in a voice that vibrated like the rest of her body. "I told you I've ridden before, and I have."

"Betts is telling the truth, Mr. Ricker. She had to hold me when we went to the circus and I was too little to go on alone. But that was really different from this."

"How's that?"

"The man in charge held onto a rope and walked the horse in a big circle. We got two turns."

Ben was still hooting long after he'd turned around.

Elizabeth eyed her brother, hoping he'd get the message that she was not happy with him.

His wide grin indicated he didn't have a clue. "Isn't this great? Look, I can make Jethro go really fast." He kneed his horse. "Giddy up." His face lit with excitement. "Look how fast I'm going, Mr. Ricker."

When Ben turned to her brother with a gentle smile, it was impossible to say who looked happier, man or boy. She watched them closely and almost fell off her horse when she realized what emotion she saw on

Ben's face. Love. He loved Josh, and Josh loved him. It was plain as the sun in the sky.

Something stirred deep inside her chest. Unexpected tears sprang to her eyes. She wiped them away before anyone noticed.

As Jethro and Hector plodded along, Elizabeth enjoyed the breathtaking view. Snow-capped mountains rose above a lush green valley. Wildflowers grew in abundance and filled the air with their rich fragrance. She loved Boston, but she'd come to love Montana, too.

As they crossed a narrow brook that rippled over rocks and fallen branches, Ben leaned close, covered her hand with his, and pointed to a fawn drinking nearby. She thought her heart would burst with happiness, from both his touch and the breathtaking view. Everything was perfect. Everything except her black and blue behind, which took a beating whenever it connected with the unyielding saddle.

When they stopped to water the animals, Ben helped Elizabeth down. She staggered as if she were drunk. It took all her willpower not to rub her backside with both hands.

"Are you all right, Lizzy?"

Something about the way he said her

name lit a flame low in her belly. "Yes, I'm fine."

"If your muscles are sore, I'd be more than happy to rub them for you."

One look at his face and she knew exactly which part of her anatomy he was referring to. "No gentleman would say such things."

He chuckled. "Aren't you glad I'm not?"

When he reached for her, she slapped his hand. With as much dignity as she could muster, she limped away. She was still smiling when he caught her around the waist and kissed her neck. She gasped, turned around, and gave him a hard shove, which didn't budge him one iota. "Are you crazy, trying such things with my brother nearby?"

"I keep asking myself the same thing. I've lost my mind for sure. But relax, your brother wasn't looking. I checked."

Flustered, she picked up a stone along the shore and studied the flecks of mica that glittered in the sunlight.

"Beautiful," he murmured in her ear, standing right behind her.

She turned the rock so it caught the light. "It is pretty."

"I was talking about you." His husky voice rang in her ear long after the words were out. The heat from his body radiated through the material of her blouse and britches. It seemed indecent to allow him to stand behind her this way. What had happened to her good upbringing? Yet, she couldn't stop herself from leaning into him, noticing the smell of bay rum and leather. His masculine scent did strange things to her insides — a scent that filled her mind with sinful thoughts.

As she stared at nothing in particular, Josh stripped down to his underwear and stomped through the cold water, splashing both Elizabeth and Ben. "Betts, why don't you take off your trousers and come in, too."

"I don't think so."

Ben's hand brushed her arm. "Yeah, why don't you?"

He was teasing, but she couldn't face him. He'd aroused in her feelings that until now she hadn't known existed.

She moved away, and as she sat on a nearby rock, she couldn't stop her face from contorting in pain.

"Lizzy, would you like to head back to the ranch?"

Her name on his lips left her dizzy with longing. When he sat close by and cupped her hand, she leaned against his shoulder. "No, I'll be okay in a little while."

"You sure?"

"Do I look that bad?"

He gave a low laugh. "Maybe you shouldn't ask me that."

Her laughter caused her muscles to tighten, adding to her discomfort. She pretended she didn't hurt all over. "Josh will never forget today."

"And what about you?"

"Today will be a memory I cherish always."

"I hope there'll be many more."

She studied his whiskey-colored eyes. They were warm and sensual. If only . . . if only she were staying in Welcome. No, this was foolish. She would leave soon. The thought that she wanted to stay tore her in two. She would never allow a man to direct her life. And she'd already decided to go to California. But that didn't prevent the ache that settled in her heart.

Her breath caught in her throat when she met his gaze. She wanted to remain in Welcome with Ben. But she would never allow herself to trust any man. *Not even Ben.*

"We'll be leaving for California sometime soon," she said, waiting for his reply, silently praying he'd ask her to stay. As she waited, she saw the play of emotions across his handsome features: confusion, indecision, and then fear.

He tightened his grip as if to keep her

near. "You'll be here a while longer?"

She hid her disappointment. "Yes." It was better this way. Neither of them ever intended to marry.

He lowered his head against hers. "Then let's make the most of the time we have left."

Like the water tumbling over rocks, passion rippled through her body. She didn't trust herself to speak, so she nodded instead.

Some time later, as the horses meandered along the base of the mountains, Ben gazed at the threatening sky. In the last few minutes, low-lying clouds had filtered in. The large ponderosa pines swayed as harsh winds whipped up the earth and pelted the horses and their riders with flying debris.

"Shouldn't we go back?" Elizabeth asked him with a tremor in her voice.

Ben gave her arm a comforting squeeze, trying to chase away the fear in her eyes. "There isn't time. We need to find shelter, and I know just the place."

Even Josh, who up until now hadn't had a care in the world, looked frightened. The clap of thunder that shook the ground a moment later didn't help matters.

"Partner, would you like to ride up front with me?"

Eyes wide with terror, he nodded.

Ben steered his mount next to the boy,

and as he reached over, Josh literally leaped into his saddle. Ben didn't bother to hitch up Jethro because he knew the horse would follow.

Thunder rumbled and lightning sluiced across the blackening sky. All hell broke loose a minute later when the sky opened up. Rain fell in sheets, pummeling them like fine gravel. Ben could no longer see where he was going, but after throwing a spare blanket over Josh's head and instructing Elizabeth to do the same, he pulled his Stetson low over his face and allowed his horse to lead the way. They were soaked to the bone by the time they entered the Gold Nugget Mine. No sooner were they inside than Josh wrapped suffocating arms around Ben's neck.

Ben reached for the lantern he kept by the mouth of the mineshaft. He struck a match, lit the wick, then patted the boy's shoulder. "If you don't open your eyes, you'll miss seeing what a gold mine looks like."

The kid slowly lifted his head and opened one eye. "A real gold mine, really?"

"You got that right."

"Wow!" His high-pitched voice rivaled the storm raging outside.

As Ben dismounted, he grabbed Josh by

the collar of his shirt to prevent him from running into the mineshaft. "Where do you think you're going?"

"To find some gold." His voice echoed around him. He froze in his tracks. "What was that?"

The echo repeated, "Was that, was that."

A shiver racked the boy's body.

Laughter rumbled from Ben and echoed in the cave. "It's your own voice vibrating in this empty cavern. It's nothing to be afraid of, but you had better stay put with us. It's dark and you could get hurt running around. Besides, I need you to help me."

"What for?"

"I want you to collect scraps of wood from the floor so I can start a fire."

Josh did as he was told. "Ben, did you ever find gold in this mine?"

"Not much, but my granddaddy found a vein about twenty years ago."

"Are you rich?"

"Unfortunately, no. Gramps didn't find that much gold, just enough to build up our herd and purchase more land."

Josh threw several small pieces of wood at Ben's feet. "Maybe if I looked really, really hard, I can find some gold, too. I'll share with you, and we can be rich together."

Ben ruffled his hair. "If only it was as easy

as that."

"If I stay where you can see me, can I look now?"

Ben didn't have it in him to ruin the anticipation on the boy's face. "Sure, but you stay right around here." There'd be time enough later to explain gold didn't just sit around waiting to be picked up.

Ben focused his attention on Elizabeth, who was smiling at him as if he'd done something remarkable. "What's that smug grin for?"

"I was thinking how good you are with Josh. I've never seen a more patient man."

Her long hair clung to her back like a damp sheet. After helping her down, he wrung out the long strands between his palms. "You'll catch a cold if you don't dry off."

He took the saddlebags down from his mount. Inside he found a worn shirt and towel he kept for such emergencies. He also withdrew a small flask of rum.

He took a swig and offered her some. The look she threw him added to the chill in the air. "Lizzy, you're a narrow-minded woman. This will help fight off the cold."

"I'd rather freeze than drink rot gut."

He chuckled aloud. "For a nondrinker, you sure know all the phrases. And stop looking at me as if I'm sloshed. I took a couple swallows to bring up my body temperature." She stood before him as if he'd offered her poison, but her beautiful eyes did more for his body temperature than the swallow of rum. "I don't suppose there's any sense my suggesting we give Josh a small sip."

She huffed and directed her gaze at him.

"The boy's shivering."

She searched his face for some time.

He rested one hand on her trembling shoulder. "Alcohol isn't responsible for the evils that men do."

The muscles beneath his fingers stiffened. "I know that."

"Do you?" he asked, staring into sapphire eyes capable of making a man forget his past. With his other hand, he stroked her arm, warding off the chill. "I'm asking you to trust me."

She swallowed and glanced away, her troubled eyes filled with fear.

"Which frightens you most? Taking a drink or trusting me?"

She met his gaze, gave him that look that showed no fear. But he now knew better. Elizabeth O'Hara wasn't the sort of woman to wear her feelings for others to see.

"Josh," she said, her voice trembling like

246

the rest of her. "Mr. Ricker has a swallow of medicine for you to take."

Josh scampered over, his eyes widening when he spotted the bottle. "That's not medicine, that's liquor, booze, hooch."

Ben hid his grin.

Elizabeth broke away from Ben's hold and knelt before the boy. "Used correctly, alcohol can be beneficial for one's health. Ben knows about such things." She cleared her throat. "Besides, even I took a small sip of Granny's apple brandy when I was recuperating from the bear attack."

"You did?"

A pained expression skittered over her features. "Yes, I did."

"But you told me never to take even a teeny tiny taste."

"In some instances, it's all right to consume a few drops. You need to trust Mr. Ricker."

"Heck, I already trust Mr. Ricker."

Ben handed the bottle to Josh. "Only take one swallow. Let me warn you. It might burn on the way down."

"Do real cowboys drink rot gut, Ben?"

Ben ran his fingers along the boy's neck. "They do for medicinal purposes."

Josh took a large swig. His face contorted. He stamped his foot against the dirt floor, but in the end, he swallowed and fanned his mouth. "That sure is strong medicine," he said, in a tone guaranteed to burst eardrums. A moment later he left to search for treasure.

Standing with her back to him, Elizabeth's entire body shook from the cold. Ben moved behind her and clasped her shoulders. "What about you? Do you trust me?"

She turned. Fire lit her eyes. "Oh, give me that bottle," she said, grabbing the flask from his hand. "I can see you won't drop the subject until I take a swallow of this devil's brew."

That said, she raised the container to her mouth and took three large gulps. She blinked away the moisture collecting on her lower eyelids. Her cheeks grew the prettiest shade of pink Ben had ever seen.

"Now was that so bad?"

She simply looked at him.

"Does this mean you trust me, too?"

"It does not mean any such thing, but I'll tell you this, you had better keep your distance, Ben Ricker."

"And why is that?"

"Because my breath will likely singe your eyebrows."

Ben wrapped his arm around her shoulder. "Now that's my Lizzy," he said before he could stop himself. If she heard, she didn't let on. My Lizzy. Those words had a nice sound. But a frightening ring.

She would never be his Lizzy. Soon she'd marry Ward. Or worse, she'd pack her bags and leave Montana. She'd head to California and never return. The scenario sounded too familiar. A hollow feeling settled in his chest.

He should distance himself from Elizabeth. Instead, he hugged her tighter. Common sense abandoned him as he whispered in her ear. "I'd love to kiss a woman who breathes fire."

She elbowed his ribs. "You're the most infuriating man I've ever known."

Humor was safe. Ben relaxed. "If I remember correctly, that means you like me."

"Yes, Ben Ricker, I like you. Are you satisfied?"

"It's a start. Here," he said, throwing his shirt and towel at her. "Strip down, then dry off, and put this on."

"I most certainly will not do such a thing."

"It's for your good. If you get sick, who's going to care for the children? Do as I say. Josh and I will turn around until you're through."

She hesitated but finally agreed.

Ben made sure Josh didn't look as they

stacked the kindling and got a fire going. Unfortunately, no one was there to watch him, and he fought the constant urge to turn around. He needed to get his mind on something else. He knew Ward would do the trick.

"How'd your big date go last night?"

"It was all right."

"From what I hear, the man's an octopus."

"He was a perfect gentleman."

"You mean unlike me."

"You said it, I didn't."

Josh pulled at Ben's shirt. "What's an octopus?"

"Hope you're happy with yourself, Ben."

Ben ignored Elizabeth's comment. "It's a big slimy creature that lives in the ocean."

"Are you saying Mr. Metcalf lives in the ocean?"

"No, just that he's slimy."

Josh seemed to accept that statement as fact, which endeared him to Ben even more.

In the silence Ben's mind wandered. He tried to focus on anything but what was happening a few feet behind him. He heard her peeling away the damp material. He'd have gladly done the job if Josh hadn't been around. He knew she was standing behind him without a stitch of clothes, toweling herself off. The erotic image left him aching with need. The last of his resolve to behave crumbled. He decided to steal a glance.

Before he could turn, Elizabeth announced, "It's okay. I'm decent."

Decent didn't do her justice. She stole his breath away, left him with his mouth gaping. The soft folds of his shirt did things he hadn't thought possible. She looked like an angel cloaked in a plaid flannel robe, the soft material draping her curves and falling well below her knees. Her small hands peeked from under the rolled-up sleeves. The fact that she was wearing his shirt pleased him immensely, filling him with a strong, possessive feeling. Ben rose and took her cold palms. He rubbed her fingers and blew on them with his warm breath. "Come sit by the fire."

Josh stripped down to his underwear and fanned his shirt over the flames. The next thing Ben knew, the sleeve caught on fire. Ben threw the shirt to the ground and stomped on it with his booted foot.

"Josh, you're going to be the death of me yet."

Josh cowered next to Elizabeth and peeked at Ben. "Are you mad?"

"I'm not happy."

"Are you gonna whip me with your belt?"

It took a moment for Josh's words to

register. His father had used a belt on him. When Ben dropped down on one knee to comfort the boy, Josh flinched at his touch. "I'd never take a hand or a belt to you. You have my word."

"Honest?" Josh whimpered.

"Yes."

Elizabeth had tears in her eyes when Ben looked at her. He wasn't sure why, but he noticed that her fingers curled around his good and tight. "You're really something, Ben."

"Is that good?"

"It's better than good."

A feeling of contentment settled deep in his soul as he sat there by the crackling fire with Elizabeth and Josh. This mine had stopped producing gold years back, but tonight he'd found something more valuable. He was in love with Elizabeth.

The idea of loving her frightened him to his very core. Because of their different backgrounds, they had no future together.

His own father had died a drunk because he couldn't accept reality. Abandoned by a wife who didn't love him, he'd dug himself an early grave with a bottle of cheap whiskey in one hand and a glass in the other. Ben remembered the desolate look on his father's face as he stared through bloodshot eyes, waiting in vain for his wife to return. Ben had learned from his father's mistake.

Needing to get away for a while, he lifted his arm from Elizabeth's shoulder and saw the disappointment on her face. Josh had fallen asleep by her side. He kissed her forehead and got out of there before he did something he'd regret. He needed time to think.

I love her, he said silently, repeating the phrase in his mind. He'd suspected as much, but until today hadn't given the notion much credence. Now he had, and it left him feeling mighty jittery.

To keep busy, he arranged a makeshift clothesline from a rope in his saddlebag. Elizabeth gently set Josh down and came up beside him. "Let me give you a hand with the wet clothes."

Their shoulders touched as they worked side by side, and it took every ounce of self-control not to pull her against him. He watched her drape her wet blouse and britches over the rope. He wondered what she'd done with her underthings. "Where's the rest of your wet clothes?"

"I've hung up everything."

Ben eyed her closely. Even in the firelight he detected a rosy glow to her cheeks. He gave her a lecherous grin. "You mean to tell me this is all you had on?"

"If you think I'm about to hang my un-mentionables for you to see, you must be crazy."

He rolled his eyes heavenward. "Here we go again," he said with a laugh. And he knew she was right. He was crazy to be in love with someone from Boston.

He might be crazy, but he wasn't stupid. He never intended to tell her.

CHAPTER 18

When Elizabeth awoke the next morning, she took a moment to enjoy the peace and quiet and to savor the wonderful warmth that surrounded her. She hugged her arms around her middle and pretended she was back in the mine with Ben. She'd felt secure in his embrace. It was a day she'd not soon forget.

Ben's treatment of Josh had earned him a special place in her heart. When her brother accidentally set his shirtsleeve on fire, he'd scampered to her side with a look of horror. For a moment she was back in Boston, ready to defend him again. Her stomach churned as she waited for Ben's reaction, but her worries vanished when she saw understanding on his face.

Once Ben quelled Josh's concerns, he'd turned to her. In the glow of the lantern, she'd seen deep emotion in his eyes that she didn't dare name.

All night she'd tossed and turned while irrational thoughts ran through her head. Had she taken leave of her senses? Surely, they had nothing in common. She'd proven repeatedly how inept she was around the farm. She'd been ready to milk the bull. What more proof did she need? She didn't belong on a ranch any more than Ben belonged in the city. Though she told herself they could never have a future together, her pounding heart disagreed. She and Ben had shared a closeness in the mine, and Elizabeth could hardly wait to see him again.

But trust? Did she trust him?

A shiver raced down her spine. Was it possible she'd already taken leave of her senses? Had she allowed herself to trust Ben? As her fingers clasped the bedding, Elizabeth's resolve to never trust any man weakened — or possibly dissipated into thin air.

She did her best to climb out of bed without waking the children. But as she straightened, she groaned. Every nerve ending in her body screeched in pain, a residual effect from her ride on Hector. She rubbed her aching backside, legs, and back muscles, tiptoed across the room, and glanced at her brother. Curled up on his side with his fist on the pillow, he looked like a sweet cherub. The expression would vanish shortly, and she braced herself for when he awoke.

She opened and shut the bedroom door without making a sound. As she stumbled across the kitchen on stiffened legs, she spotted a small bouquet of lilacs on the counter. There was no note, but she knew the flowers were meant for her. Ben's thoughtfulness added to her overflowing heart. She brought the bouquet to her nose and inhaled the sweet fragrance, plus the stronger scent of something else. Brandy. Her nose wrinkled in disgust.

When she lifted the glass container, she understood where the noxious odor had come from. That infuriating man had actually put her flowers in an empty brandy bottle. The nerve of him. He was deliberately trying to antagonize her.

Elizabeth listed Ben's traits: patient, thoughtful, and when she gave the matter more thought, added infuriating to her list. She removed the lilacs from the bottle and slipped them into a glass. "There, that's much better."

"What's much better?"

Startled, she jumped and turned around, her heart thumping a steady beat against her ribs.

Ben's deep brown eyes set her insides ablaze. "Do you do that much?"

"What?"

"Talk to yourself. It's not a good sign." His wide grin stretched across his face. "It could mean one of several things. You might be missing a few of your marbles."

She frowned at him.

"Or, according to my granddaddy, it might mean you're about to come into a large sum of money."

"That would be nice."

"Or it could mean you're going to kiss a cowboy."

"Your grandfather was wrong."

"Oh, was he?"

She nodded. "Definitely. I've heard the saying many times. When a person talks to himself, it means he's either going to inherit a large sum of money or kiss a fool."

"You're the one who's wrong."

In a blink of an eye, she found herself crushed against his chest. When his mouth covered hers, he wedged his tongue between her lips. The spark that ignited in her belly spread fire to her arms and legs. Without one thought to impropriety, she threw herself at him, all her common sense gone. She threaded her fingers in his hair and pulled his head closer, making certain he couldn't escape even if he had a mind to. As Ben lifted her against him, she felt his arousal pressing against her stomach. She wiggled shamelessly.

From deep in his throat came a low, deep moan.

As if the sound had brought him to his senses, he lowered her until her feet were touching the floor again. Dizzy and out of breath, Elizabeth wasn't sure she could stand on her own. Ever so slowly, he pulled away, closed his eyes, and tipped his forehead against hers, his breathing ragged. "I shouldn't have done that, Lizzy."

"I wanted you to."

He heaved a sigh. "I know." He studied her face as if he were memorizing what he saw. "What you want, I can't give you. You need someone who'll marry you and whisk you off to the city. I'm not that man."

As she took a moment to digest what he'd said, he wrapped her in his arms and held her tight, his heart beating the same desperate tune as hers. Disappointment replaced the happiness she'd felt earlier. Her heart shattered into a million tiny pieces.

Why did she feel so miserable? Ben didn't mean that much to her. But then she realized the truth. God help her. Without a doubt, she was completely in love with Ben.

"Lizzy, if you don't stay away from me, I'll take advantage of you."

That made her angry. "I wouldn't allow you to take advantage of me."

"Your kisses tell me differently." He ran a hand through his hair. "You're inexperienced."

"And you aren't?"

"I'm experienced enough to know I shouldn't get involved."

She refused to think of him with other women. "Don't tell me about it."

He smiled. "They didn't mean a thing to me. You do. That's why I feel I should warn you. I'm not the marrying kind."

"Neither am I," she reminded him.

"I think you are. Run as fast as you can. Earlier today I promised myself I'd keep my distance, but as you can see, I didn't." He kissed the tip of her nose. "Lizzy, I want you."

The husky tone of his voice lifted the fine hairs at her nape. She inhaled deeply. He'd said she mattered to him. Her mind refused to dwell on anything but that important fact. She mattered to him.

"I care about you, too."

Worry streaked across his face. "You don't know what you're saying."

"Ben Ricker, you are an arrogant man. For all you know, I'm as experienced as you are." She thought about what she'd said.

The laughter in his eyes made her throw caution to the wind. "You can wipe that know-it-all smirk from your face. I wasn't planning on telling you, but seeing as we're on the subject, I've had plenty of experience. There, are you satisfied?"

His grin widened. "You expect me to believe that."

She thumped her finger against his chest. "I don't care whether you believe it."

He gave a deep belly laugh. "Why doesn't that surprise me? Not once have you admitted not knowing anything, from your cooking experience right down to your horseback riding skills. This time you're courting trouble. If you aren't careful, you'll end up in my bed." He made his point by giving her one long, passionate kiss.

By the time he'd finished, she knew he was right.

Worse yet, she was beginning to like the idea.

After breakfast, Elizabeth took out her sewing and went to sit on the porch beside Granny, who was patting Bernie and the puppies. "Mornin', Lizabeth."

"Your hair sure is looking pretty today."

A gentle smile crossed her features. "Cecelia curled it again. That child's a pure joy to have around."

Elizabeth sat down and started sewing a button in place. "What's that you're makin'?" Granny asked.

"Another shirt. I'm almost done. Queenie got me orders for three more. She's supposed to send someone over with the money this morning."

Granny ran her fingers behind Bernie's ear. "I've done a little embroidery, but I never had me much time to fuss with sewin'. The animals and work around the ranch kept me busier than a lone rooster in a crowded hen house."

Elizabeth chuckled at Granny's comment. Once the button was on good and tight, she knotted the thread and cut it off near the cotton fabric. "Done," she said with a growing sense of satisfaction. "Another ninety cents to add to my bankroll."

Granny eyed her with concern. "What you gonna do with all the cash you're earnin'?"

Elizabeth had planned to head west, probably go to California and start her own business. Now she wasn't so sure. She didn't want to leave Ben. "I've been thinking of maybe buying myself a sewing machine and opening my own shop."

Granny frowned. "That mean you're gonna leave us, Lizabeth?"

"Not for a while yet."

"You don't need to leave, you know."

"I can't stay indefinitely."

"Why don't you stay and cook for us?"

"You know the answer to that as well as I do. Everyone would wither away from starvation." The two women shared a laugh. But deep inside, Elizabeth's heart was breaking.

"You've brought a peck of happiness to this here old ranch house. And to me."

Elizabeth would miss the old woman. She folded the shirt she'd just finished and covered Granny's hand with hers. "You've enriched my life, too."

"Mind tellin' me 'bout somethin'?"

"What's that?"

"Who in the devil's Robert T. Hines?"

Elizabeth was shocked to hear Granny say the name. Before she could comment, Granny continued, "I didn't mean to eavesdrop, but I overheard you mentionin' him to Queenie."

"He's Cecelia's stepfather and Josh's father. My mother married him a few years after my dad died of consumption. Robert T. Hines was a real gentleman until the door closed behind him. In the privacy of his own home, he was master of his domain. He was a tyrant. I grew to hate him," she

263

ended on a whisper.

"What happened to your mother?"

"She died a year ago during childbirth. Until then, Robert T. Hines was tolerable, and he pretty much left Cecelia and me alone. Afterwards, we bore the brunt of his wrath. It almost killed Cecelia. She didn't dare take a breath for fear of angering the man. And when he drank, he turned into a beast. He beat Josh's backside black and blue with a belt because Josh spilled a glass of water on the table. I took the children and ran before he could do any more harm."

"And he's been lookin' for you?"

Once more, Elizabeth was surprised at how much Granny knew. "He tried, but that's over now. I'm hoping the children and I are finally free of him."

Granny patted Elizabeth's knee. "I'm right glad to hear he isn't likely to bother you ever again."

Before Elizabeth could inquire where Granny had gleaned her information, she saw a horse and rider approaching. A white-haired man dismounted and walked onto the porch. "Ma'am, I'm John Kemper." He extended his hand.

Elizabeth put her sewing on the chair and took his palm. "I'm pleased to meet you."

"Queenie promised my shirt would be

ready today. She gave me the money for the other two, said I was to bring them back with me."

"Yes, I'll go get them and be right back." As Elizabeth hurried inside, she couldn't hide her excitement. Three more shirts. That meant another two dollars and seventy cents to add to the twenty-eight dollars she'd already saved. She'd have the money for her new sewing machine in no time.

She took the shirts from the shelf in her bedroom, wrapped them in paper, and headed back to the porch.

Mr. Kemper opened the package to examine his shirt. "It's right nice work, ma'am. I might be needing a few more. I'll get back to you when I get paid."

Elizabeth couldn't believe her good fortune. Her new business was going better than she'd thought possible. After the man left, she flashed the bills at Granny. "Look, he gave me three whole dollars."

Granny frowned and patted Bernie. "Don't expect me to be happy 'bout you savin' money to leave."

Elizabeth was hoping to stay, but that depended on Ben, and she couldn't very well tell Granny that. Without saying another word, she headed into her bedroom to add her money to her growing stash.

For years she'd been made to feel useless, and her self-esteem had suffered, but now she'd begun to feel a sense of purpose. She needed to prove to herself that she could stand on her own two feet. This money was a giant step in the right direction.

Elizabeth hurried into the bedroom and slid a box from under her bed. She shoved aside the material and sewing notions in it and felt around for the envelope that contained her money. Not finding it, she checked the other side of the cardboard container. It wasn't there, either. Certain that she'd missed the envelope, she emptied the contents of the box onto the floor and still found nothing. She checked between the folds of each piece of fabric. She even checked under the bed in case the money had somehow fallen out. Finally, she gave up.

Her money was missing.

Ben arrived to find the children seated in the kitchen and Elizabeth pacing back and forth.

"If none of you took it, then who did?"

Josh gave Ben a wide smile. "Maybe Ben did it."

"What have I done now?"

"My money is missing," Elizabeth informed him with a flushed face.

"Are you sure you didn't just misplace it?"

She looked at him as if he'd lost his mind. He was beginning to get used to that expression. "I've looked all over. It's gone." She was close to tears.

Josh leaped off the chair. "Maybe a robber crept into the house when we was sleeping." He wrapped his small arm around Elizabeth's waist. "Don't worry about a thing. Ben and me will form a posse. I'll ride Jethro and lasso the culprit." His grin lit his face. "Right, Ben?"

Ben smiled at the boy. He hated seeing Elizabeth so upset. He couldn't imagine anyone on his ranch stealing her money. It was too ridiculous to consider.

He set the bottles of apple brandy he'd brought in from the bunkhouse on the kitchen counter and went to put his arm around Elizabeth. As he turned, he noticed the look of disgust directed at him. When her gaze darted from the bottle and back to him, he knew the cause of her distress.

He chose to ignore that issue and focused on the matter at hand. "How much money are we talking about?"

"Twenty-eight dollars."

Josh whistled. "Wowwee."

"Lizzy, try to calm down. No one here would take your money. We know how hard you worked for it. I'm sure it'll show up."

She would have none of it. "I've searched everywhere. It's gone."

Ben pulled her against him and tried to comfort her. A long strand of her hair fell over his face. Its fine smell stirred his desire. What started out as a gesture of friendship turned into much more. He forgot about the children. He forgot about his good intentions. Instead, he lifted her chin until she was looking up at him and focused on her perfect mouth as his lowered of its own accord.

Elizabeth broke his concentration when she gasped and took a quick step back. He was in worse shape than he'd originally thought. She'd gotten into his blood, and only one thing would satisfy him.

"For a minute I thought you was gonna kiss Betts. Yuck, why'd you want to do that, huh?" Josh stuck out his tongue and grimaced.

Ben exchanged knowing looks with Elizabeth. "You might say I lost my head for a minute."

He missed her touch, her smell, and he knew his life would never be the same after she left. But she'd leave, eventually. When she did, she'd be taking his heart with her.

The children bounded from the room, and

Ben slid a chair from the table, turned it around, and straddled it. "What's a guy have to do for a cup of coffee around here?"

Elizabeth took down a cup and filled it with the dark brew. Ben smiled up at her. "Your coffee's great."

She took the compliment in stride.

He quirked his brow. "You're supposed to say thanks."

"I was waiting for the rest."

"Huh?"

"You know," she went on with a flourish of her hand. "How it's saved you money because you've used it in place of axle grease on the wagon."

He planted an astonished look on his face. "Lizzy, how did you find out?"

She laughed and rested her hands on his shoulders.

"That feels so good. Just a little lower."

As her fingers worked their magic on his tightened muscles, he closed his eyes and enjoyed the moment. "What kind of envelope was the money in?"

She kneaded his back. "Plain old ordinary envelope, why?"

"I figured I'd keep my eyes open for it."

Chapter 19

Ben grabbed two planks and heaved them on the wagon, then repeated the process several more times. Sweat rolled off his face and down his neck.

Lefty joined him a moment later. "I did as you asked, boss. We can start carting the wood inside for storage."

Ben nodded his approval. "By the time we deliver the lumber, it'll be nice and dry. Green wood is a bitch to work with, and our customers will appreciate our efforts."

It would be easier to keep an eye on the lumber inside his barn. Although in the last few days Ben had seen no signs of trouble, he could sense it in his bones. He needed all the luck he could muster. He was increasing his odds by storing the cut timber inside the barn. Earlier today he'd done the math. If all went as planned, he'd have Ward Metcalf's money in plenty of time. After that, the profits would be his.

From a distance Ben heard the sound of approaching hooves. He shielded his eyes from the sun and peered at a black stallion and its rider. Ben stepped toward the stranger.

The man dismounted and extended a gloved hand. He spoke around a cheroot clamped between his teeth. "Duke Witham here. I heard the Gold Nugget ranch was hiring."

Ben shook his hand and introduced himself. The stranger, five feet tall with a barrel-shaped chest and shifty gray eyes, didn't look capable of doing manual labor. A jagged scar ran from his left eye down his cheek and disappeared at his hairline. Ben didn't believe in judging a man by looks alone, but he was tempted to do just that.

"You from around here?" he asked.

"No, sir."

Duke didn't elaborate, but Ben didn't press the issue. He didn't care about the stranger's personal life. All that mattered was whether he could put in a good day's work. His first impulse was to send the man on his way. But they could use the help, and he wanted to give Zack a break. Besides, the old man hated anything that had to do with wood.

"Have you worked in a sawmill before?"

"Can't rightly say that I have."

Ben appreciated his honesty.

"But I'm a quick learner," he went on, "and I'm willing to work without pay for one day to prove myself."

Put that way, Ben had nothing to lose. He hesitated for only a moment. "Tell you what. You put in a day's work, and I'll pay you what I think you're worth. How's that sound?"

He grinned around the cigar that still hung from a corner of his mouth, exposing one gold tooth. "Sounds damn good to me."

"Duke, I do have one stipulation. I like my men to be spiffy dressers. Before you leave, I want you to go over to the house and order two shirts from our cook. Tell her you'll pay for them come payday."

Confusion showed in Duke's eyes as he took a puff on his cigar and nodded his agreement. "Can I start tomorrow?"

"Be here at 5:30 A.M. with your gear. You can stay in the bunkhouse if you like."

"Sure thing."

Before Duke left, Ben took a gander at those cold gray eyes. He didn't trust the man and wondered if he'd made a mistake. He shoved the uneasy feeling aside and walked back to where Lefty and Zack were working. He grabbed several boards and

272

threw them into the wagon.

Zack frowned. "I tell you, it isn't right. We're cattlemen, not lumberjacks. Your poor grandfather's rolling over each time we add another damn log to this damn pile."

"At least Granddaddy's getting plenty of exercise. It's good for his rheumatism."

Zack didn't crack a smile but instead grumbled and threw more wood on the wagon.

"Besides, I just hired someone to take your place. Starting tomorrow, you can go back to being a full-time cowpoke."

The news shut Zack up for a moment, but the silence was short-lived. "Tell me you aren't talking 'bout Shorty who just left here? I thought I'd need to get the stepladder for him to climb onto his horse."

Ben scowled. "You didn't, did you? And as usual, you're exaggerating. I'm guessing Duke to be at least five-foot-five."

"It was more like four-foot-five, and I'm giving him a few inches 'cause I'm such a nice guy."

Lefty chuckled under his breath.

Ben did his best not to smile. "Now, don't you go encouraging him."

Several minutes later Lefty cocked a brow. "Did you hear about Elizabeth's money disappearing?"

"Sure did," Ben replied.

Zack dabbed at his forehead with his red handkerchief. "If you ask me, it's a dog-goned shame. She worked damn hard for that money. Wonder where it went to."

Lefty paused. "It would take a mean son-of-a-bitch to do such a rotten thing."

"You know how women are," Ben said with authority. "Always misplacing things. It's bound to turn up."

Zack's scowl lifted. "It wouldn't surprise me none if that's just what happened."

Lefty said, "That's exactly what I was thinking, too. A nice lady like Elizabeth deserves better than someone making off with her hard-earned cash."

Ben glanced at their concerned expressions. "Wouldn't surprise me if the money turned up right where she left it."

"Where was that, boss?"

"She told me the money was in an envelope in a box under her bed."

"That so," Zack said, scratching his chin. "Don't reckon she could have overlooked it?"

They shared a laugh.

"You know how women are," Ben repeated. "She's probably misplaced it. The money's likely right there under her nose."

■ ■ ■ ■

Elizabeth searched every inch of her bed-room several times. She double- and triple-checked the box under her bed and finally had to accept facts. She'd never see her money again. Even the children were con-cerned, and she'd made light of the matter because Josh and Clyde had both started carting their most prized possessions around in pillowcases.

She tried to look on the bright side. The orders for shirts were coming in every day. She'd still start her own business, only now it would take longer. The thought filled her with gloom. Before she could dwell on her misfortune, someone knocked on the kitchen door.

She swung the screen door open and saw a mean-looking man with a scar on his face.

"Good day, ma'am." The man removed his hat and smiled around a thick cigar. "Are you the cook?"

"Yes."

He grinned and flashed a gold tooth. "Good, I want to order two shirts."

That news made her feel much better. "What color?"

The man gave the question a moment's

thought. "I don't know. Does it matter?"

No one had ever posed that question to her. "I guess not. Do you want long or short sleeves?"

Again, he hesitated. "Which does Mr. Ricker prefer?"

She was really confused. She considered asking him why but decided not to chance insulting him. "I don't honestly know. I've seen him in both."

The stranger took a puff on his cigar. "Tell you what. Make me two of each."

"Two with short sleeves, and two with long?" She wanted to make sure she'd heard him right.

"Yeah, that way I'll know I have the right ones."

She didn't have a clue what he was talking about. His deliberate leer left her feeling edgy. "I'll have to take a few measurements, so you'll have to come inside for a couple of minutes."

He did as she asked. She hurried because she didn't want him around her. He stared at her while she worked, and the way his eyes kept track of her as she wrapped the measuring tape around his large chest caused sweat to roll down her back. Her hands were clammy with perspiration by the time she finished.

She wrote his measurements on a slip of paper and walked him to the door. "Do you want cotton, Mr. . . . ?"

"Name's Duke Witham. Cotton's fine with me, but what does Ben Ricker prefer?"

"I'll check with him." Without a doubt, Mr. Witham had to be the strangest man Elizabeth had ever met.

Ben had an errand to run that afternoon, so he put Lefty in charge.

"Boss, will you be gone long?"

"I expect to be back in about an hour."

"Good, 'cause I need someone to cover for me a little while this afternoon."

"No problem. I'll be back soon."

On the way, Ben caught Zack creeping around the ranch, looking as if he was up to no good. Ben tiptoed up behind him and tapped his shoulder.

Zack must have jumped three feet. "You trying to kill me? My old ticker can't take this, you know. Why are you sneaking around like that for?"

Ben grinned. "I was about to ask you the same thing."

The old man looked guilty as hell. "You want to know what I was doing?"

"You got it."

"Can't an old man go for a walk without

277

everyone and his brother making a big thing out of it?"

Looking somewhat flustered, Zack scooted into the woods. Ben chuckled to himself. Life sure would be dull without Zack around to tease.

Forty-five minutes later, Ben replaced Lefty. "Will you be eating at the house tonight?"

"I thought I would. Elizabeth's making another attempt at beef stew."

Ben stopped dead in his tracks. "I hope she forgoes the biscuits. My teeth can't take any more abuse."

Lefty hooted along with Ben. After a moment, Lefty asked, "Is there something going on between you two?"

"Why'd you ask?"

Lefty waved his hand around. "You're answering questions with questions. I have my answer. Besides, I've seen how you look at her. I think even Granny can see, and you know how poor her vision is."

"It's that obvious?"

"Yes. When you going to do something about it? Zack tells me Ward Metcalf has been sticking mighty close lately."

"He asked her to marry him."

"Holy shit. What'd she tell him?"

"Nothing. He never gave her a chance to

reply. He expects an answer when he returns in a few days."

Lefty looked at him suspiciously. "How did you find out all this?"

"I overheard them talking."

"Eavesdropping sounds more like it."

"Maybe."

"You love her?"

Ben didn't say a word.

"You don't need to answer. I can see it on your face. What I can't understand is why you aren't taking her someplace special and doing a little proposing of your own."

"I can't marry her."

"If Ward Metcalf has his way, that'll be a fact. Give him a run for his money."

"I'm not about to make the same mistake my father made."

"What does Elizabeth have to do with your father?"

"Don't you see the irony?"

"Frankly, no."

Ben took a slow ragged breath. "My mother came from Boston. She couldn't hack the life out here, and ran back East with another man."

Lefty mulled over what Ben had said. "As your friend, I've got to say something you aren't going to like." He paused and laid a comforting hand on Ben's shoulder. "When your mother left, she did some serious damage to you and your father. Have you ever considered that maybe she wasn't the sort of woman to stick with one man? Maybe her leaving had nothing to do with being from Boston. I don't think you're giving Elizabeth enough credit. I hope you wake up before it's too late."

Lefty's comments hit hard. The muscles in Ben's jaw tightened. As he contemplated an angry rebuttal, some of what Lefty had said started to sink in. He took a calming breath and grabbed another plank. "If I plan to make the bank payment in time, I better get to work."

After Lefty walked away, Ben couldn't help rehashing his friend's words. Could Lefty be right? As a child, Ben had hated Boston. As a man, he despised the city, yet he'd never even been there. Maybe it was time he laid blame where it was due.

His mother.

That evening Ben arrived for supper wearing his finest shirt and newest jeans. He'd combed his hair, spit-shined his boots, scrubbed beneath his fingernails, and even had Zack trim his hair. He showed up thirty minutes early with a bouquet of wildflowers. He was prepared to clean his plate and ask for seconds regardless of how bad the beef stew tasted.

He'd even memorized a long list of compliments that would have put Ward Metcalf to shame. Ward wasn't the only man who knew how to praise a lady. Above all, he was going to keep his wise comments to himself.

When Elizabeth looked at him, she was going to see a refined gentleman. He'd even tuck his napkin in his collar and drink tea with his little pinkie waving in midair if that's what it took. He laughed at the ridiculous notion and reminded himself that that kind of thinking would get him in trouble.

He entered the kitchen and spotted her setting the table. "Evening, Lizzy."

She looked at him. Her cheeks flushed, her mouth in a perfect bow. He wanted to touch her so much, he ached inside.

"Can I help you with anything?"

She seemed surprised at his offer. "I have everything under control. Thanks."

Ben brushed past her and sat down. She seemed aware of his light touch, and she scurried away from him but briefly glanced in his direction. Ben smiled when she did. "You're looking mighty pretty this evening."

"Thank you." She pushed a loose curl from her forehead and studied him for a moment. "I like that shirt, Ben."

The way she'd said his name started a slow burn deep in his belly. He could look at her sapphire eyes for hours and not get bored. He watched with fascination when she nervously licked her lips. As he debated whether to stand and gather her in his arms, Josh and Clyde raced into the kitchen. "Hi, Ben. When we gonna go riding again?"

Elizabeth shot Josh a look. "What did I tell you about asking for things?"

"What's wrong with that? Ben doesn't mind. He goes riding anyway, and I bet he gets really lonely all by himself. I'm doing him a favor."

"Yeah, what's wrong with that?" Ben repeated with a wide grin and a wink. "My partner needs to ride his wild bronco once in a while."

"Yeah," Josh shouted with great enthusiasm.

"You boys go outside and wash up."

"I've been thinking of fixing up this kitchen." Ben didn't know where that had come from. He was more surprised than Lizzy to hear himself say it.

"Really?"

"This house needs running water. It wouldn't take that much work or money. I could dig a ditch from the well to the counter, put in a sink, and attach a hand pump. Would you like that?"

"It would make things a lot easier around here."

"It certainly would." The idea grew on him. Why hadn't he thought of this before now? "After I pay off my loan, I might even install indoor plumbing."

"I bet Granny would love that. It can't be easy for her to go outside for her necessities."

Ben was so caught up in his conversation he hadn't realized he'd crushed the stems he was holding. He examined what had started out as good-looking bouquet.

Lizzy glanced down and took them from his hand. "Are those for me?"

He felt like a damn idiot. He'd mangled the flowers. "They looked better when I picked them."

She took down a Mason jar and filled it with water. With great care, she arranged the blossoms as if they were long-stem roses and took a moment to inhale their fragrance. She looked all teary-eyed. "When these die, I'll press them in a book so I can keep them forever."

Ben figured it meant she liked the flowers. Apparently, Lizzy was more sentimental than he'd thought. If that was all it took to make her happy, he'd make the effort more often.

When she set his plate on the table, he took her hand and gave it a gentle squeeze. The smile she bestowed on him warmed him clear to his toes. He decided right then what he was going to do. Ward Metcalf wasn't due back for several more days. Ben planned to make the most of what time remained.

"Did you happen to find your money?"

Lizzy smiled mysteriously. "I want to wait until everyone has eaten to share my good news."

By the happy look on her face, Ben was certain she'd found the money.

Lefty entered a few minutes later. "Good evening, Elizabeth. Did you find your cash?" He was wearing the shirt Lizzy had sewed for him. Ben seemed to be the only man around who didn't own one of her hand-made creations. He felt left out.

Lizzy gave him a puzzled smile. "I just told Ben I plan to make an announcement after supper."

Lefty seemed damned pleased as he took the chair beside Ben. Ben examined his wide grin and wondered what he was up to. "Did you have enough time to do whatever you had in mind this afternoon?"

"Yes." Lefty didn't elaborate, and Ben didn't ask any more questions.

Granny arrived with her hair curled, wearing a dab of lipstick. She squinted toward Ben. "Who you gawking at?"

"I was thinking you're about the prettiest grandmother I've ever seen."

Granny mumbled something about his being a damn fool.

Zack arrived in time to hear Ben's comment. "She's a sight for sore eyes. She's got my old ticker galloping away." He grabbed his chest as if he were having a heart attack. Granny's eyes lit with amusement. Ben waited for her to tell Zack he was a damn fool, but it never happened.

As the old man escorted Granny across the room, he whispered something that had her smiling like a schoolgirl. He pulled out her chair and after she'd sat down, made a point of yanking his chair closer. Ward Metcalf could take lessons from the old man.

When Zack finally stopped staring at Granny, he turned his attention to Lizzy. "Any sign of your loot yet?"

"I have an announcement to make after we eat."

Zack slapped his leg, looking happier than a kid on his birthday. "I have a feeling it's good news."

Cecelia arrived, and the children took their seats a few minutes later. Ben had saved a chair for Lizzy next to him, but Josh leaped onto it. "We're partners, you and me, right?"

Ben smiled down at the kid. "You've got that right, partner."

Lizzy was about to pick up the serving bowl of stew when Ben jumped up. "Let me do that." He carried the dish to the table while she removed the biscuits from the oven. Seeing her bent over gave Ben ideas not suited for the supper table. He unfastened the top button of his shirt.

When she approached, he took the platter of biscuits from her, making sure his fingers lingered over hers for as long as he dared. They shared a look that made it clear to him his touch had stirred her awareness. The temperature in the kitchen shot up again.

As she pulled out her chair, Ben leaped up again and pushed it back in.

Granny frowned at him. "You're making me dizzy with all this jumping up and down. Sit, so we can eat."

Ben sat back down. When it was his turn to take a biscuit, he grabbed two and smiled at Lizzy. "These sure smell great."

Josh elbowed Ben's ribs. "Bet you're

286

gonna make some more horseshoes with Bett's biscuits, huh?" The boy laughed long and hard. Ben did his damnedest not to join in. Could he help it if he had a sense of humor or that he flashed a quick grin?

When Ben bit into the biscuit, he was amazed to discover it was quite good. "These aren't half bad."

Lizzy's eyes narrowed at his compliment.

The stew was a pleasant surprise. The vegetables were cooked, and there were no bugs on the bottom of his plate. It tasted fair and didn't leave a floury taste in his mouth.

"This stew actually tastes good." The incredulous tone of his voice was evident even to his ears. "I mean, I never expected it to taste like this." That, he decided, wasn't any better than his first statement. He considered trying to undo the harm by telling her how relieved he was not to see spiders swimming in his dish, but he wasn't sure if she'd take that as a compliment, either. Instead, he dug in and asked for a second serving. He even soaked up the gravy at the bottom of his plate with an extra biscuit. If that didn't mean he liked the meal, he didn't know what did.

Once the dishes were cleared and the table wiped down, Lizzy stood ready to make her announcement. Ben was prepared to hear she'd found the envelope containing the money. She looked so happy, he knew he'd done the right thing. When he glanced around the table, he saw that Zack and Lefty seemed as happy as he. Everyone here loved Lizzy. It was easy to understand why.

Lizzy pulled a white envelope from her pocket. "Look what I found while putting clean sheets on my bed this afternoon. The money was under my pillow all this time, and I didn't even notice. Isn't that wonderful?"

Confused, Ben eyed the envelope. He couldn't understand how it had gotten under her pillow. Maybe one of the children had switched its location.

Granny seemed more surprised than Ben did. He wondered what the puzzled look on her face meant.

"That's great news," Lefty and Zack said in unison.

Ben stood to give his congratulations, but Lizzy waved at him to sit back down.

"This isn't all my news. About half an hour later, I found another envelope between the clean clothes in the laundry basket."

This time no one said a thing, except Josh. "I prayed you'd find the money and look

288

what happened. Do you think if I pray for a horse, I'll get two?"

Lizzy smiled down at him. "After today, I don't dare say."

For the life of him, Ben couldn't figure how the money had ended up in the laundry basket. He offered Lizzy an innocent smile and meshed his fingers together on the table.

Cecelia glanced at her sister. "You found two envelopes?"

Lizzy shook her head. "No." She smiled at everyone. "I found a third envelope in the stew pot under the kitchen counter."

At least, Ben knew how that one had gotten there.

CHAPTER 20

After supper Zack, Lefty, and Ben headed
to the porch with glasses, a bottle of brandy,
and each with an envelope containing
twenty-eight dollars. They each grabbed a
wooden rocker. A laugh rumbled from deep
in Zack's chest.

"What's so funny, old man?" Ben asked.

"You two, that's what. How dumb can you
get? Hiding your envelope in a stewpot.
That doesn't make one lick of sense. And
you," he continued, gawking at Lefty and
tapping his temple, "Elizabeth does wash
every day. You'd have to be loco to think
she might have misplaced it there."

Ben gave Zack a pointed look. "You think
you're any smarter? She stripped the bed
this morning. Don't you think she'd have
noticed her money under her pillow when
she did that? As I see it, none of us were
any too bright."

Lefty opened his bottle and placed a

booted foot against the porch railing. "Elizabeth said her money was in an envelope with her name and address on it."

"Too bad she didn't keep the cash," Zack said. "I wanted her to have it."

"She's a prideful woman," Ben added.

Zack nodded. "Stubborn, too."

"That's a fact." Ben glanced at his two companions and lowered his tone. "I think I know how we can help Lizzy out."

"You saw her face, boss. She won't take a cent from us."

"No, but she isn't about to turn down orders for shirts. Now is she?"

By the widening grins on the two men's faces, Ben knew they understood. "Queenie's been collecting orders."

Zack stretched a leg over the railing. "Seems to me Elizabeth's doing well without our help. Just today I heard Queenie got her two more orders."

Ben lowered his tone. "And where do you think those came from?"

Zack slapped his thigh. "You shrewd bastard. Where have you been hiding the shirts?"

"In the bottom bureau drawer in my bedroom."

"Aren't you afraid she'll see them when she brings the wash up to your room?"

"She leaves my things on my bed, and I take care of them myself later."

Zack scrutinized Ben's clothing. "Too bad you can't wear the shirts. If you don't mind my saying so, the one you have on right now is ratty."

Lefty looked confused. "Why don't you just order them for yourself?"

"She'd see right through that."

"How many do you have?"

"Seven, so far, but I have another two on the way."

Zack looked skeptical. "Why are you really doing this?"

"I want Lizzy to see she has a future here. I want her to build a business in Welcome. I want her to stay here with me where she belongs."

Zack scowled. "What's gonna happen when she finds out it's all a hoax?"

"I hope she doesn't find out."

"Aren't you afraid Queenie will tell Elizabeth who her best customer is?" Lefty asked.

"Queenie doesn't know. Pete's in cahoots with me. I give him my order, and he passes it on to Queenie."

Lefty chuckled. "Next time you see Pete, order three for me."

"I could use a few, too," Zack added.

"You can tell him yourselves tomorrow

when he comes over to check the mare."

Ben popped the cork on the bottle of apple brandy and filled their glasses. He took a swig and almost choked. "Have you noticed anything strange about this brandy?"

Zack and Lefty both took swallows.

The old man rolled his eyes. "It tastes like dishwater."

Lefty poured out the contents of his glass onto the ground.

Ben went into the kitchen for another and noticed the chagrin on Lizzy's face. "If you have something to say, why don't you say it?"

"I noticed how fast you downed your first bottle."

"That bottle wasn't any good. I think I'm losing my taste for the stuff."

She seemed happy with that. "Maybe you should consider, as you probably say in Montana, going on the wagon."

"I don't have a problem."

She chewed on her lower lip. "I know that."

"Do you?"

"Two drinks can turn into several more until there's no end."

Ben stroked her face. "Not every man who takes a drink turns into a son of a bitch. I know firsthand the harm liquor can do. After my mother left, my father drank himself to an early grave. I'm not about to repeat his mistake."

He saw the compassion in her eyes. "I didn't know."

He wanted to share everything with her. His past, his dreams, and his future. Until now, he hadn't realized he was going to ask her to marry him.

"Ben, are you feeling all right?"

"Of course." He folded her in his arms. "How'd you like to go for a picnic? Just the two of us."

"I'd like that very much."

"Good. As soon as I train the new man, I'll take some time off."

He wanted to say more, but Zack's raspy voice came from the porch. "What's taking you so long?"

"I guess I better go. I'll talk to you later." Before heading out, he traced her mouth with his finger just to make sure she was real.

A moment later, he caught Zack eyeing him when he handed him the bottle. "Oh, oh! One look at your hound-dog expression, and I can guess why you've been dallying." Zack stabbed his finger into the air. "Watch yourself, boy, or you'll end up hog-tied and lovin' it."

Lefty flicked off the bottle cap with his thumbnail. "I think someone's tampered with this bottle, too."

Ben set his glass down by his rocker. "I have a sneaky suspicion who's responsible."

For the next forty-eight hours Ben supervised at the sawmill during the day and kept an eye on his herd at night. He hadn't slept more than four hours straight in the last week. Fatigue was catching up with him.

He yawned and watched Duke run a board through the saw. What the man lacked in size, he made up for in speed. Each time Lefty carried three planks to the wagon, Duke took one, but he made two trips for each one Lefty made.

"You're a good worker," Ben said, thinking Duke might stop to talk a spell. Ben didn't know why, but he still felt uneasy around Duke. Finding out more about him might settle his mind.

Duke scurried past him, grabbed another thick plank, and set it on the saw bed. He glanced up, puffed on his cigar, and mumbled, "Thanks."

Ben had never seen a man smoke as much as this one did. Zack, who had an opinion about everything, theorized the cigar smoke had stunted Duke's growth. According to Zack, Duke slept with a lit cigar clamped between his teeth, and smoke oozed from his pores. Since Duke's arrival, the old man had stopped complaining about Ben's lumber business and now spent his spare time coming up with ridiculous notions about Duke. Before coming out to the mill, Ben had gone into the bunkhouse to have a word with the old man. When he saw the stepstool beside Duke's bunk, he warned the old coot to clean up his act. Zack assured him he would, which only added to Ben's worries.

Lizzy arrived a moment later with a tray of cookies and a pitcher of lemonade. She wore a blue gingham dress that emphasized the color of her eyes. A white lace ruffle circled her neck and accented the slender column of her throat. He remembered the taste of the soft flesh beneath her ear and the exact spot he'd kissed to tease a moan from her.

Elizabeth assumed she'd never see her missing money again, but she no longer cared. Its disappearance had been a mixed blessing. When she lost the twenty-eight dollars, Lefty, Zack and Ben had come to her aid. She couldn't think of their thoughtfulness without blinking back tears.

She was mending a pair of Josh's trousers when Pete rode up in his wagon. "Good day, Elizabeth."

"Hello, Pete."

"Got some good news for you. A customer at the Golden Harp wants some shirts made."

"How many?"

"Six."

She expected him to say two, maybe three. "My goodness."

He handed her an envelope.

Ben happened along at that precise moment and gave the envelope a cursory glance. She looked shocked when she opened it and found seven dollars inside. "What's this?"

"Money."

"I can see that."

Pete exchanged a look with Ben. "The customer is prepaying this order."

"But why?" No one had ever done this before.

"He wanted to."

"Oh." She paused to catch her breath. "There should be five dollars and forty cents in the envelope, not seven dollars."

"He said it was extra for a job well done."

"Have I made shirts for this gentleman

before?"

"He knows your work, and he feels your shirts are worth more than what you charge."

At this rate, Elizabeth would have the money for a new sewing machine soon. She'd questioned the wisdom of investing in such expensive equipment, but she no longer did.

"Pete, I'd like you to check Clyde while you're here," she said, thinking it high time she learned more about the boy's problem.

"Is Clyde sick?"

"No, but I think he's deaf."

Elizabeth did her best to restrain Clyde long enough for Doc Cartwright to examine his ears. "I'm no expert in this field," Doc said, "but I see nothing out of the ordinary in his ear canal. However, he didn't even flinch when I shouted, and he was unaware of the bell I rang behind him. I suspect you're correct. The boy is deaf."

Elizabeth took this as good news because it would explain Clyde's erratic behavior. "At least his mind isn't impaired."

Doc scrubbed his hand over his chin. "I didn't say that. The boy doesn't act like a normal youngster."

Elizabeth tightened her grip around

Clyde, who grunted like an animal. "He's a bright boy. No one's ever taken the time to work with him."

"You may be right, but don't get your hopes up. You can let him go. I've finished my examination."

Clyde ran from the room.

Elizabeth thought of something that might help. "Back in Boston, one of our elderly neighbors used an ear trumpet to pick up sounds."

"That works only if the patient has diminished hearing. In Clyde's case, I suspect he hears nothing at all."

"He acts out and makes strange noises because he can't communicate with us. I'd like to try to teach him sign language. I was hoping you'd know what I should do first."

Pete looked thoughtful for a moment. "I have a book on signing that you can have. What you're trying to do for the boy is admirable. I don't know whether Clyde is capable of learning. But if anyone can get through to that boy, it'll be you."

Ben needed to speak with Granny in private. He knocked on her door and entered when she told him to come in. "How's my favorite girl doing?" He sauntered across the room and pressed a kiss on her forehead.

"How come you aren't up to your armpits in sawdust instead of jawing with an old lady?"

"I'll be outside soon enough."

"How's it goin'?"

"Good." He paused to glance into her faded gray eyes. How much longer before she lived in total darkness? Despite his concerns, he smiled when he noticed the springy curl bobbing over her forehead. "I see Cecelia's been fixing your hair again."

"That child's a blessin'."

"You'd miss her if she went away, wouldn't you?"

" 'Course."

"And Elizabeth, you'd miss her, too?"

"If you're tryin' to make a point, get to it."

"I've been doing a lot of thinking lately, about what life was like before Lizzy and the children came here to live."

"You mustn't forget 'bout Bernie and her pups," Granny said, stroking the hound's long ears.

Ben chuckled. "I couldn't forget about this mangy dog even if I wanted to with you around to remind me." He chose his next words carefully. "I need to discuss something that might not set well with you."

"What might that be?" Granny looked

guilty even before Ben could ask his question.

"Granny, I don't want to insult you, but what I'm about to ask needs asking." He cleared his throat and paced across the room.

"Don't bother askin'. I took Lizabeth's money." She held her head high and stared straight ahead. "At the time, it seemed like the right thing to do."

Ben issued a long sigh. "When I saw your face at supper the other night, I knew something was wrong."

"When Lizabeth said she'd found her money, I near dropped dead on the spot."

"You know what you have to do now?"

" 'Course, but I didn't steal the money. I borrowed it so she would stay."

"I suspected as much."

"Do you think Lizabeth will go away when I give her the money back?"

"I certainly hope not."

"If you have a brain in that head of yours, you'll see that she don't."

CHAPTER 21

Elizabeth was dicing carrots when Jeb, one of Ben's new hired hands, ran into the kitchen, gasping for breath. "There's been an accident at the mill."

The dish she was holding fell and shattered. "Did something happen to Ben?"

"No, ma'am, Lefty's been hurt. He's bleeding bad."

"Where's Ben?"

"I don't know."

"I may need Granny's help." She hurried from the kitchen and returned with Granny a moment later to find Jeb pacing.

"You two go on ahead." Granny grabbed a stack of towels off the counter. "Take these with you, Lizabeth. When you get to Lefty, loosen his shirt. Put his head up. Me and Cecelia will hook the horse to the buckboard and be there shortly."

"We best hurry, ma'am. Or Lefty will die

before we get to him," Jeb said with certainty.

"Hogwash." Granny threw Jeb a warning look. "Lefty's tough. He's got Montana blood flowin' through his veins."

Sick with fear, Elizabeth grabbed the towels from Granny and took off toward the sawmill with Jeb at her heels.

As she neared the makeshift shed that housed the saw, she spotted Lefty on the ground, his head at an awkward angle like a broken doll. She ran to his side and dropped to her knees.

"Lefty," she whispered, praying he could hear her.

His face was gray, his skin clammy. Her fingers trembled as she felt for a pulse. Was there a faint one?

She prayed Granny would arrive soon. Elizabeth spotted a water bucket several yards away. She jumped to her feet, dunked one of the towels she'd brought along, and ran back. As she laid the wet cloth against Lefty's forehead, Jeb arrived, out of breath.

"Is he alive, ma'am?"

"I don't know." She slipped a few towels under Lefty's head. When she undid the buttons on his shirt, she saw crimson bruises and a deep gash on his right side. She stuffed two more towels against the wound to staunch the bleeding. Then she ran her fingers along the sides of his head to check for injuries.

Lefty groaned softly.

She heaved a sigh of relief. "Granny will be here soon. She'll know what to do."

His eyelids fluttered open for a moment.

"Does it hurt bad?" she asked.

Jeb knelt beside her. "I spotted Duke when I came over the rise. When he saw me, he took off like the devil was after him. I figured he was up to no good, so I decided to have a look around. That's when I spotted Lefty."

Elizabeth heard the sound of wagon wheels. A heavy weight lifted from her chest.

"Granny's here," she said to Lefty.

He didn't stir. When she put her finger beneath his nostrils, she couldn't tell whether he was still breathing. Her heart clenched.

She ran to the wagon to help Granny down, but the old woman leaped off and grabbed hold of Elizabeth's hand. "You'll have to direct me. I don't know which way to go."

By the blank look in Granny's eyes, Elizabeth knew she could no longer see. She took her arm and led the way.

Granny scrambled onto the ground. She

ran gentle fingers at the base of Lefty's throat. "I feel a pulse." She continued down to his chest.

Lefty winced.

Granny put her mouth against Lefty's ear. "You're going to make it. I won't let you die. Lizabeth, I need to bind his chest 'fore we move him or a rib could poke through his lungs. Get the sheet I brung."

Elizabeth ripped the sheet she found in the back of the wagon into long strips. She handed Granny the cloth and spoke to Cecelia, who seemed unable to move. "We need you to help us slide this bandage under Lefty's back." Elizabeth's sharp order forced the child into action.

While Elizabeth, Cecelia, and Jeb lifted Lefty, Granny started to wrap the material around his chest. Except for an occasional moan, Lefty seemed unaware of what they were doing.

Granny angled her head. "Jeb, soon as you help get Lefty in the wagon, go fetch Pete at the Golden Harp."

"Yes, ma'am."

"Tell him to hurry."

When Ben rode in some time later, he was surprised to see Pete's horse tied out front. Panic consumed him as he dismounted and ran into the kitchen, where he found Cecelia weeping.

"What's wrong?"

"Lefty got hurt at the mill."

Ben didn't wait for an explanation. He ran through the living room and took the stairs two at a time. His bedroom door was ajar, and the whispers coming from inside increased his apprehension. He removed his hat and entered.

"What happened? Will he be all right?" he asked, taking in Lefty's ashen color.

Pete glanced up. "He took a severe blow to his rib cage. I've given him a thorough going over, and I think he's going to pull through. It's a good thing Granny and Elizabeth got to him when they did." Pete put his supplies back in his bag. "I've given him laudanum for the pain. I suspect he'll sleep for the rest of the day and into the night."

The next morning, Ben went to check on Lefty. Lizzy, who'd been up most of the night caring for him, was sound asleep in the chair beside the bed. Lefty's coloring had improved. His breathing was still shallow, but according to Pete, that was to be expected. Once he was certain his friend was on the mend, Ben tiptoed toward Lizzy and kissed her cheek.

She came to with a start.

"I didn't mean to wake you," he said. "I just couldn't help myself."

Her smile warmed him. "I'm glad you did."

"The picnic we talked about will have to wait." His heart was bursting with love. He considered asking her to marry him right then, but he wanted everything to be perfect with moonlight and stars.

He pulled her to her feet, wrapped his arms around her waist, and took a moment to enjoy the closeness.

Lefty stirred and uttered a low moan. Holding hands, they went to check on him.

"How are you feeling?" Ben lowered his head, hoping to hear a reply.

Lefty's eyes opened a fraction. "I hurt all over."

"You will for a while. Pete left some laudanum for when the pain gets bad."

"Sorry."

"For what?"

"You were counting on me."

"Now I'm counting on you to get better. What happened to the saw?"

"I caught Duke swinging a sledge hammer at it. I was his next target." Lefty winced and shut his eyes.

Before leaving, Ben gave Lizzy a quick hug

and a kiss. "I don't know when we can be together again."

"Will I see you at suppertime?"

"There's a lot of work to do, but I'll sure try."

Some time later, Ben saw Zack coming out of the bunkhouse.

"How's Lefty doing?" Zack asked.

"He's damn sore."

"He's lucky he wasn't killed." The old man blinked back tears and glanced away a moment to regroup.

"It's a good thing Jeb showed up when he did," Ben said.

Zack fisted his hands. "I spent half the night at the mill, trying to repair the damage Duke done."

"Let's go have a look."

The magnitude of the destruction was worse than Ben anticipated. The metal frame was nicked and dented. Several pulleys were smashed. Half the blades were broken or bent. His stomach churned with rage.

Zack looked worried. "Do you have any spare parts?"

"No. I'd planned to buy an extra pulley and a few blades in case we needed them. But I put it off because money was tight."

"How long will it take to order parts?"

Ben wondered the same thing. "Too damn long."

"Why would Duke do this?"

"Hell if I know."

Zack spit on the ground. "I'd wager a week's pay he's the son of a bitch who's been cutting our fences."

"I've been thinking the same thing." Ben glanced at the saw. He could lose everything. "I need to get this fixed in a hurry. Ward Metcalf won't give me an extension on the loan." Fear settled in his chest and mushroomed until it threatened to suffocate him. He couldn't lose the ranch. It was his whole life; Granny's too.

It was all he had to offer Lizzy.

Zack spat on the ground. "I never did trust Duke. I'll sleep better knowing he's gone."

"I don't doubt that."

"Next time you hire an ugly critter like him, I'll move into your room and let you have my bunk."

"You're sure ornery when you want to be."

"I'm merely stating facts." Zack inspected the broken strap at close range. "Maybe we can make a belt."

"It has to fit tight."

"If it takes too long to order, there'd be

no harm in trying. I could check with the cobbler in Butte. See if he has any ideas."

"It might be worth a shot."

Zack picked up the damaged pulleys and scowled. "Too bad Duke ran off."

"Why's that?"

"I'd like to shove these up his nose."

CHAPTER 22

The next day, after sleeping a few hours, Elizabeth tiptoed into Lefty's room to replace Cecelia. "Thanks, Pumpkin, I feel much better."

Elizabeth smiled as her sister scampered away. Cecelia had blossomed into a happy, easygoing child. Not once had Elizabeth regretted leaving Boston, and now, she was more convinced than ever she'd done the right thing.

She picked up her sewing from the basket and started to tack a collar in place. As her nimble fingers flew over the fabric, her mind was on the man who'd stolen her heart. Ben had mentioned he wanted to have a serious discussion with her. The sensuous look in his eyes had left her weak-kneed and longing for the type of intimacy that brought a blush to her cheeks.

She pondered whether upstanding ladies thought of such things and quickly dismissed the thought. She wanted Ben to hold her, kiss her, and she didn't want him to stop. She loved him and suspected he felt the same way. With all her heart, she hoped their discussion would involve that very topic, along with plans for a future together.

Did she trust Ben enough to put their lives in his hands? She couldn't afford to make a mistake. Cecelia and Josh's happiness depended on her decisions. Did she have the ability to think clearly?

Not so long ago, she'd have laughed at anyone who suggested she'd even consider getting married. But before she'd take that step, there were matters to be resolved. She smiled at her foolish thought. Ben had not even proposed, and she was fussing about the details of an agreement that might send him running.

A soft whisper interrupted her thoughts. "Elizabeth."

She put her sewing down and walked over to the bed. "How are you feeling?"

"Like I was trampled by a bull." Lefty inhaled a shaky breath. "Have they found Duke?"

"Not yet."

Sweat beaded his forehead.

"Can I get you anything?"

He licked his parched lips. "Water."

Elizabeth lifted his head and helped him take a sip of the cool liquid. "Maybe if you eat something, you'll feel stronger."

"Maybe."

She helped him lay back down and left to ask Cecelia and Granny to prepare a tray with oatmeal and weak tea. She returned with a basin of water and a washcloth.

Lefty eyed her with suspicion. "What's that for?"

"I thought I'd help you get cleaned up."

"No way." He took the cloth from her hands and brushed it over his face and arms. "There, I feel better already."

Though Elizabeth saw little improvement, she kept her thoughts to herself and was glad when Cecelia arrived with his breakfast a few minutes later.

"If you two ladies will help me up, I'd be much obliged."

"Do you think that's wise?"

He leaned his elbows into the mattress and grimaced. "We'll soon find out."

The hardest thing was standing. Once Lefty was upright, he took a few steps without much difficulty. When he reached the chair, he grabbed hold of the arms for support and lowered himself. The veins in his arms stood out from the effort. Closing his eyes, he settled into the chair and leaned his head back.

"There, I did it," he said, heaving a deep breath. "I might never get back up, but I'm not going to worry about that right now."

Cecelia helped Elizabeth strip the linens and put on clean sheets. After Cecelia left, Elizabeth sat on the edge of the bed and spooned oatmeal into Lefty's mouth. His face had taken on a healthier color.

"I appreciate you taking such good care of me," he said.

"I don't mind."

He glanced toward the window, his face contorting in pain. "Ben needs me right now, and I can't do a darn thing."

"Ben will manage." She felt a deep sense of pride when she thought of Ben. He was a good man, someone she could trust, someone she hoped to build a life with.

Lefty shivered and goose bumps popped out on his arms.

"You're cold," Elizabeth said. "Let me get you something to wear. You don't want to catch a chill."

"When Zack comes to visit, tell him to bring me over a shirt."

"Who knows when that might be. I'm sure Ben has something you can wear until then." She scurried across the room and flung open a drawer filled with socks and

underwear. The next drawer held a con-
glomeration of things, but not a single shirt.

"Elizabeth, don't . . ." came the feeble
voice behind her.

She looked at Lefty askance. "Why not?
Ben won't mind if you wear one of his
shirts. Lord knows you aren't going to ruin
it. They're in such shabby condition to
begin with." She ignored Lefty's protests,
yanked open the bottom drawer, and almost
fell on her backside when she saw its contents.

Several shirts stacked in a neat pile. Why
were these here?

When the pieces of the puzzle fell into
place, she was shaking with anger and disappointment. She recognized each one because she remembered taking the orders
from Queenie. The red plaid and green-
striped shirts would be too small for Lefty.
She brushed her fingers against the soft,
blue cotton material of a shirt that would fit
a massive chest. When she'd sewn this one,
she'd envisioned a beast of a man as its
owner.

When she got her hands on that beast,
there'd be hell to pay.

Later that afternoon Elizabeth noticed
Granny sitting on the porch, with a forlorn

look on her face. "Would you like some lemonade, Granny?"

Granny stared straight ahead at nothing in particular and shook her head. "Ain't been a good week for me."

Elizabeth pushed the rocker closer to the old woman, sat down, and held her fragile hands, giving them a tender squeeze.

"The shadows are gone," Granny said.

At first, Elizabeth didn't understand. "What do you mean?"

Granny sniffed several times. One plump tear splashed onto the bib of her overalls. "I can't tell day from night no more. I ain't never goin' to see Bernie lookin' at me. Or the sun comin' up. I ain't ever goin' to see nothin' again."

Elizabeth remembered the cantankerous old woman she'd met her first day at the ranch. Granny had lost her spunk, and Elizabeth felt helpless. Seeing the empty look in those tear-filled eyes made her feel like crying, too. "What can I do to help you get through this?"

"I've been sittin' here feelin' mighty sorry, tryin' to tell myself I still got lots to live for. I ain't believin' it."

"Granny, you have Ben. You have the children and me . . . You have Bernie," she added, knowing how Granny felt about the dog. "We all love you."

Granny stared straight ahead, seemingly unaffected by what she'd said.

Elizabeth pressed a kiss against the parchment-like cheek. "I'm here to help you every way I can."

After a few minutes of silence, Granny blinked away tears. "I have Ben, but I'm gonna tell you somethin' that might change your mind 'bout lovin' me."

Before Elizabeth could assure Granny that nothing would change her feelings, the older woman reached in her overall pocket and withdrew an envelope with Elizabeth's name and address on it. "It was me who took your money."

At first, Elizabeth thought she'd heard wrong, but the evidence was right in front of her in a trembling hand. Why would Granny do such a thing? She looked inside the envelope and counted thirty dollars. "I only had twenty-eight dollars."

"I gave you interest for borrowin' it."

"Oh. But you don't have to do that."

"It ain't open for discussion."

Granny stared blankly toward the barn and chewed her bottom lip in silence. Elizabeth could see she was embarrassed. She also saw the pride and stubbornness etched on her face. "Surely, you needed the money for something important."

Granny's lower lip trembled. "I needed to keep you from leavin'."

At first, when Ben thought of getting married, he'd break into a cold sweat. But the idea had begun to grow on him. Even the fact that Elizabeth was from Boston didn't worry him half as much as it had. Ben had reached a decision. Once he paid off his loan, he'd ask Lizzy to be his wife.

As he came up behind Lizzy in the kitchen, the urge to pull her against him was hard to ignore. But the children were watching his every move. He settled on giving her an innocent smile, masking thoughts that were anything but innocent.

"Hello, Lizzy," he whispered, lowering his head slightly and teasing his senses with the smell of lilacs.

She dropped the plates she was carrying with a clang on the checkered tablecloth. Without sparing him a glance, she sashayed back across the room and returned with utensils, which she heaved alongside each dish. For someone who'd turned setting the table into an art form, she'd sure changed her ways.

He attributed her foul mood to fatigue as he slid his flowers into a glass, plunked them on the table, and took a seat across from Zack and the boys.

Ben winked at Josh, who seemed unfazed by his sister's strange mood. "Howdy, partner."

"Me and Clyde's been learning important stuff from Zack."

"What's Zack been teaching you boys?"

"Zack said to wait till after supper and surprise everyone then. But I can give you a hint. When Zack was in Butte today, he bought us each a present. We spent an hour learning how to use them. The man who made mine has the same name as you."

"Josh, the bright fellow is a Mr. Richter, not Ricker," Zack said, looking mighty proud of himself.

Josh elbowed Clyde, who grinned at Ben and waved his hand side to side, his sign for hello. Ben was amazed with the boy's continued progress.

Ben waved back, then pretended to be deep in thought. "Let me guess. I bet it's a pair of new socks, right?"

"Course not."

"Or maybe a shovel so you two can muck out the stalls?"

The boys exchanged conspiratorial grins.

As she neared him, Elizabeth cast him an annoyed look. Since everything had been fine between them this morning, he attributed her foul mood to fatigue. Or maybe it was the time of the monthly curse. Ben was no expert on the subject, but he'd heard horror tales from several of the married men at the Golden Harp. The next time she looked at him, she replied to his sympathetic smile with an icy glare that sent a chill down his spine.

Josh reached across the table and poked Ben's arm. "You gonna take another guess?"

He regarded Lizzy a moment, but she avoided his gaze. What was wrong? Before he could dwell on the matter, he felt a small hand shaking his arm. "You gonna guess?"

He shifted his attention to the boys. "I think I've finally figured it out. Zack bought you each a broom so you can sweep the floors."

Josh folded his arms across his chest. Clyde mimicked his actions. "That's the dumbest thing I ever heard. I'm not giving you no more clues."

All through the meal, Ben tried to figure out what had transpired since morning to change Lizzy's attitude toward him. "The beef soup is good." Truth was he'd barely tasted the food but felt a compliment might be in order.

"Thanks." She dug her spoon into the hot

broth and spent considerable time deciding which carrot to lift to her mouth. As soon as she'd accomplished the simple task, she made a chore of sliding cubed potatoes around her plate.

Ben's stomach knotted. "Lizzy, I need to talk to you, now."

He saw hurt and confusion in the blue eyes that met his. "But we haven't had dessert yet."

"Forget about dessert," he replied in a voice filled with frustration. He pushed his chair back and wrapped insistent fingers around her arm. "I'm sure Cecelia can handle dessert, right?" He waited long enough for the child to nod. Then, without giving Lizzy a chance to protest, he hauled her to her feet and started across the kitchen.

He swung the door open and came face to face with Ward Metcalf, one hand poised ready to knock, the other holding more roses than Ben had seen in his lifetime. Without waiting for an invitation, Ward strutted in, grabbed Lizzy's free hand, laid the flowers at her feet, and planted a kiss on her palm. "My dear, how grand to see you again." The waxed mustache wiggled upward as he smiled.

A graphic expletive tumbled from Ben's

mouth, causing Lizzy to spear him with another disgusted look.

Under his breath, Ward mumbled something about someone being an uncouth swine. Ben challenged his rival with a brazen grin and did his damnedest to remain unfazed by the unexpected visit while holding on tight to Lizzy's hand.

Right there, in the middle of the kitchen, Ward dropped to one knee. He pulled a small velvet box from his pocket, flicked it open, and exposed a ring with a diamond the size of one of Granny's prize-winning peas.

"Elizabeth O'Hara, I'm asking you in front of everyone present to be my wife."

Chapter 23

According to Ben's pocket watch, Lizzy had been outside for twenty-eight minutes, the longest twenty-eight minutes of his life. While the children ate apple cobbler, Ben pushed his dessert around his plate. When Lizzy finally entered the kitchen, he could hear Ward's fancy surrey wheeling away. Trying not to be too obvious, he glanced at her left hand and was relieved to see a bare ring finger.

Josh spoke around a spoonful of cobbler. "I can hardly wait to show you my surprise. You won't believe . . ." When the boy spotted his sister, he stopped mid-sentence and jerked his chin in her direction. "If you marry Mr. Metcalf, I ain't leavin' Granny and Ben. And I don't care what that nincompoop says, I ain't never ever gonna work in his bank."

Lizzy's eyebrows took a dramatic leap.

"You'd best watch what you say, young man."

"But Zack told Lefty 'bout that nincompoop sniffing your skirts. Why would he want to do that for?"

Lizzy's cheeks turned crimson. "Mr. Metcalf did no such thing. And you're never to use that word again. Do you hear me, Joshua? Now eat your dessert so I can finish up with the dishes."

Ben forced a cough to hide his grin, but he needn't have worried. Lizzy never spared him a glance before turning to the counter. He rose and came up behind her. "Lizzy, the dishes can wait. I need to talk to you outside for a minute."

"I have absolutely nothing to say," she replied, her tone set in stone.

"You're stewing about something, and I think it'll do you good to get it out of your system."

With a resigned sigh, she led the way to the porch. Once the door slammed behind them, she whirled around and pointed a finger at his chest. "You make me so angry. I could . . . I could just strangle you."

The thought of her hands around his neck appealed to him. "Sounds like a damn good way to go."

"I'm serious."

"I know. Before we straighten out this matter, I need to know what you told Ward."

"That doesn't concern you."

"It might. Lately, I've come to think of you as my girl."

She pushed a strand of copper hair from her face. Taking a shallow breath, she glanced down, and finally met his gaze. "I told Ward I couldn't take his ring."

"Was it because of me?"

"You are an arrogant man."

He grinned down at her. "Thanks."

"That wasn't supposed to be compliment."

"Oh." He wanted to taste her lips so much that he found himself leaning forward. As he neared the most tantalizing mouth he'd ever encountered, he saw a little flour on her left cheek, no doubt from the cobbler dessert she'd made. He remembered how she'd looked dusted with the fine white powder after her first baking attempt. "Good enough to eat."

She shook her head in confusion. "What?"

"I said you look good enough to eat."

She uttered a short, nervous laugh. "You shouldn't say such things."

"Even if it's true?"

"You're trying to change the subject."

"Maybe." He stole a kiss and pulled away

before she could protest. "Now, tell me what I've done."

"You're a conniving, good-for-nothing fibber."

"Is that all? For a minute I was afraid you thought poorly of me." He smiled down at her and rested a hand on her shoulder, which she instantly brushed aside.

"Ben, you can't laugh your way out of this. I don't think I'll ever trust you again."

"How did I betray your trust? I wasn't even around today." He saw the tears in her eyes and felt like a heel. "I'd never knowingly hurt you."

"Wipe that innocent expression from your face. It looks as out of place as teeth on chickens."

He smiled at her choice of words. Lizzy was sounding more like Granny every day — a real farm girl. This time when he reached for her hand, she didn't pull away. True, her grasp was limp as a wet rope, but he held on tight anyway. "Are you going to tell me what I did so I can defend myself?"

"Lefty was cold, and I didn't want him to get chilled." She spared him a look reserved for rodents. Her lower lip puckered, and she blew out a short breath. "I saw the shirts in your bottom drawer."

"You weren't supposed to find them."

"You're a despicable, low-down scoundrel."

"I did it for you."

"You tried to trick me, and it worked. It was a mean thing to do. You hurt me . . . deeply."

"I never meant to hurt you. I wanted you to succeed, but . . ."

She poked a firm finger in his chest. "And you didn't have enough faith in me to succeed on my own so you drummed up a bunch of fake orders. Then you came sauntering around, big goofy grin on your face, and I was dumb enough to think it was because you were happy to see me, but all the time you were having a good laugh. Who else knows about this?"

"Just Zack, Lefty, and Pete."

"At least you had the decency not to lie about that."

"I don't lie."

"No, you stretch the truth without a thought to the consequences. I'm surprised you didn't write another article for the newspaper, seeing how you're so good at that."

"I don't regret writing that other article."

"It was full of fabrications."

"It brought us together."

He wound his arm around her shoulder

and steered her to the stoop where he persuaded her to sit beside him. "I was afraid if you didn't get enough orders, you'd take off, and I'd never see you again."

"You were trying to control my life. Both my father and my stepfather were good at controlling the people around them. When things didn't go their way, they manipulated my mother until they got what they wanted. You manipulated this situation until it suited you."

"I couldn't take the chance of losing you. Besides, I wanted you to feel good about yourself."

"And how do you think I feel now?"

"You should feel loved. I certainly wouldn't go to all this trouble if I didn't care for you."

Before she could reply, a familiar tune came from Zack's harmonica as the old man rounded the side of the house with Josh and Clyde in tow. The discordant music, like a tomcat's incessant wail, bore into delicate eardrums. Ben stared in disbelief at Josh blowing into his own mouth organ with such force that it damn near drowned out the loud booms coming from the drum in Clyde's hands.

"Oh My Darling, Clementine" had never sounded worse, but when Lizzy leaned into him, pressed her mouth to his cheek, and whispered, "Oh my darling, Ben," he'd never felt better in his life.

Ben even gave Josh a thumbs up, which was a mistake because long after Zack had disappeared the boy sat on his lap, playing the incessant serenade.

The next day, Elizabeth tapped on Granny's bedroom door. "Can I come in?"

"Ain't locked, is it?"

She crossed the room in a few determined strides. "I've been thinking about your predicament."

Granny directed a mean scowl at her. "Poppycock! I'm blind. Calling it my predicament won't change the fact. Ain't no sense dancing 'round the issue."

Seeing the old woman's shoulders hunched forward twisted Elizabeth's heart. She took a breath for strength and continued, "Precisely what I was thinking. You've gone blind, but you knew that was going to happen. As I see it, you should be glad it's over and done with. Before this happened, all you had to look forward to was losing your eyesight. I'd think you'd be glad to get that behind you."

Granny gave Elizabeth a bewildered look. "Are you daft? What kind of crazy reasonin' is that?"

Elizabeth forged ahead. "Now the worst is behind you. For months, a dark thundercloud hung over your head. Now that the storm has passed, you have the rest of your life to look forward to."

"You got more than a few kernels missing from your cob, Lizabeth."

"I was scared silly when I first came to Welcome. But once I accepted my situation, things didn't turn out so bad."

Granny cleared her throat. "Your cooking was terrible."

"Yes, but I survived. And when I look back, I can smile. Maybe being blind won't seem so bad after you've had a while to adjust."

"This ain't the same as cookin'."

"I know." She hugged the old woman and blinked back tears. "I'm certainly not making light of your serious situation . . . er, blindness, but I know you'll do well if you set your mind to it. I still remember how you looked when I first arrived. You were an ornery old lady, and no one would have dared to cross you. You had me shaking in my shoes."

"I was angry."

"I want to see that spirited woman I met the first day get her dander up and fight.

330

This isn't what anyone wanted for you, but it doesn't have to be the end of your life. I know this is rough, but you can overcome it. You have so many people who love you. You aren't alone."

Chewing her lower lip, Granny set her gaze toward the window. The pained expression twisting the wrinkled face added ten years to her frail appearance. Finally, heaving a weary sigh, she whispered, "I ain't never been so scared in all my doggoned life." Tears flowed unchecked down her cheeks.

Elizabeth pulled Granny against her. "I'm here to help you. The children are, too. Maybe together, we can get through this."

As Elizabeth glanced around the room, she spotted Granny's pipe and tobacco on the dresser. "Why don't you come downstairs and have a smoke?"

"I ain't feeling like doing much of anythin' right now."

"What do you say I have Cecelia come in here to doll you up? Nothing like a new hairdo to get a woman's juices flowing."

"My juices dried up years ago."

"If you could see the way Zack eyes you when you're all spiffed up, you'd know his haven't."

She rubbed at her eyes. "Now I know for

sure your corncob's missing several rows, but have the child come up anyway. I wouldn't mind a spit curl or two dangling over my forehead. Who knows, it might pick up my spirits."

Elizabeth kissed Granny's cheek and started across the room. As she reached for the doorknob, she looked over her shoulder. "I've been thinking about making a cake for supper."

"What kind?"

"Only kind I know how . . . pan-cake."

Granny's brows knitted together. "On second thought, the hair can wait. I'm escortin' you to the kitchen. I'd rather not have to dig my piece of cake out of the pan."

Gone was the weariness as she rose and stepped toward Elizabeth. She reached out a hand, which Elizabeth held in a firm grasp.

" 'Bout time you took some notes on how to do things 'round here. Land sakes, every woman should know her way 'round the kitchen. Pigs 'round here are 'bout ready to bust their guts from all the mistakes they been swilling down."

"I thought fat pigs were a good thing."

"Yes, but my waistline's been shrinking. It's time I gave you a hand. You never tasted nothin' like my white cake."

Elizabeth squeezed Granny's hand. "I can

hardly wait."

"Lightest cake you ever tasted. Before we start, you better head to the barn and find four long nails."

"What for?"

Granny's face wrinkled in a teasing smile. "When I take my cake from the pan, it'll float clear to the ceiling if we don't anchor it down."

Elizabeth knew everything would turn out just fine.

Later that afternoon Elizabeth was working on another shirt. This one was special because it was for Ben. Though he already had several of her shirts, most of those didn't fit him. As she stitched a side seam, she remembered his words. *You should feel loved.* A warm, tingling sensation settled in the pit of her stomach. This shirt was her gift to him, her way of saying she forgave him. Unlike her stepfather, Ben had tricked her because he cared. Once he'd explained his reasons, her anger had dissipated like steam from a boiling kettle.

Unfortunately, Zack and the children had made it impossible to discuss what was in their hearts. Hers brimmed with love.

A short while later she was humming "Oh My Darling, Clementine," a song she'd begun to think of as theirs, when she caught sight of a tall figure approaching on horseback.

When he reached her, the dark-haired stranger tipped his hat. "Good day, ma'am. Can you tell me where I can find the lady that sews the fancy shirts I've been hearing about?"

Elizabeth's heart dropped to her knees and her temper soared. A red mist settled over her eyes. Throwing Ben's shirt aside and pricking her finger in the process, she shot to her feet and gave the stranger a look that would send a grizzly scurrying. "What for?"

"I got an order for her." He dared to smile.

She frowned up at the giant, hoping he'd leave. Only an idiot would believe the innocent look on the clean-shaven face.

"How many shirts are you ordering?"

"I'd like to start out with a dozen."

So angry her hands shook, it was a moment before she'd calmed down enough to speak.

How dare Ben do this to her. Again!

"That many, huh? In a variety of sizes, right?"

"Yes, how did you know?"

"Pete sent you, right?"

"As a matter of fact . . ."

"I've heard enough. Wait here a minute. I've something to show you."

Fueled with rage, Elizabeth dashed into the house, grabbed Granny's unloaded shotgun, and returned with the weapon pointed at the phony customer. His jaw hit his chest when he spotted the gun aimed at him. "Ma'am, I believe there's been a mistake."

"Oh, there's been a mistake all right, and you've made it. I suggest you turn tail and run before I make another mistake." She clamped her teeth together and tried to look mean.

The man waved both hands in front of him. "Don't worry, I'm leaving, and you can bet I won't be back."

"See that you aren't."

He took off in a cloud of dust.

Some time later, Elizabeth was coming out of the hen house with a pail of eggs when she spotted Ben with his back to her. Glancing into the pail, she chose a fat egg and took direct aim.

"Ben." She used her most feminine voice.

He turned, with a wide grin. It did her heart good to see that grin vanish when the egg hit his forehead with a loud crack, depositing its contents over his startled face. "What in the hell did you do that for?"

The next egg struck his chin. Yolk and egg white oozed onto his neck and shirt. He rubbed a hand over his jaw, swore prolifically, and took off toward her at a run. Before he could stop her, she managed to crack two more eggs over his head.

He yanked the bucket away and cuffed both her hands behind her. "Tell me what's going on, or I swear you'll be sorry."

"I'm never speaking to you again."

"Good, remember that while I pay you back."

"You're a mess," she pointed out.

"Ah, you aren't speaking, remember?"

"You should see yourself." Threads of egg white hung from his eyebrows. Yolk ran from his cheek down over his chin.

"I'm a mess, huh? Not as messy as you'll be when I'm through with you."

Elizabeth felt a moment's panic. "You're a despicable man. You deserve what I did."

"And you deserve what I'm about to do to you."

Holding both her hands in one of his, he reached into the bucket and held up three eggs for her inspection. "My, my, one of Granny's chickens outdid herself with these. Bet they're double yolks. Would you care to place a bet?"

Elizabeth tried to wrench her hands free.

"No? It's your last chance. I'm surprised, Lizzy. I'd taken you for a betting woman."

She watched him lift the eggs over her head. She tried to escape, but he was too strong. She heard the shells crack and felt the thick goop flowing over her hair and down her forehead.

A deep chuckle rumbled from his throat. "Too bad you didn't bet, you'd have won. Turns out they weren't double yolks after all."

He worked his hand over her scalp and down the side of her face, tweaking her nose and leaving behind a yellow dot. "This is more fun than I thought." When his sticky fingers settled at the nape of her neck, she felt him undoing several buttons. She fought him with everything she had, but he continued to loosen her collar. Even as she kicked his shin, he dug into the bucket again.

"It pains me to have to do this, but I feel that I must." With mock compassion on his face, he dropped another two eggs down the back of her shirtwaist, then pulled her into an embrace that had the eggs oozing down her spine.

"I'd say we're even, wouldn't you? And just to show I've no hard feelings, I'll help you to clean up."

He released her and dug into his pocket

for his handkerchief. When he attempted to dab the egg from her hair, she swatted at his hands.

"You should see yourself," she told him. "You're a sight."

"You aren't looking any too good yourself."

A dollop of egg white landed on her nose. Ben swiped his hand along the side of her face and pulled her against him. "Now, care to tell me what I did wrong?"

"You forgot to call off your latest customer."

"What customer?"

"A tall, dark-haired man came around to order shirts this afternoon. But he took off when I waved Granny's shotgun at him."

Ben grinned. "I had nothing to do with that order. That man was a bona fide customer."

CHAPTER 24

The following day, rocking in a chair on the porch, Granny yanked her pipe from her pocket and stared blankly toward the barn. "Lizabeth, tell me what you see."

"In the lilac bush to our right, the largest robin I've ever seen is staring at us with his lady friend. She's brown, like cinnamon. He's the dashing one of the pair. By the way he puffs out his chest, I'd say he's well aware of the fact. Through the open barn door, I see Ben stacking lumber alongside Zack. Even Josh and Clyde are helping."

"Barn must be pretty near full by now."

"Looks that way to me."

"Good thing Zack was able to finagle a belt for the saw. He's a smart man, you know."

Elizabeth considered teasing her about having a beau, but she decided to say nothing. "Ben looks tired." It was no wonder, with him working round the clock. Warmth flooded her heart as she thought of the man she'd grown to love.

"Somethin' goin' on 'tween you two?"

"Maybe."

"What kind of answer is that? Either it's goin' on or it ain't."

"Ben and I need to talk, but I think so."

Granny nodded. "He's a mighty fine man, my Ben. You couldn't do no better."

"I'd like to think so."

"You better know so."

"I do." Elizabeth had grown to trust Ben, and the fear of repeating her mother's mistakes no longer consumed her.

Granny leaned forward in the rocker. "Who's comin'?"

"It's Josh."

"Ben's mighty fond of that boy."

"Ben treats him better than his own father ever did."

Josh took the stairs in one leap and pointed toward Granny's pipe. "Can I help with that?"

Elizabeth caught her brother's attention. "Granny can't see you pointing."

"I wanna know if I can light your pipe. Can I, huh?"

Granny turned her head toward Elizabeth. "Do you mind?"

Elizabeth considered saying no, but the

eager look on her brother's face stopped her. "Only if Josh promises never to light matches unless an adult is around."

"I promise, I promise."

"Get a match from over the stove," Elizabeth told him as he disappeared inside. He was back before she could blink.

Granny anchored the corncob pipe between her lips and waited. In his eagerness, Josh pushed too hard and the wooden match snapped in two. He ran back in the kitchen and returned two seconds later with several more.

"Make sure you put those back when you're through," Elizabeth warned him.

Without glancing up, he nodded. He struck the match against a rough board and smiled when a flame appeared. As he lifted the lit match to Granny's pipe, she mumbled out of the corner of her mouth. "Now, you be careful, you hear? Being blind's bad enough. Last thing I need is you catching my hair afire and me being bald, too."

"I'm being really, really careful." He touched the flame to the tobacco, and Granny took several short pulls on her pipe.

After a moment, smoke rose in the air. "You did a darn good job, Josh."

"Can I take a puff?"

"Absolutely not," both women said.

"Nobody lets me have any fun around here." With his head down and his shoulders hunched forward, he slowly walked down the stairs.

He kicked a stone in his path and was halfway across the yard before Elizabeth remembered the matches. "Josh, did you forget something?" She fully expected him to ask what, but he surprised her.

"Oh, yeah." He glanced at the matches hidden in his palm, then scampered back into the kitchen.

When Elizabeth entered the kitchen later that day, she counted four bottles of apple brandy on the countertop. Although some women would have given up by now, she wasn't that easily daunted. Until now, her tactics had gone unnoticed. By diluting the liquor, she guessed she'd thrown out enough brandy to inebriate half the men in the state of Montana.

She grabbed the bottles and headed out the door. This called for drastic measures. Never short on ideas, she came up with a humdinger. While laughing at the clever thought, she fell over a large wooden crate fifteen feet from the kitchen door. Curious, she set the bottles down and took a closer look. The words *Virginia City, J.L. Mott Iron Works N.Y.,* were stamped on the side of the crate, but nothing else to hint at what might be hidden inside.

Cecelia stuck her head out the door. "What's that, Betts?"

"Darned if I know." Elizabeth tried to push the container, but it didn't budge.

"Why are those bottles on the ground?"

Elizabeth ignored the question and tried to peer inside a tiny crack between two boards.

"Can we open it?"

"Check with Granny."

Cecelia returned a minute later. "She's asleep."

Elizabeth inspected the box and ran her fingers along the rough surface. "I think Granny would want us to open it."

"It might be Ben's."

That was certainly a possibility, but not one Elizabeth wanted to entertain. "Since it's by the kitchen door, it's fair to assume it belongs to Granny. If we open it, we'll be doing Granny a favor. When she wakes up, she'll want to know what's inside. Now help me find something to pry open this crate before I die of curiosity."

An hour later, all Elizabeth had managed to do was scrape her arm and wedge a splinter under her thumbnail. Cecelia had long since gotten bored and taken off with Bernie and the puppies. Elizabeth rarely gave up on anything, but she admitted defeat — for now.

Instead, she focused on pushing the porcelain top off the first bottle of brandy. Her fingers ached by the time she freed the last cork, emptied half of each bottle and refilled them with water. As she took a whiff of the contents, she realized she'd grown immune to the pungent odor. In fact, the strong alcoholic smell she remembered seemed nonexistent, suggesting the liquor had deadened the nerve endings in her nostrils.

Considering the damage to her olfactory senses, she could well imagine the destruction to a drinking person's digestive tract. More determined than ever to curb Ben's drinking appetite, Elizabeth poured three tablespoons of salt into every bottle before slipping the cork back on as best as she could. When she'd completed the chore, she dabbed at the sheen on her forehead and picked up the bottles. Without looking up, she started toward the kitchen door and ran smack into Ben Ricker's immovable chest.

She hoped he wouldn't question her about the bottles of brandy in her arms. "Granny got a package today."

"It's a crate."

She chewed her lower lip. She was so nervous a drop of sweat trickled down her backbone. "Yes, I see that, but what do you think is inside?"

"It's mine. I know what's inside."

"Oh. Are you going to tell me?"

"You really want to know?"

"Yes."

"I'll tell you later. But first, you've some explaining to do."

She blinked twice. "What do you mean?"

"You know what I mean."

For lack of a better solution, she pretended not to understand.

He nodded toward the bottles in her arms. "What are you doing with those?"

"Oh, these?"

"Yes, those."

"I . . . er . . ."

"The jig is up, Lizzy. I saw what you did."

"Everything?"

"Yup. I watched you pour, refill and add the s-a-l-t." He emphasized the last word.

"Oh."

"I've been on to you for days."

She thought of all her wasted efforts. "You let me do all this work for nothing. You knew all along?"

"I didn't know for sure until I spotted you

five days ago. Each day you emptied the bottles, and every evening I refill them with tea."

"Oh." Every aching muscle in her hands responded to that news with a painful twitch.

"As an expert of sorts, it amazes me you didn't notice the pale color or the absence of smell." He shook his head in a way that implied he questioned her intelligence.

She felt like a fool, but it was anger that took hold when she thought of how he'd been watching her — for days! "How could you do this to me?"

"How could you do this to me?"

"I didn't want you to drink too much, so . . . well . . . I decided . . ."

"You decided I couldn't be trusted to use alcohol sensibly. You put me in same despicable category as your stepfather."

"No, Ben. I would never do that. I thought . . ."

The hurt and disappointment in his eyes stopped her. "You thought I was no better than he. A slap in the face would hurt less." He turned away from her and stepped toward the crate.

She'd never thought of it that way. "Ben, I had no right to do what I did." This too was a matter of trust. Not once had she witnessed Ben drinking to extremes. "Am I forgiven?"

Ben kept his back to her. "I'll need to chew on it a while."

Her heartbeat sped.

He tapped his fingers along the crate's wooden slats. "What if I told you this crate is filled with bottles of cheap whiskey?"

For a moment she was taken aback. "Your whiskey would be safe with me. I'll even help you carry it inside if you like. But that's not what's inside that crate. The Ben I know does not drink to excess. He'd have no need for such a vast quantity." She ran a finger along his mouth set in a frown. "I'm sorry, Ben."

He gave her a long hard look, which softened when he stepped forward and gathered her against him. As his chin rested on the top of her head, she felt his chest heave, then heard a rumble of laughter. "If you could have seen yourself . . ."

"Enough, Ben."

His laugh intensified. "You're one hell of a conniving woman."

He was about to kiss her when Josh and Clyde charged around the corner and bounded onto the large crate. "What's inside the box?"

Elizabeth grabbed her brother's arm. "Get

347

down this minute before you break something!"

Josh hopped off the crate, and Clyde followed. "Geez, this is the biggest box I ever
saw in all my whole life."

"Partner," Ben squeezed the boy's shoulder, "can you keep a secret?"

Josh gave an enthusiastic nod. Clyde did,
too.

Ben whispered something in Josh's ear.

"Really!"

"Yes. Really."

"Wow!"

Elizabeth's curiosity grew, but she wasn't
about to let on. "I'll be fixing supper if
anyone needs my help."

No one said a word as she slipped unnoticed into the kitchen. Once inside, she
peeked out the window and was greeted by
Ben's knowing grin inches from the other
side of the pane.

While Josh played a barely intelligible ver-
sion of "Oh My Darling, Clementine" on
his harmonica, Clyde beat his drum loud
enough to drown out the creaking from the
wooden planks as Ben pushed down on the
crowbar.

To Ben's left, Zack stood shaking his
head. "You're getting to be one hell of a

high-falutin', citified sonofabitch, if you ask me."

"No one's asking."

The musical torture stopped, and Josh's crisp voice rang out. "What's a falutin' citi-fied . . . what was it you said, Zack?"

"Never mind." Ben was amazed the boy could hear above the racket. Once the discordant clamor resumed, Ben turned his attention to Zack. "See what you've done, old man. Watch what you say around the boy."

Zack scowled then mumbled under his breath. "Nothin' wrong with the way things are. We don't need some fancy indoor privy. Granny's a tough old bird. Mark my words, she'll never go for this foolishness."

"I can't have Granny stumbling around outside."

"That's why I strung a rope from the kitchen door to the outhouse. A hell of a lot less expensive than your solution."

"Yes, and I appreciate what you've done. It'll be a while before we have the time to install this. Until then, Granny will need the rope."

Ben avoided looking at the discontent on Zack's face. When the door slammed, he was glad to see Lefty sauntering toward them. Chest bound tight, Lefty walked with a stiff gait, but it was good seeing him up and about again. "How are you feeling?"

"Better, thanks." Lefty stopped next to the crate and ran his fingers along its chipped edges. "Looks like a beaver's been gnawing on this."

Ben looked toward the window and caught a fleeting glimpse of Lizzy's face. "I'm guessing a curious beaver with red hair."

Zack rubbed his fingers over the stubble on his chin. "Thought you were broke."

Ben yanked another board off the crate. Zack didn't cotton to change, and he suspected Granny might complain when she first found out, but she'd get used to it. Besides, Ben hadn't bought the sink and water closet strictly for Granny. He was certain Lizzy would appreciate a few conveniences.

As Ben lifted the straw packing from over a cast-iron sink, Zack studied the contents of the box. "You paying for all this with your good looks? If so, you're in big trouble."

Lefty gave a low chuckle.

Ben speared his friend with a warning look. "Don't you go encouraging him." He yanked another board loose. "I struck a deal with Will Smith down in Virginia City. He let me have this in exchange for building materials for the addition he's putting on his store. Besides, according to Lefty's calculations, we have enough dry lumber in the barn to pay off my loan to Ward and a little left over. I've hired men to bring the planks into Virginia City tomorrow afternoon. Day after next, I'll have my money and my life back and you two will have a bonus."

"Even so, we still don't need all this highfalutin' . . ."

"Come January, you'll probably be the first in line with a towel slung over your shoulder, ready to take a hot bath in my new tub."

"That'll be the day."

"That's what I'm afraid of."

"You think you're so gol-darn smart . . ."

Ben didn't wait for the rest of the old man's tirade. He lifted the heavy sink from the crate and headed towards the kitchen. As he backed into the room, he was greeted by Elizabeth's beaming smile.

"A real honest to goodness sink," she said in a way that warmed his heart.

"You like it?"

"Oh Ben, of course I like it."

Ben set the sink on the floor. "Before winter, we'll have indoor plumbing."

Her eyes brightened. "With a tub?"

He grinned. "Yup."

She hugged him tight. "Oh, Ben."

"I hope you'll stay here for a good long while." He pulled a folded piece of paper from his pocket. "Someone asked me to give you this."

"What is it?"

"Open it, and you'll see."

She unfolded the note and looked up at him. "Did you have anything to do with this?"

"The man you scared off the other day is opening a store in Welcome. After the way you greeted him, he didn't dare come back, but when he heard I'd be seeing you, he gave me his condolences and this order for a dozen shirts."

"This is wonderful."

"There's more good news. Three other families read the newspaper article I wrote. They've decided to stay. It seems Welcome is a growing community."

He could tell she was pleased. He wanted nothing more than to spend the rest of his life with her. And soon he'd have his life back and a bright future. "There's a full moon tonight. Would you like to go for a ride after the children are in bed?"

"Absolutely."

He claimed her mouth and was about to deepen the kiss when Granny arrived.

"What's all the commotion 'bout?"

With his arm still around Lizzy, Ben sauntered toward Granny and smacked her cheek with a wet kiss. "I have a big surprise for you, Gran."

"Well, spit it out."

"First chance I get, I'll be installing an indoor privy and a sink with running water."

Her forehead wrinkled. She gazed at him with disbelief. "Hogwash. What we need that for? Near as I can figure, either you've gone daft or you're just plain crazy."

CHAPTER 25

"But Betts, I don't wanna go to bed. I wanna go riding with you and Ben."

"You can come with us some other time, but not tonight."

Josh kicked back the covers and lay with arms crossed over his chest.

"If you don't stop this right now, your bottom will be too sore to sit atop a horse any time soon."

He made a face. "I'm sure Ben wants me to go. Check with him. Pleeeeeeease."

"The subject is closed." She attempted to kiss the top of his head, but he ducked.

"Good night," she said firmly, and shut the bedroom door. "Lefty, are you sure you're up to this?"

"Don't worry about a thing. If Josh doesn't behave, I'll hog-tie him."

She heaved a weary sigh. "You may need to."

A shrill voice came from the other room.

"What's hog-tie mean?"

With a groan, Elizabeth lifted her eyes heavenward.

"Go ahead and get ready. I'll handle this. Hey, pal," he said, disappearing into the bedroom.

Tonight she'd finally be alone with Ben. Her stomach fluttered with anticipation. She brushed her hair and let it fall down her back. As she glanced in the mirror, she noticed the rosy glow in her cheeks and the sparkle in her eyes. Tonight would be a turning point in her life.

Half an hour later, Elizabeth heard a knock. She couldn't imagine who'd be here at this hour. When she swung the door open, she was surprised to see Ben. "Why are you knocking?"

"Because I'm calling on you, and it wouldn't seem right if I barged in like I owned the place."

"But you do own the place."

"Small technicality."

"I made you something," she said.

"There's only one thing I really want," he said in a low tone that left no doubt what he meant.

She thrust the gift at him but dropped the bundle. They bumped heads when they both bent down to retrieve it. She'd have toppled over had he not caught her around the waist.

He ripped the brown paper from the shirt. "This means a lot to me," he said, his voice husky and sincere. Before she could stop him, he'd yanked off his other shirt and stood half-naked.

Her pulse roared in her ears as she admired his muscular chest sprinkled with curly brown hair that swirled around his navel and dipped out of sight in the waistband of tight jeans.

He shrugged into the new shirt and turned away to tuck in the tails. She swallowed past the wad of cotton in her throat.

The look in his eyes was unmistakable. "We'd better get out of here before I carry you upstairs to my bedroom."

She felt lightheaded with need, the need to feel his body against hers. "Ben, you shouldn't say such things." Did her tone give away her true feelings?

"Lizzy, you better get used to hearing them. I've wanted to make love to you ever since I saw you bathing in the stream."

"When was that?" she asked, clearly shocked, as he ushered her out the door.

"Oh, no. I'm in for it now."

While holding her hand, he swung up on his horse and before she could protest, lifted her onto his lap.

"Ben, you haven't answered my question."

"I didn't see anything. Well, not much, anyway."

When she turned around, she saw the teasing glint in his devilish eyes. "Don't blame me. You're the one who stripped naked less than one hundred feet from where I stood. I merely made the most of the opportunity."

"No gentleman would watch a lady bathing."

"I've been accused of many things, but being a gentleman is definitely not one of them." She saw the flash of white teeth.

"You're incorrigible." She elbowed him in the ribs, but it was a playful nudge, and revenge was the furthest thing from her mind when his lips settled below her ear and trailed warm kisses along her neck.

"Where are we going?" Her voice came out in a pathetic squeak.

"For a ride in the moonlight," he whispered, doing wonderful things to her earlobe.

"I thought I'd have my own horse."

"Are you complaining or complimenting me on my ingenuity?"

"I'd rather not say."

She leaned into him. One arm circled her waist. His other arm was dangerously close to her right breast, brushing against her while he held onto the reins with his right hand.

The horse plodded along. The full moon overhead lit their way. Except for the hoot of an owl and an occasional rustle of leaves, silence grew thick and wove a spell around them.

She saw no need to speak as Ben's heart thudded wildly against her back. Her own heart drummed an uneven beat, forcing her to take short gulps of air. She'd never felt this way before: warm, protected, and definitely aroused.

Ben halted his mount by the stream, then swung down, wrapped his hands around Elizabeth's waist, and lifted her from the horse with no effort. With legs spread wide, he positioned her back against his long, lanky frame. Leaning into him, she gazed at the rippling water that shimmered like fine diamonds in the moonlight.

She couldn't hold her feelings back any longer. "Ben, I love you."

He moved swiftly, and she found herself facing him. "I've dreamed of hearing you say those words," he whispered before claiming her mouth in a kiss that took as well as gave, that teased, that taunted, that left her breathless.

Elizabeth had never expected to feel this way about any man. She'd thought herself incapable of trusting a man with her heart and soul and loving him as though nothing else mattered. But she believed in him fully, with the same certainty that the sun would rise tomorrow.

Ben reached for the buttons at the back of her dress. She marveled at how quickly he unfastened them. A light breeze flittered along her bare flesh as he eased one sleeve off her shoulder. "Lizzy, tell me to stop."

Instead, she threaded her fingers through his hair and held him tight.

But he broke the connection and pulled her sleeve back in place. "I didn't mean to take advantage of you."

"Ben, what do you want from me?"

"Eventually, everything. But tonight, I'd like to sit next to you, hold you for a while, kiss a little, then bring you back home . . . unspoiled."

As he spoke, he sauntered toward his horse, and reaching into his saddlebags, he retrieved a blanket and a medium-size box. He then knelt on one knee and spread the thick blanket over the ground. She took a step toward him, and he reached out to her. "Come sit. I've a surprise for you."

At the touch of his warm fingers, butterfly

wings fluttered in her stomach. She sat and folded her hands in her lap and watched him gather twigs and leaves, then strike a match and blow down on the kindling until flames flickered to life. He moved with a fluid grace that was both gentle and strong.

"What are you doing?"

"Curious, huh?"

"No."

"Reach in that box for me."

She removed a small tin, several bars of chocolate, and a jar of luscious-looking strawberries. Once he'd positioned the tin over the flames, he broke the dark chocolate into small pieces. As the chocolate melted, he turned back to her. "Have you ever tasted strawberries dipped in chocolate?"

She nodded. "Once, at the Jameson Tavern in Boston." She was surprised that Ben would think of such a thing. "Where did you ever get such an idea?"

He gave her a peck on her cheek. "I found an article in one of Granny's magazines about a fancy restaurant that served this exact same thing."

He made a production of dipping the strawberry in the melted chocolate. "Open up," he said, and delivered the succulent morsel to her mouth. His fingers lingered against her lips. The flames under the metal tin were nothing compared to those in the pit of Elizabeth's stomach.

"My turn," she said, plucking a berry from the jar and leaning over Ben until she was able to reach the tin of chocolate. By then, she was half sprawled over him with her breasts against his chest. He groaned softly. A small warning went off in her head, but she was too busy to notice or simply too happy to care.

"Lizzy, you're playing with fire."

He felt warm, inviting. "I do believe you're right." She lifted the strawberry to his mouth, and at the point when he was ready to bite down, she popped the berry into her mouth.

"You'll pay for that."

"I'm not afraid of you, Ben Ricker."

He captured both her hands in his left one, and with the fingers of his right hand lifted a strawberry from the jar, double dipped it in chocolate, and dropped it in his own mouth.

"Hmm, that was definitely the best berry I've ever tasted."

She met his smug smile with one of her own. "The one I stole from you was far better."

He quirked an eyebrow. "Maybe I should offer this one to you. Nah." He slid his tongue slowly over the chocolate. "If you promise to behave I'll give you a bite."

Something about the way his tongue moved over the juice on his lower lip stole her breath. "I'll be good," she promised, in a voice that sounded nothing like hers.

As his fingers delivered the fruit to her mouth, she clamped her teeth over the berry along with his fingertips. He pretended to cry out in pain, yet made no effort to pull away. She licked the chocolate from his fingers, and he leaned in close. His breath caressed the side of her face.

"Maybe we should go back now," he said, but made no effort to move away.

She tossed her head back and gave him access to her neck, which he nibbled and kissed until she didn't care what happened next as long as he continued to hold her.

"Let's get out of here before we do something we'll both regret come morning." He looked at her questioningly, and she knew he was giving her a chance to come to her senses.

Elizabeth was tired of being sensible, tired of always doing the right thing, tired of being responsible and carrying the weight of the world on her shoulders. If they stayed, she'd have only herself to blame, but she didn't want the night to end. "Let's have a few more berries before we go. It's my turn."

As she reached into the jar, he ran his hand along her shoulder and down her arm. "If that one's for me, coat it really good."

She dipped the plump strawberry once, twice, three times and aimed it at his mouth.

His crooked grin made her love him all the more. "You better not lose your train of thought this time. Remember, I like my women docile and obedient."

She intentionally missed her target, and instead ground the berry into his face.

One second she was sitting, the next she found herself thrown back against the blanket, one of his long legs pinning her down. "Didn't you learn anything from that egg episode?"

She knew she was in for it. "You're right, it's time to go home."

"Not just yet. You wanted strawberries, remember?" The tiny lines at the corners of his eyes crinkled.

"Thank you, but I've had enough strawberries for one night."

"Oh no, you haven't. Here, have another." He poised the berry above her. The sticky juice dripped onto her chin and down the side of her face.

She tried to wiggle free but failed. In the moonlight she could see red stains on his skin. A few seeds stuck to his cheekbone, and a smear of chocolate ran diagonally across his mouth.

When the strawberry collided with her nose, he laughed. The more she struggled, the louder he roared. "Now look what you made me do. Let's see if I can get it right the next time."

"Ben Ricker, don't you dare."

The next chocolate-covered strawberry was on a direct course with her forehead when their eyes met and held. Indecision played across his handsome face. She watched his Adam's apple bob once, then twice. He cleared his throat. "You were right. We better get the hell out of here." But he didn't remove his leg from over her. The berry in his hand slipped to the blanket unnoticed.

"Ben . . ." She paused to consider what she was about to say and found she had no doubts. "I want to stay."

The desire in his eyes was unmistakable. "Are you sure?"

She didn't have to ponder the question. She loved this man. The smile she gave him was all the encouragement he needed.

When his mouth settled over hers, every cell in Elizabeth's body came alive. Any remaining concerns about making love without the bounds of holy wedlock slipped away like feathers in a gale. His soft lips tasted of strawberries and chocolate. Her senses reeled as if she'd consumed a quart of Granny's apple brandy. Though she'd never known the feel of a man's hands on her body, she welcomed Ben's bold advances and encouraged him when he reached behind her and started to unbutton her shirtwaist.

Before he could finish, she pushed his fingers away and undid the remaining buttons herself, then allowed the bodice to slip from her shoulders. She took immense pleasure in the appreciative look in his whiskey-colored eyes.

He trailed a line of warm kisses along the lacy trim of her chemise, curling the toes in her tightly laced shoes. Elizabeth shivered, though she was anything but cold.

Sometime later, he rose to his knees. "Lizzy, let me undress you."

At the sound of his deep voice, goose bumps exploded on her flesh. Her lack of experience made her nervous, but she took a breath for courage and slipped her hand around Ben's neck. "Only if I can remove your shirt first."

The smile that followed was one she'd never seen before. "Nothing would make me happier."

With unsteady fingers, she fumbled with each button, and finally the shirt lay open. The gorgeous chest she'd seen earlier was hers to explore, and she took great care to touch every single inch. Purely by accident her thumb raked across his right nipple, which beaded under her inquisitive touch. He moaned and captured her mouth in a searing kiss.

Between long tantalizing kisses, he unlaced her shoes and slowly bared each foot, taking great pains to massage the arch and every toe before lifting her skirts and boldly running fingers up her calves. How his mouth ever came to rest on her knee, she'd never know, but rest it did. Her heart rumbled louder than the subway back in Boston. Deep inside, muscles twitched with an intensity that frightened her.

"You mustn't," she whispered, trying to push his head away, not sure what he'd think if she allowed him to continue.

"My sweet, innocent Lizzy." His lips lingered against the inside of her right knee for a few more seconds before possessing her mouth again. "It's not too late to change your mind."

"I love you, Ben. I don't want you to stop," she replied with certainty. She waited for him to tell her he loved her too, but the words never came. What were words anyway when deep in her heart, she knew the truth?

He slowly peeled away each article of her clothing, lingering here and there to drop a kiss. When she lay completely naked on the blanket, he studied every inch of her as one would a work of art in a museum. "I've dreamed of seeing you like this."

Elizabeth too, had thought of this moment but felt none of the embarrassment she'd expected. He shrugged out of his shirt. So caught up in the feel of his chest, she'd never finished what she'd started. "I should be doing that."

"Next time."

She watched with wonder and a little fear when he reached for the waistband of his jeans and started to undo his fly. Her breath caught in her throat as his fingers reached for the second button. She glanced away and had the decency to blush.

The last vestiges of ladylike behavior evaporated when her curiosity got the better of her, and she found her gaze riveted on the fingers undoing the last button. The gasp she uttered at seeing what sprang free a moment later was unanticipated. She'd told herself she knew what to expect. After all, she'd seen Josh naked. Clearly, she'd underestimated. Never in her wildest dreams had she ever expected . . .

Well, there was no way . . .

"Lizzy," he whispered, stretching alongside, his manhood pressing against her legs. He smiled and gave her a long kiss. "I wouldn't hurt you for the world." He slanted his mouth over hers and brushed a finger over the nipple of her left breast. It beaded to attention.

"My sweet Lizzy," he murmured, a moment later taking the rigid peak in his mouth, suckling until she was dizzy with longing. He then traced a path downward with his tongue, teasing the sensitive flesh around her navel. She moaned his name and grabbed handfuls of his hair. Moments later he rose above her and after gently parting her legs, he started to slip inside.

She traced the corded muscles of his neck. "I want you to make love to me."

Tiny beads of sweat dotted Ben's upper lip as he gently pushed forward. Instinctively, she arched her hips. The pain was sharp but brief, and she couldn't control the cry that tore from her throat.

He froze, his eyes opening.

She chased away his concerns with a smile.

He rained kisses over her forehead, her nose, each cheek, then took a leisurely tour of her mouth, plunging his tongue repeatedly where it tangled with hers.

On a sigh, she whispered his name, "Ben, oh Ben."

"My sweet, sweet Lizzy," he groaned, his voice deep and hoarse. Slowly, ever so slowly, he started to move. The exquisite rhythm of flesh rubbing flesh awakened dormant muscles. Flames of desire licked at her center and danced along her spine as she angled her hips and met him thrust for thrust.

He shouted her name. She murmured his. Their arms and legs entwined. Their hearts soared as one beyond the trees, the moon, the stars, and up to heaven and back.

Some time later when Elizabeth could speak again, she murmured against Ben's shoulder, "I love you so very much."

He leaned up on one elbow, his dark sensuous eyes hinting at what was in his heart. "You've become my world."

But he didn't say the words she wanted to hear, and that was the only thing marring an otherwise perfect moment.

CHAPTER 26

In the moonlight Elizabeth's long red hair glowed like spun gold. As Ben glanced down at the woman he loved, he remembered the silken strands slipping over him just moments earlier. He'd heard tales of wives who endured their husband's lovemaking with their eyes shut and their mouths set in grim lines, waiting for the ghastly ordeal to end.

But not his Lizzy.

Despite her inexperience, she'd welcomed the joining of their bodies. He'd dreamed about this moment, but never had he expected such a strong release. His heart was so full it spilled over with love for his dear, sweet Lizzy.

Once he squared things with Ward Metcalf, money would be scarce for a while. Soon he'd be able to provide a decent life for everyone. Besides running water and an indoor privy, he intended to buy Elizabeth one of those new-fangled iceboxes he'd read about.

Elizabeth loved him. And he loved her.

No man could ask for more.

Though he'd planned to propose only after he had his money in hand, suddenly he couldn't wait one more minute. "I love you, Lizzy. I want you to be my wife."

"I was beginning to think you'd never say how you felt," she murmured in his ear as she kissed the side of his face.

"The words come hard to me."

"I love hearing you say you love me."

"Then I'll have to practice. I love you, Lizzy." He sighed and took a breath. "If my father could see me now, he'd say I'm a bigger fool than he was."

"And how would you reply?"

"I'd tell him you're never going to run out on me."

"If I accept your proposal, I'll never leave you."

He'd never considered that she might say no.

"I won't repeat my mother's mistakes. I will not marry and play the part of a docile wife. I will not keep my mouth clamped shut regardless of the trouble brewing around me. I will marry you, Ben Ricker, only if you assure to me that we'll discuss all important matters in our lives. I have a stake in our future, and I want my voice heard."

"Haven't I always listened to you?"

"You've listened, but I don't think you always take me seriously."

He kissed her forehead, then glanced into her eyes. "I give you my word that I won't make important decisions without first hearing what you have to say."

"And you won't mind if I continue sewing shirts?"

"I thought with the extra money coming in, we might be able to hire a cook." He wished he could retract that last statement, but when she smiled, he knew she loved him, warped sense of humor and all. "Will you marry me?"

"Yes," she said, pulling him closer.

When he took her in his arms and they made love again, Ben knew he'd cherish her until the day he died.

Ben took the long way home, determined to stretch what little time remained of their wonderful night. With Lizzy against him, the full moon overhead, and love in his heart, he figured life didn't get any better than this.

When he heard her humming the notes to "Oh My Darling, Clementine," he nudged her. "Not you, too?"

"I can't seem to get the tune out of my head."

"It's no wonder, with both Zack and Josh playing the piece nonstop. But you know what? Tonight, I even like the song."

He hugged her closer and in a boisterous voice sang the lyrics etched forever in his mind. They sang the song twice and were about to move on to "Little Brown Jug" when Ben detected the smell of burning wood.

He didn't know how he'd missed the orange glow in the sky, but it looked as if dawn was rising over the ranch.

"Hold on," he warned. He kneed his horse forward and prayed his suspicions were wrong.

As they came to the rise overlooking the ranch, he saw his barn ablaze. Flames leaped from the roof and each window and door. It was too late, yet he couldn't accept the fact. He had to save the barn and the lumber inside. Afraid this might be their last time together, he tightened his hold on Lizzy.

He had no recollection of helping her down from the horse or how he'd ended up next to Lefty and Zack. He didn't remember picking up a shovel. But he found himself,

shovel in hand, heaving dirt over the crackling flames.

The barn roof collapsed.

Still he sprayed pitiful amounts of earth
over the raging inferno. Even after the back
wall tumbled, he didn't stop. Behind him,
he heard Lizzy and the children crying.

Granny's ripe curses rent the air.

Someone grabbed his arms. "It's no use,"
whoever it was said, but he elbowed him
away and dug the tip of the shovel in the
ground again. He shoveled dirt until every
muscle in his back knotted in pain. His neck
grew tight, and it was an effort to lift his
head, but he refused to quit.

Tears filled his eyes when the sides of
burning structure fell in. The horrific sound
of moaning timber filled the night and
echoed in his mind long after the dust had
settled.

He stood for countless minutes, taking in
the destruction. Inside he could make out
the piles of burnt timber, the charred
remains of several saddles, and possibly the
stall where he'd bedded his horse.

"Are the animals all right?" he asked no
one in particular.

Lefty and Zack nodded. Tears ran unchecked down the old man's face. Ben
turned away, his gaze transfixed on the

glowing wooden skeleton of what remained of his barn. He wiped his eyes with his palm. The shovel slipped from his grasp. He pushed aside the hands reaching for him, tore across the yard, leaped onto his horse, and escaped his nightmare.

He'd lost much more than his barn tonight.

His entire life had gone up in those flames.

CHAPTER 27

Ben returned after dawn to face facts. His ranch and land were as good as gone. In another week, Ward would swoop down on the place like a vulture to claim what was rightfully his.

Ben had failed.

He wasn't ashamed to admit he'd cried last night, cried for what might have been, for Granny, the children, and especially for his Lizzy. He had nothing to offer except a bleak future. He was broke with no means of supporting himself, much less a family.

What would happen to Granny?

Ben would find a room for her somewhere, and until something better came along, he'd work at the Anaconda Mine to pay for food and lodging. It would be rough on Granny to leave the ranch, but she'd have to adjust.

In the week that remained, he'd work the mill day and night. He'd use the cash from the lumber to buy Lizzy that sewing machine she was always talking about. He couldn't send her away empty-handed. It was the least he could do for the woman he loved.

No matter how hard he tried, he felt no regrets about last night. Though he probably should.

When he'd made love to Lizzy, he intended to claim her as his wife. In time, he hoped she'd forgive him. For as long as he lived, he'd remember the touch of her lips and the feel of her silken hair falling like a velvet curtain over both of them. Memories of their lovemaking would keep him warm until he drew his last breath.

At the sound of crunching gravel under boot soles, Ben turned and saw Lefty, his long face downtrodden. With a despondent shake of his head, his friend lifted his arms and dropped them back by his side. "I don't know what to say."

Ben heaved a long, weary sigh. "There's nothing to say."

"Guess you're right."

" 'Fraid so." As he climbed over the burnt remains of his barn, Ben felt like an old man. The acrid stench of smoke and failure choked him. "How's Granny?"

"Seems all right."

Ben nodded absently and drove soot-coated fingers through his hair. "All our work . . . gone."

"Maybe we can rebuild."

"My loan comes due next week."

"Can't you get an extension?"

"I didn't borrow the money from the bank. The loan came from Ward. No way in hell he's going to give me a break."

"Son of a bitch."

Shoulders drooping, Ben climbed over the charred remains and started across the yard. "You better look for another job."

"We still have a week."

"No way in hell we'll come up with four thousand bucks before then." Ben kicked a stone in his path and watched it tumble over a corncob pipe half buried in the ground. His stomach roiled as he glanced at the remnants of his barn.

"Lefty, how do you think the fire started?"

"Damned if I know."

"Maybe someone left a lantern burning?"

"No way. After Josh finally settled down, I thought I heard some noise, so I checked the barn."

"Was Granny sleeping when you went to bed?"

"When I walked by her room, her lamp was still on. A while later I thought I heard her going downstairs."

Ben's shoulders sagged under the weight of his suspicions.

"Oh, speaking of Granny, she said for you to come see her as soon as you returned."

When Ben entered the kitchen a moment later, he couldn't bear the sad look on Lizzy's face. He quickened his pace and kept his head low.

"Ben . . ."

He bolted into the living room and headed up the stairs, well aware of the stark look in Lizzy's eyes. She wouldn't like what he had to say, and he didn't have the strength to say it yet. Like flies on manure, his problems had multiplied. And he could handle only one at a time.

Lefty had checked the barn, and the sky was clear, so unlike the Golden Harp Saloon, lightning wasn't to blame. A careless, blind old lady taking a smoke seemed the only rational explanation.

Ben knocked and opened the door that was slightly ajar.

"Been waiting for you," Granny said, her voice choking with emotion.

"Lefty said you had something to tell me."

"Couldn't sleep a wink after the fire. I got somethin' to tell you, all right, somethin' that's gonna shock the livin' daylights outta you."

Ben knelt beside her rocker and wrapped his arm around her. "I think I already know."

Granny's back stiffened under his gentle touch. "You know?"

He leaned his head against hers and nodded.

"You let me go on worryin' for weeks, and you knew all along?"

Ben couldn't follow what she was saying. How could she worry for weeks about a fire that happened only hours earlier? "I only figured it out a few minutes ago."

Granny looked puzzled. "How'd you do that?"

"I found your pipe."

Granny directed a scowl at him. "What's that gotta do with anythin'?" Her eyebrows meshed. "You darn fool, you think I started that fire?"

"Isn't that what you were trying to tell me?"

She mumbled a few choice words under her breath. She ran her hands over the knees of her overalls, spent some time gazing blankly out the window. The fingers of her right hand fidgeted with the clasp on her suspender.

"Granny," he whispered, rubbing the pad of his thumb over the frail skin covering her knuckles, "After what I've been through in the last twenty-four hours, nothing you can say will shock me."

"First you think I set the fire. Now you think I can't shock you?"

Ben blamed stress for her crotchety mood. "It's pretty damn hard to shock a man who's just seen his life go up in smoke."

"Glad to hear that. 'Cause I killed someone."

He sprang to his feet. "You what?"

"Picked up a gun and shot him through the chest."

"Who?"

"Donald, that no-good from Boston, came creeping round the privy, thinkin' I was a defenseless old lady. An old hag, he called me, can you imagine that? He even boasted about keeping the reward money for himself. Donald figured he'd kill me first, then Lizzy. He planned to kidnap the children and take them back to Boston."

Too astounded to speak, Ben watched her rise from her chair and scurry across the room to the dresser. She reached in the top drawer under some clothes and threw what looked like a man's lumpy white sock on the bed.

Dumbfounded, Ben stood and took a few steps. "Granny, are you telling me you were the one who shot the man we found back a spell?"

"I tried to tell you when you first come in, but your head was filled with too much nonsense."

"Where did you get the gun?"

Granny reached under her pillow and pulled out a two-shot Derringer. "When no one was looking, Queenie gave this to me on my birthday." She nodded toward the bed. "Look in that sock over yonder," she said. " 'Cause I reckon you're in for another shock."

Ben dug deep and pulled out a wad of crumpled bills.

"It's my nest egg. Over the years I've managed to put away a few dollars. Before wrapping his hands around my neck to silence me, Donald bragged about the reward hidden in his money belt. Thanks to his contribution, I got close to eleven hundred dollars in that sock. Use the money to build another barn."

He'd worried what would become of his grandmother should something happen to him. This windfall eased his mind. Eleven hundred dollars was a lot of money.

But not nearly enough.

"Betts, whatya think caused the fire?"

Elizabeth brushed away the tears from Josh's face. "I don't know."

"Can a fire start all by itself?"

The fire had been a traumatic experience for the children, especially Josh, who followed her around like her shadow. "No. It takes a spark of some kind."

"Could a very tiny, bitty little spark burn a whole barn?"

"I suspect a tiny spark could become a big one, and yes, in time devour an entire building."

She studied her brother's face. The hollow look in his eyes frightened her. "Why are you asking all these questions?"

He lowered his head and shrugged. "I dunno. Maybe lightning came down and caused the fire, just like the saloon in Welcome?"

"There was no lightning last night." At least none she could tell Josh about.

"You don't know everything. It coulda been lightning." A string of drool slipped over his trembling lower lip that he dashed away with the back of his hand.

"Why is this so important to you?"

He slid slowly into the chair by her side. "I was just wondering." His foot swung back and forth. "If someone puts out a little flame, can it come back to life all by itself?"

Elizabeth didn't want to voice her suspicions. "Josh, did you have something to do with the fire?"

"I . . . I . . . tried to light Granny's old corncob pipe, but the flame burnt my finger so the pipe fell . . . me and Clyde put out the fire . . . it must have started back up. I didn't mean to do it." The tears came in earnest as his small body crumpled against her.

That's how Ben found them a few minutes later when he walked into the kitchen looking worse than she felt. She wanted to crawl in a hole and hide for the next fifty years. But the man she loved deserved the truth.

She kissed the top of Josh's head. "Sweetheart, we have to tell Ben what happened."

Josh burrowed deeper into her skirt.

Gone was Ben's easygoing smile when he collapsed in the chair next to her. "We have to talk."

"I know. But first Josh has something to tell you."

It took a few minutes to persuade her brother to let go of her. Another two to get him to open his eyes, but nothing she said could make him talk or look at Ben.

Elizabeth held Ben's hand. The flesh that had come to life under her touch last night felt cold and unyielding. "I have something terrible to tell you."

His face, cast in stone, showed no emotion.

She took a breath for courage. "Josh started the fire in your barn."

"How?" He directed the one hollow-sounding syllable at Josh.

Slowly her brother lifted tear-filled eyes. "Me and Clyde put out the fire, but we musta missed a teeny flame." Before she could stop him, Josh scooted off her and climbed onto the lap of the man who looked already dead. "I'm sorry, Ben. Please, forgive me."

As Josh's tears fell down the front of Ben's shirt, Ben's arms came to rest around him. "It was an accident . . . don't worry about it."

Elizabeth grabbed a napkin from the table and dabbed furiously at her eyes.

"Now be a good boy, and go outside so I can speak to Elizabeth." Ben set Josh down and watched with bleak eyes as he slowly retreated from the room.

Elizabeth went into her bedroom and returned a moment later with an envelope. "Ben, I know it isn't much, but I want you to have this."

Ben stared straight ahead.

"It's my sewing money. I've been thinking

about this since you left. You said yourself my business was about to take off. I want to help you."

"I can't take your money." The cold, hard truth showed on every crease of his soot-smudged face.

She needed him. He needed her.

Surely, he'd allow her to help once they discussed everything together. "I know this is rough on you," she continued hurriedly, not wanting to hear anything he had to say. Eventually she ran out of words, and she stared down at the man she loved with tears in her eyes.

"Lizzy . . ."

She raised her hand to stop him. "Ben, it's only a barn. I know it was filled with wood, but look around you." She waved her hand toward the window. "There's lots more lumber. We'll rebuild together. In time everything will be all right."

He pushed sooty fingers through his hair. "I wish it were that simple. In seven days, I'm going to lose this ranch. Don't look at me like that. I have nothing left to give. You should leave, the sooner the better."

"But Ben, we love each other."

"Love isn't enough."

"It is for me."

Because he remained silent, she continued, "You asked me to be your wife."

"There's no way I can marry you now."

"You swore you'd listen to what I have to say before making any important decision. Our future is important. Why aren't we discussing this . . . together?"

"There's nothing to discuss."

"But you said . . ."

"Forget what I said. I didn't mean any of it."

"I don't believe that, Ben."

She grabbed hold of the table to steady herself. He wanted her to lean on him and rely on his strength. Instead, he stepped back so he wouldn't be tempted to touch her. "A man will say damn near anything to a woman after a roll in the hay."

"I won't leave you. I know you don't mean the hurtful things you're saying."

"Our lovemaking was no more than a romp." He forced himself to go on. "And no wife of mine will ever work outside the home."

"Are you telling me everything you said was lies?"

Because he knew she wouldn't leave unless she hated him, he struck an arrogant pose and forced a cocky grin. "By now, you should know I don't lie. Though sometimes, I do stretch the truth a bit."

For three days, every attempt Elizabeth made to reason with Ben failed, so she decided to take matters into her own hands. Lefty had let it slip that Ward Metcalf was the man who held Ben's future in his palm.

"Whoa." The command, issued in a raspy voice, brought the supply wagon to a standstill. Zack lifted one shaggy eyebrow and squinted. "It's a waste of time, I tell you, to go butting heads with that no good son of . . . well, it's a waste of time."

"Ward will listen to me. We're friends."

Zack waved a bony finger at her. "You don't know the man like I do. The only way you'll get Ward to change his mind is if there's something in it for him."

She hopped down from the wagon. "I should be done shortly."

Zack flicked the reins. "I'll be at the mercantile if you need me."

With what she hoped was a confident stride, she marched into the bank with her string purse swaying from her wrist.

When Ward spotted her, he crossed the room and took her hand in a firm grip. His mustache twitched upward. "My, my, what brings you here, Elizabeth?"

"I have some business to discuss with you."

He rested his hand under her elbow and led her to his desk, where he pulled out a chair. "Can I get you a cup of tea?"

Elizabeth needed a moment to regroup. "Yes, that would be nice."

She brought a gloved hand to her brow and dabbed at the perspiration. A moment later Ward returned with a serving tray that held a cup and saucer along with a small bowl for sugar and another for cream. She dropped a cube of sugar in her tea and stirred, then met Ward's anxious gaze.

He leaned back and meshed his fingers over a silk vest. "What can I do for you?"

"Did you know Ben Ricker's barn was destroyed by fire?"

"Seems to me someone mentioned it."

"I was hoping you'd allow me to make a payment."

"Does Ben know about this?"

"No. I want to keep this business transaction between us."

Ward swiveled around in his chair and reached into the oak cabinet behind him. He removed a file with the name *Ricker* printed in bold letters. "Elizabeth, I must admit you surprise me. You didn't strike me as a woman of means."

She realized he'd misunderstood. "I'm certainly not wealthy."

"Well, then, how can you pay off Ben's loan?"

"I was hoping you'd allow me to make payments." She withdrew an envelope from her purse, containing every cent she'd saved.

"How much money are you planning to put down?"

She handed him the bills she'd counted earlier that morning. "Seventy-eight dollars and thirty-six cents."

His smile slipped a fraction. "That trifling sum is a fraction of the money owed me. When can you hope to pay off the rest of the loan?"

She ran her tongue over her lower lip and gazed into the eyes of a hawk. "I don't know, but I'll tell you this. My business is booming, and I'll give you every penny I earn." Her hand shook so much she set her cup down, fearing she'd spill the hot beverage down her front.

The way Ward looked her over knotted her stomach, yet she met his unblinking gaze head on.

"I have a solution to Ben's problem," he said with a gleam in his eyes that set her nerves on edge.

"I knew I could count on you."

"I think you better hear my terms first."

The icy fingers around her chest tightened. "I'm waiting, Ward."

"You fascinate me, Elizabeth. You're bold. You're a fighter. A man could go far with you by his side."

"What are your terms?" she asked, her patience stretched thin.

"Marry me, Elizabeth, and Ben won't owe me a dime."

Chapter 28

Ben turned his back as she approached. Elizabeth told herself he hadn't seen her, although she feared he had. She watched him push a log along the saw bed, the sharp teeth of the blades slicing through the thick lumber like butter. She waited for the noise to die down.

She couldn't believe she'd agreed to marry Ward. At first, she'd flat out refused him, but the more she thought about it, the more she realized she didn't have a choice. Had she not come to Welcome, Ben would not be in danger of losing his ranch. She felt responsible, and marrying Ward seemed the only solution to right a wrong.

As she looked at the sweat glistening on Ben's broad back, her stomach turned over. It would be torture to live in the same community as the man she loved and never again be able to touch him.

And she'd have to give up her sewing, too.

How would it look for the wife of a prominent banker to take in mending for money? She regretted subjecting the children to a loveless marriage — a controlling marriage.

She'd wanted so much more for them and for herself.

This would be her last chance to change Ben's mind. And though she didn't hold much hope, she needed to try.

"Ben, I'd like to speak with you," she said, once the deafening noise stopped.

A vein along his jaw twitched. His gaze skittered over her before turning away. "What?" The one word was issued in a harsh tone. Since the fire, he hadn't displayed any feelings toward her. Nor had she seen the hint of a smile or any of the warmth she craved.

"I was hoping you'd reconsider sending us away."

He glared at her impatiently. "We've been through this before. There's no place left for you to stay."

"But . . ."

"In another four days this ranch won't be mine."

If he still loved her, she couldn't see it in his cold eyes.

"Leave, Lizzy. There's no reason not to." The fraction of warmth penetrating his voice gave her hope.

"You're a mule-headed, unreasonable man," she said. "I know you're about to lose the ranch and this land. If I could do anything to prevent it, I would. But I love you, and I'd rather live in one cramped room with you than in a mansion with somebody else. I'll sew and you'll get a job. Together we can save enough money to start over somewhere."

He heaved another log onto the saw bed. "Are you through?"

Before she moved on with her life, she needed to know one thing. "Ben, do you love me?"

Time stopped. Blood roared through her veins, echoing in her ears until she grew dizzy. Nervously, she licked her lips.

He turned. Unblinking eyes met hers.

"I'm telling you to go. That says it all."

Elizabeth didn't need to be hit over the head with an iron frying pan. The look on Ben's face went beyond the pain of losing his ranch. He didn't love her. With what little pride remained, she lifted her chin and walked away.

Later that afternoon when Ben approached the ranch house, he saw Lizzy's wagon piled high with boxes. Early tomorrow morning,

Lizzy and the children were leaving. When she'd mentioned she might marry Ward, he'd assumed the words were an empty threat. But Zack had set him straight. His Lizzy would be another man's wife — Ward's wife.

Originally, his greatest fear had been that Elizabeth would abandon him, and here he was sending her away.

Ben walked into the kitchen. Josh ran to him, wound his arms around Ben's legs. "I promise to never smoke again. I'm your partner. Please don't send me away." The boy's tears soaked through the denim of Ben's jeans.

Ben persuaded the boy to let go, then gathered the child in a tight hug. He squeezed his eyes shut and memorized the feel of the small arms wrapped around his neck. He wanted to give Josh the world, but that wasn't possible. As he held the boy to his chest, a realization struck him, hard — he couldn't love this child more if he were his own flesh and blood.

"Josh," he began, then cleared his throat to steady his voice. "You'll always be my partner. I'll miss you like the devil, but I can't afford to keep the ranch going any longer."

The boy pushed back slightly. "You and

me can get some gold and then we'll have lots of money, and I'll help you build another barn."

"That old mine hasn't produced enough gold in the last ten years to pay for a new pair of boots."

"I bet I could find some."

Ben swallowed past the tightness in his throat as he took in the eager, wobbly smile on Josh's tear-streaked face. "If we had more time, the two of us could give it a try just for fun. But you leave tomorrow. In another few days Granny and I will have to go, too."

As hard as it was for Ben to believe what he was saying, reality was knocking at his back door. In a few more days, he'd be out on his ear with Granny to look after.

Josh pursed his lips. "I ain't gonna go live with that nincompoop . . ."

"Josh," came Lizzy's stern warning.

Ben added the sound of her voice to his memories. Soon, memories would be all he'd have left.

"Mr. Metcalf won't let Clyde come live with us."

Josh's words knifed through him. "I know you love Clyde, but I'm sure you'll see him around. Lefty and Zack will keep an eye on him for you."

"But Clyde's almost my brother. It ain't right to keep us apart."

Ben looked down and marveled how such a small boy could have made such a large impact on his life. "Sometimes things don't turn out the way we want. If I could make everything right, I would. Remember this, we may not see each other every day, but trust me, you'll always be with me, right here." He tapped his chest. "Now dry your tears. You're a cowboy, aren't you?"

Josh brushed the moisture from his cheeks and nodded.

"Real cowboys don't cry."

The boy's lower lip quivered as he bravely looked Ben in the eye.

Ben gave his shoulder a pat. "That's much better, partner. I'm counting on you to be brave and not give your sister a lot of lip."

Deep in sleep, Ben thought he felt Lizzy's warm hands on his bare shoulders. He sighed, content to share his bed with her.

He felt someone shaking him and realized he wasn't dreaming. He opened his eyes and saw Elizabeth standing over him.

"Josh and Cecelia were not in bed when I woke up. Jethro's missing, too."

Ben hurriedly dressed. "I bet he's gone to

the mine. Josh was hell-bent on finding gold."

"I hope you're right."

"If he's not there, we'll find him."

Ben saddled his horse in record time. As the first rays of sunlight sliced through the leafy canopy overhead, he could see the entrance to the Gold Nugget mine. Nearby, Jethro was munching on low-lying shrubbery.

"Thank goodness," Lizzy muttered.

Ben's gaze settled on the buckboard hidden behind a stand of trees where a man of short stature heaved heavy crates onto a wagon. Ben pulled back on the reins and silenced Lizzy by cupping a hand over her mouth.

"I think you should wait here." He pointed to the culprit concealed in the shadows.

She gave him that stubborn look he'd seen from day one. "The children are down there. I'm going."

He didn't have time to argue. Yanking his rifle from the saddle scabbard, he whispered, "At least hold this, and don't be afraid to use it."

Not wanting to alert the intruder, they went on foot the remaining distance. As he and Lizzy crept along the winding path, he recognized the man: Duke, his reprehensible hired hand.

Ben took the last few yards at a run and knocked Duke to the ground.

The no good, son of a bitch called out, "I give up."

When Ben loosened his hold, Duke took a wild swing, and his fist connected with Ben's jaw. Ben wrapped his hands around the man's shoulders, slamming Duke's head onto the hard-packed dirt.

Ben yanked him to his feet, twisted his arm behind him and dragged him toward the Gold Nugget mine. Boulders blocked the entrance. He cocked his sidearm gun. "Are the children in there?"

Duke flashed his gold tooth. "You're too late. I set a charge of dynamite guaranteed to blow your mine from here to kingdom come."

"But the children are in there . . ." Ben started to choke up.

"They got in the way. Blame your granddaddy, not me. If he hadn't stolen what was rightfully ours, none of this would have happened. I was merely evening the score."

Ben slammed his fist into Duke's jaw. "That's from me and my granddaddy."

Once Duke was tied to the wagon, Ben whistled for his horse. Lizzy was so distraught, she'd dropped onto her hands and knees and was clawing at the pile of rocks. For several minutes Ben dug right alongside her, but finally, his common sense kicked in. Some of the boulders that blocked the entryway were too large for one man to move. It was futile to attempt to work alone.

"Lizzy." He placed a finger under her chin and forced her to look at him. "We need to go for help. We're wasting precious time. I'm not leaving you here alone."

Ben couldn't tell whether she understood, but Elizabeth didn't resist when he pulled her to her feet and lifted her onto the saddle. The seemingly endless ride back to the ranch gave Ben time to think. If he hadn't sent Lizzy away, Josh and Cecelia would still be safe at his ranch, instead of trapped under a pile of rubble.

He cursed his stupidity. Without Lizzy and the kids, his life would have no meaning. Even if he had his ranch and all the money in the world, life still wouldn't be worth a plugged nickel without the ready-made family he'd come to love.

CHAPTER 29

Hours later, despite his growing fatigue, Ben worked shoulder to shoulder with the other men from Welcome. Even the newcomers had turned up to lend a helping hand. Though no one voiced their worst fears, Ben sensed the despair around him.

The womenfolk had arrived in wagons about an hour after the men to set up a table with coffee, cold water, and food. Queenie brought along a water barrel with damp towels so the workers could wipe off the sweat that clung to them.

And though Ben had emphatically told Granny to wait at the ranch, she arrived a short while later with Clyde holding the reins. It was a wonder they weren't both killed. She and Lizzy now sat huddled together under the shade of an old oak tree.

Six hours later, Pete pulled Ben aside and gazed at him the way he had the day his father died. "It doesn't look good."

Ben wanted to tell him to go to hell. "If you're saying those children aren't alive, you're wrong."

Pete pulled his timepiece from his pocket and shook his head. "I pray to God you're right."

A cheer rang out behind them. Both men ran to find out what the commotion was about.

Lefty stuck his arm between the boulders. "I think we've broken through. And it looks as though only the opening of the mine collapsed."

Lizzy and Granny ran toward them. "Can you see them? Can you hear them?"

Ben knelt down, brought his mouth near the opening and shouted the children's names, but no reply came.

"Doesn't mean a thing," he told Lizzy, though it did, and his gut wrenched with fear. "They might be in too far to hear our voices."

The men picked up their pace, but it took another two hours before they'd cleared a space large enough for a man to crawl through.

Ben was torn between staying with Lizzy and leading the way. "Stay here," he told her. "I'll bring them out safely. I promise." If it wasn't already too late.

Elizabeth didn't argue. "Hurry, Ben. I'll be right here when you come out."

Granny stood still, her lower lip quivering. Ben hugged both women before he dove into the dark tunnel, followed by several men.

Ben and Lefty led the way with lit lanterns. Behind them came Pete with his black bag of medical supplies and Zack carrying a pick and shovel in case they encountered more destruction. As they hurried deeper into the mine, Ben was relieved to discover the explosion had affected only the entrance. The air smelled fresh. If Duke hadn't harmed the children, chances were they'd survived the blast.

"Josh, where are you, partner?" Ben shouted, every cell in his body straining to hear a reply.

Lefty followed suit. "Cecelia, honey, say something if you can hear us."

The men stood and listened.

"We're here," came Josh's voice from a distance. "You better hurry, 'cause Cecelia's really, really scared."

They found the children with their ankles and wrists bound together. Lefty cut them loose and lifted Cecelia in his arms. Josh latched onto Ben and wouldn't let go. "It wasn't me that started the fire in your barn."

"Don't worry about that, now. You're all right. That's all that matters." Ben tightened his arms around the boy.

He reached over and wound an arm around Cecelia's neck. "I love you both so very much."

"Ben, I didn't start the fire," Josh repeated, his voice sharper, more high-pitched.

This time, Ben paid attention. "Then who did?"

"Duke said he threw lamp oil over the hay."

"That son of a . . ." Ben caught himself in time. He'd seen the shame on Josh's face when he thought he'd started the fire that destroyed the barn and all the lumber inside. "I'm glad to hear that, partner. Bet that's a load off your mind."

"Duke said your granddaddy stole the mine from his granddaddy in a card game. Cecelia and me caught him stealing your gold. Now that you have some gold, maybe we won't have to leave."

"That depends on whether I can persuade your sister to give me another chance." As Ben lifted the child in his arms, he looked closely at Josh's bruises and his left eye, which was swollen shut. Dried blood caked his split upper lip. "Did Duke hit you?"

"I punched him back." Josh wound his

arms tight around Ben's neck. "It don't hurt much . . . now that you're here."

The boy's devotion touched Ben. He'd let the law deal with Duke. He needed to attend to more important matters.

Moments later, Ben crawled through the opening. When Lizzy saw Josh's bruised face, she dropped to her knees and ran her fingers over the side of his head as though he were a delicate porcelain doll.

Josh pulled away. "Don't go doing no sissy stuff. I'm a cowboy."

"It looks worse than it is," Ben said, trying to ease her worries.

The gathering crowd cheered when Lefty appeared carrying Cecelia, who soon vanished in a group hug.

Pete insisted on examining both children. After listening to their breathing with his stethoscope and taking their pulses, he cleaned Josh's cuts, applied ointment, then proclaimed both kids fit as fiddles.

Some time later, Ben stood off to one side with Josh and Lizzy. She stretched on tiptoes and planted a soft kiss on the corner of his mouth. "Thank you, Ben."

His heart galloped like stampeding hooves. "For what?"

"For being there when I needed you most."

Ben glanced down at the little guy in his arms and the woman he loved and was overwhelmed with emotion. For hours he'd feared the worst. But he was given a second chance. When he thought how close he'd come to losing the children and Lizzy, tears blurred his vision.

Josh gawked at him. "Ben, are you crying?"

Ben tried to look nonchalant. "I got something in my eye."

Josh studied him a moment. "I thought you said cowboys didn't cry."

Ben gave Lizzy a long, meaningful look. "Seems I was wrong about a lot of things."

The townspeople left, and Zack drove the wagon with Granny and the children back to the ranch. Lizzy stayed behind because Ben had asked her to. The cave-in had brought her closer to her neighbors, and the way they'd banded together was not something she'd ever forget.

She'd changed since arriving in Welcome. The same men she'd judged as good-for-nothing drunks the day she came to town had worked countless hours to save Josh and Cecelia. She owed these people, yet they'd waved away her words of gratitude, saying she was one of them. And they took care of their own.

She'd choose living in Welcome over Boston any day. Though Welcome would never have a subway, it had so much more. She put Ben, Granny, and her newfound friends at the top of her growing list.

"Come with me," he said, taking her arm and leading her to the opening of the mine.

"You want me to climb in there?"

"Yup."

"Is this your idea of a joke?"

He gave her a gentle kiss and nudged her forward. "Trust me."

"The last time I trusted you, you broke my heart."

"I regret that deeply."

After a moment's hesitation, Elizabeth scrambled over the rocks and glanced at the lanterns blazing inside the stone cavern. She couldn't guess why Ben had brought her here.

Ben climbed in behind her and pulled her to her feet. "I have something to tell you that's worth repeating."

"Why are you whispering?"

"You'll see." He shouted, "I love you." His deep voice echoed. "Love you . . . love you . . . love you . . . love you . . . love you . . ."

Then he took her hands and entwined

their fingers. "I've been a fool. Forgive me for turning you away. I'm asking you to give me another chance."

When she was certain he meant every word, she nodded.

A relieved smile hiked a corner of his mouth. "If I promise to love, honor, and listen to every word you say from now until the day I die, will you marry me, Lizzy?"

Later that week, low-lying clouds darkened the Montana sky, but to Ben it was still a beautiful day. Soon Lizzy would be his wife, and though the gold mine hadn't made them rich, it had saved the ranch and provided enough extra cash to build another barn, buy more cattle, and buy Lizzy a new sewing machine.

He heard hoofbeats and looked up to see Zack heading toward him at a gallop. Zack pulled the horse up, leaped off, and ran toward Ben. He hadn't thought the old man could move that fast. Zack bent at the waist and gulped in ragged gasps. "There's trouble brewing in town."

"What's up?"

"A man calling himself Robert T. Hines was poking around asking questions. No one told him anything, but he still intends to stick around a few days and have himself a look around. On the ride over here I got an idea that might send Hines packing."

"What do you have in mind?"

Later that afternoon, Ben sat by himself at the Bear Claw Tavern watching Robert T. Hines sipping his soup like a true gentleman. Sticking out of a satchel by his feet was a rolled-up *Wanted* poster of Elizabeth that Hines had been showing to anyone willing to look.

He watched with interest when Benny, the boy who worked for the printer, came through the door. The child was twelve with blond hair, blue eyes, and a face fit for a cherub.

"Mister, care to buy a paper?" Benny asked his uncle Lefty, as if he'd never before laid eyes on him.

"Keep the change," the next customer said, allowing his gaze to travel over the printed page.

At the next table, Pete and Queenie both bought newspapers and soon were exclaiming about the sad turn of events.

"Such a young thing," Queenie said, in a voice loud enough to carry.

Pete settled his glasses over his nose and read the headlines. " 'Cave-in claims three lives.' " He patted Queenie's pale hand. "If they'd stayed in Boston, they might still be alive."

Queenie pressed a hankie to the corner of her eye.

Ben shook his head sorrowfully. "Damn shame what happened to those kids. I hear Elizabeth O'Hara was a real beauty."

"Kid, I'd like a paper." Hines threw two bits on the table and grabbed the *Butte Sentinel* from Benny's hand.

Below the lowered brim of his Stetson, Ben studied the man he'd come to loathe. He expected to see some regret on his face but found none as Robert T. Hines scanned the front page, stood, and dropped the paper on the table.

It had been Zack's idea to have the bogus front page printed, telling of the tragic fate of Elizabeth O'Hara and her two siblings, Josh and Cecelia, who perished in a cave-in at the Gold Nugget mine.

When Robert T. Hines boarded the early train heading east later that day, Ben knew he wouldn't be bothering Lizzy or the children ever again.

EPILOGUE

Ten months later

The following July, Ben sat with his arm looped over Lizzy's shoulder, trying out the new porch swing he'd built to accommodate his growing family. The gentle creak of the overhead chains as the wooden seat swung back and forth was just what a tired cowboy needed after a hard day's work. He suspected it might calm a crying infant, too. In a few more weeks, they'd have a chance to test his theory.

From inside came the murmur of voices as Granny and Cecelia prepared supper. Despite being blind, Granny had flourished with the constant attention.

Ben settled his hand over Lizzy's distended belly. "How's the little guy doing?"

"Feels as if he's rustling steer." She hesitated a moment. "Will you be disappointed if it's a girl?"

He tipped his head against hers. "I don't

411

care whether it's a boy or a girl, but I do wonder what our baby will be like."

A playful smile lifted the corners of her mouth. "I certainly hope the baby doesn't have your sense of humor. One in this family is enough."

"Nothing's wrong with stretching the truth once in a while. Let's hope the kid doesn't have your stubborn streak."

"Me, stubborn?"

"You always barge in, won't admit defeat, no matter the circumstances."

Josh and Clyde leaped onto the porch. Clyde squeezed in next to Elizabeth.

Josh scooted to Ben's side. "Maybe the new baby will take after Clyde or me."

Ben shook his head and pulled Lizzy close beside him. Though he gave the boys a worried look, he didn't have a care in the world. He'd learned he could overcome anything with his family *forever* by his side.

ABOUT THE AUTHOR

Diane Amos lives with her husband, Dave, in a small town north of Portland, Maine. They have four grown children, five grand-children, a fat tabby named Millie, and a miniature Dachshund named Molly. Diane is an established Maine artist. Her paintings are in private collections across the United States. She is a Golden Heart finalist and winner of the Maggie Award for Excellence. For more information about Diane and her books, check out her Website at www.diane amos.com.